We're All in This Together

We're All in This Together

A Novella and Stories

Owen King

BLOOMSBURY

Published by Bloomsbury Publishing, New York and London
Distributed to the trade by Holtzbrinck Publishers

All papers used by Bloomsbury Publishing are natural, recyclable
products made from wood grown in well-managed
forests. The manufacturing processes conform to the
environmental regulations of the country of origin.

Library of Congress Cataloging-in-Publication Data

King, Owen.
We're all in this together : a novella and stories / Owen King.—1st U.S. ed.
p. cm.
ISBN-10 1-58234-585-6
ISBN-13 978-1-58234-585-7
1. United States—Social life and customs—Fiction. 2. Grandparent and
child—Fiction. 3. Mothers and sons—Fiction. 4. Teenage boys—Fiction.
5. Maine—Fiction. I. Title.

PS3611.I5837W47 2005
813'.6—dc22
2005006926

First U.S. Edition 2005

1 3 5 7 9 10 8 6 4 2

Typeset by Hewer Text Ltd, Edinburgh
Printed in the United States of America
by Quebecor World Fairfield

CONTENTS

For Kelly,
the prettiest girl in Yuma

Reports that say that something hasn't happened are always interesting to me, because as we know, there are known knowns; there are things we know we know. We also know there are known unknowns; that is to say we know there are some things we do not know. But there are also unknown unknowns—the ones we don't know we don't know. And if one looks throughout the history of our country and other free countries, it is the latter category that tend to be the difficult ones.

—Donald Rumsfeld on the question of
Iraq and WMDs, February 12, 2002

We're All in This Together

DON'T MOURN!

When you are a kid, adults are always telling you about their revelation, the moment when the mist cleared and they saw what it was they wanted, or finally understood what it was that never made sense before.

For instance, my grandfather told me that he decided to be a union organizer after he saw the man who lived next door at the boarding-house come home one morning after a late shift at the paper mill, remove his shoes at the door, and pass them off to his wife, who then slipped them on and continued out on her way to another job. As the man handed off his shoes, my grandfather realized that what the man was actually handing off was his dignity, and that a life without dignity was no different from a life without love—because how could a man without dignity bear to love another person, when he must hate himself so much?

Dr. Vic claimed that he fell in love with my mother when he looked out his office window one sunny afternoon to see her striding up to the elderly Catholic priest who sometimes prayed on the sidewalk in front of the Planned Parenthood office for hours at a time. The old priest appeared to be swaying slightly; Emma helped him from his knees over to a bench. After that, she went back inside, and came out a minute later with a cold bottle of water for the holy man. Dr. Vic watched it all, and wondered how many times that old crank had warned my mother that she was on the path to hell, and there she was anyhow, doing the decent thing to save him from a case of sunstroke, or worse. Until then I only thought she was beautiful, said Dr. Vic, but that proved it.

At a rally for striking longshoremen in Portland, my grandmother said she heard Papa relate the story about his neighbors who had to share a single pair of shoes, and while she felt compelled by his words, she didn't fully devote herself to the cause until after the meeting—when he came down from the platform and shook her hand. Nana had seen other union men talk, and dramatically whip off their coats, and stomp around in their braces while they railed against the bosses. She even met one of these big stomping sorts once, and it was like shaking hands with a liver. When she was introduced to my grandfather, though, Nana realized immediately that Papa was different: in spite of his suit, my grandfather wasn't a college boy, or a politician—he was an actual stevedore, just like her brother and her uncle. She could tell this by the fine dirt in the creases beneath his eyes, what her mother used to call "Working Man's Scars." Then Papa stuck out his hand, said, "How do," and Nana grasped it. He had clean hands, dry hands. She was moved to think of how hard he had worked to get himself clean. Finally, she thought, here was a young man who believed in something.

What I take from these stories is the impression that until that certain moment—the awakening, the sign—each of us is waiting outside the life that we are meant for, like a stranger with nothing to do but sit on the steps until the Realtor arrives. Then she does appear, charging up the walk, a fury of possibility and jingling keys. She throws open the door, and hurries you inside, and you know, right then. This is the place, the one place you really belong.

Except, I think now that for most people, it's more complex than that. In the moment of realization, maybe the mist doesn't actually clear, but thicken, taking on color, smell, and taste. Maybe the house is for sale because it's haunted; maybe every house is haunted.

When Papa saw the man give his wife the pair of shoes, he saw that something was wrong, but maybe he summed too quickly, and underestimated the depth of a man's dignity. When my mother brought the old priest a bottle of water, maybe Dr. Vic bet too high on Emma's generosity, and too low on the hard-earned pessimism of a single mother and motivated activist, who undoubtedly worried a good deal more about the news stories that would follow the death of a priest on the sidewalk in front of the clinic, than she ever did about the man actually dying. And was there ever a time—years and years after she took the clean hand of the dirty soapboxer that day on the docks—that my grandmother wondered just what my grandfather's effort amounted to, now that they lived in a time and in a place where it seemed that the filthiest thing you could say about a person was that they were liberal, that they had a bleeding heart?

Obviously, something was on Nana's mind when she died. After January, she never again left the guest bedroom, and one morning in early March, I found her cold. A sour, ponderous expression lay on her face, a grimace of real dissatisfaction, as if she had been expecting a surprise, but just maybe not the one she received. Her eyes were open, too, and fixed on the framed portrait of Joseph Hillstrom that hung on the wall.

In those last seconds, what did she see in the eyes of labor's truest martyr? Did she see the cool expression of a sincere organizer? Or did she see the passionless stare of a killer?

Four months later, in the middle of summer, and with the grass already grown full and burnt brown on Nana's grave, I saw something that surprised me, too. At the time, I understood it couldn't be real, that it was a hallucination. But, these days, I know better than to believe my eyes. Sometimes up really is down; sometimes the ground is the water, and the sky is a cliff.

In the morning, before setting out, I eat a bowl of oatmeal and write my mother a quick note. Have a lovely day with your conscience. *There's nothing unusual about this; my mother and I are regular correspondents. Without knocking, I stride into the bathroom while she is in the shower and smack the yellow legal pad against the frosted glass so she can read it. I record her silence, the trickle of water down the drain, and the squeaking of her feet, as a minor victory.*

When I roll my bike out of the garage, Dr. Vic sticks his head out the window of his BMW and asks if I want a lift on his way to work.

"Sorry, but I don't take rides from strange men," I say. I usher my mother's fiancé on his way with a sweeping gesture.

Dr. Vic responds to my challenge with perfect, maddening acquiescence: he gives a pleasant nod, and simply coasts down the driveway, when any normal person would slam on the gas and lay down a patch of screw-you-kid rubber.

But I am feeling good as I pedal out onto Route 12, heading for the tall white house on Dundee Avenue where my mother grew up and Nana died. The wind and the summer smells of grass and tar make me feel fast, and on that markerless stretch of road I can pretend I am between almost any two places in the world. Leaving always gives me a high feeling, and the bad part—the coming back—is a whole day away. Route 12 dips and rises. I lean into a bend and the first sign of town comes into view. The Beachcomber, a beleaguered ranch motel, crouches across from the mouth of the interstate ramp, catering to late-night drivers who are too tired to make it south to Boston, or north to Bangor and Canada.

That's when I see it—see them. I glance at the motel and there are three men standing on the boardwalk in front of a room, loading the trunk of a taxi. There is nothing distinct about these men: they are all white; they all appear to be in the normal range of weight and build; they are all dressed in suits and ties. In other words, they are three men, three normal men, boarding a taxi. The taxi is a member of the local fleet, a creaky-looking station wagon with plastic wood panels.

When the trio climbs in, I observe the undercarriage of the cab sag slightly beneath their collective mass. Then I am around the corner and turning into town.

I pass another block before I apprehend very clearly what it is that was so striking about the three strangers: that is, the three men weren't strangers at all. Those men were my mother's old boyfriends. They were Paul and Dale and Jupps, all of them, together. In another block, I work out the many reasons why this is not possible, not the least of which happens to be that none of my mother's boyfriends ever knew each other. Besides, Paul lives way up north, and this is tourist season, his busy time, and as far as we know, Jupps didn't even live in the United States anymore. On top of that, the only time I could ever recall having seen any of them wearing a tie was Dale at Nana's funeral, and that had been a bow tie.

No, of course not. Of course, I didn't see them.

What I saw didn't even qualify as a hallucination; it was too boring. My vision was more like some kind of sad little kid wish, like an imaginary friend, or your Real Father. Not the crazy drunk that your mother's ex-boyfriend once had to beat the shit out of with a snow shovel, not the jerk-off felon who never gave you anything in your whole life except a polydactyl toe and a five-dollar bill for your tenth birthday—not him, not that imposter—but your Real Father, *the superhero. Your Real Father is sorry to have put you through all this, but he couldn't risk it, because if his enemies ever discovered his secret identity, his family would have been in terrible danger. But now everything can be different—because he* needs *your help—and the invisible spy plane is idling in a grassy field outside of town and it's go, go, go! The fate of the world may depend on it!*

In the time it takes to consider the matter logically and, in turn, dust off the old (but not that old) Real Father Fantasy, I have traveled another two blocks. I have also started to cry. I slam on the brakes and start back to the motel, standing on the pedals and pushing uphill. But the gravel parking lot is empty; the men and the taxi are somewhere up the road, out of sight.

I am still sniffling when I reach my grandparents' house and find a small gathering in the front yard. My grandfather and the neighbors, Gil Desjardins and his wife, Mrs. Desjardins, stand before the 15 × 15-foot billboard that Papa has recently posted on the lawn, and which lists, succinctly, his deeply felt political beliefs concerning the most recent election, between Al Gore and George W. Bush.

I roll onto the grass and pull up beside them. Between their shoulders I make out slashes of pink paint, and even before reading the latest accusation, the situation is evident: for the third time in a month, the vandal, the fascist paperboy, Steven Sugar, has attacked.

"Somehow," says Gil, "that the paint is pink, that makes it worse, doesn't it?"

Mrs. Desjardins flicks away a pink chip with her fingernail. She clucks sympathetically.

Papa crosses his arms and contemplates the pink message in silence.

Mrs. Desjardins purses her lips at me and gives my bicep a squeeze. She wears a kimono and a thin black ribbon fastened around her old woman's neck. It is accepted that Gil's wife is odd.

"Whoever would have guessed a bourgeois newspaper could lead to such a rumpus?" Her gaze falls on me expectantly.

I shrug.

"Oh, for shit's sake, Lana," says Gil.

"It is bourgeois. The New York Times *is bourgeois."*

"That may be, but if you say 'bourgeois,' you sound like an asshole. In fact, I've been told that 'bourgeois' is a code word that assholes use to recognize each other when they're in unfamiliar places. If you even spell it in Scrabble, it makes you sound like an asshole."

"I believe you're being obtuse again, Gilbert," she says, not sounding displeased.

At the center of the group, Papa has hardly shifted. I see now that what the vandal has sprayed across the billboard this time is the inexplicable—and yet, somehow, terribly damning—epithet **COMMUNIST SHITHEEL**. *Papa reaches out and uses his knuckle to trace the letter* C. *The thin-lipped expression on his face is unreadable. "It's enough to make a person think—" he starts, and lets the thought hang.*

My grandfather gently moves his knuckle around the letter O.

"Well, Henry, don't kill yourself. I'm going home to read the dictionary and try to take a piss."

Gil starts scraping his walker back in the direction of his house. When he reaches the edge of the driveway, he encounters some difficulty in trying to jerk the legs over the lip of the pavement, and I rush over to help. He throws his arm over my shoulder and I guide the walker up onto the driveway.

"Thanks, George," he says, pausing to catch his breath. Then, seeming less to speak to me than to himself, "Man's too old to get wound up like this. Especially over this. As if there's any real

difference between the two of them. One's a fool from Tennessee who wants to tell us how to live, and the other's a damn fool from Texas who wants to tell us how to live. Either way, we were going to end up with a fool. No difference." He crutches down to the sidewalk, his wife beside him and rubbing his back. They disappear around the hedge.

I return to my grandfather. With his palm pressed gently against the billboard, he looks almost prayerful, not unlike the photograph in a recent newsmagazine I have happened to see, of a penitent at the Wailing Wall in Israel.

"Papa," I say. I feel a sudden need to be reassured that I am not crazy. If there is anyone who can explain what I saw—what I thought I saw—it is Papa. "On the way here, I was on my bike, and I saw this cab . . ."

He turns and blinks at me.

Until now, I suddenly realize, Papa has not even been aware of my presence, does not even realize that the Desjardins have left, maybe doesn't even know they were here in the first place. Which is why, when he sees me now, sees my raw eyes and flushed cheeks, Papa construes their meaning in the only way that must seem possible to him.

The old man steps forward and embraces me, hard. "Don't worry, George," he says, "the paint will come off."

I open my mouth, close it.

We spend an hour soaking the pink paint off the billboard, and then my grandfather and I drive to the sporting goods store and browse until we find the right weapon.

1.

For armor, I went looking in the junk closet in my grandparents' garage. When I opened the door a cascade of twenty-year-old Halloween decorations and disassembled fishing poles poured out, along with a lot of other interesting things: moth-eaten life preservers, sheaves of ancient AFL-CIO newsletters wilted up like onion skins, a few ratty lures, a tire gauge with a cracked face, a Richard Nixon mask. I sat on a milk crate and put the mask on my hand, made it talk to me. I was in no hurry. "Maybe he'll just forget," said Tricky Dick. "McGlaughlins have long memories," I said. "But you're a Claiborne," said Dick, "I recognize you by the devilish toe." This surprised and silenced me. I sat in the cool dark of the garage and tried to think of some silly song for Nixon to sing. Maybe he had really forgotten, maybe he had come to his senses, I thought, but a moment later, through the wall, I heard the old man's voice calling for me.

I sighed, shook off the mask, and dug the softball equipment out from the bottom of the closet, a too big chest protector and a pair of cracked shin guards that reeked of mold. There was, however, no catcher's mask and no jock.

Around the back of the house, on the patio, I reported to my grandfather.

"Well, there's nothing to be done about it," he said. "I'll just have to aim low."

Papa was stoned, and eating peanuts. He took one salty piece at a time, rolling it between his fingertips, and finally plopping the peanut into his mouth. The automatic rifle lay balanced across the arms of his deck chair.

Gil, who besides living next door was also my grandfather's best friend, made a disapproving noise from the back of his throat. He was attempting to fire the black stub of a roach held in a twisted paper clip, flicking a lighter and sucking wetly.

My grandfather made an impatient hand-it-over gesture. This elicited another critical grunt, but then Gil passed over the works.

The afternoon, bright and dry, spun with pollen and carried the sound of children screaming from the public pool. Nearby, the five-hundred-shot ammo boxes were stacked up in a pyramid, like a display of beer cases at the supermarket. I put a hand in the pocket of my shorts and checked my package for reassurance.

Papa thumbed the light and drew deeply. The joint hissed to life, and he exhaled with relish. He raised a gray eyebrow at me. The corner of one bloodshot eye twitched. "What's the problem?"

I shifted my weight from foot to foot and tried to formulate a response that didn't sound too cowardly. The chest protector sagged around my torso. When I imagined being shot at, I saw myself running in circles, faster and faster, until my evasive maneuvers had gained the impossible quality of an accelerated film reel, and I was like a fool in a silent movie, doing a hotfoot jig on a bed of firecrackers. Then, an instant later, I saw myself take a direct hit in the sack, and plummet to the ground in a boneless heap, dead, balls pulverized.

I decided to abandon any pretence of courage. "Why don't you shoot at Gil, Papa?"

"With that walker? He's too slow."

"Thanks, kid."

"I said, 'I'll aim low.' " His eye was still twitching.

"High or low, Henry, it seems to me that the boy has ample reason for concern. His face and his ball bag are exposed.

"Your prudence is well earned, George." My grandfather's best friend waited a moment before adding an afterthought: "If it is wrong to be prudent about one's ball bag, then I, for one, would rather not be right." To punctuate this declaration, he threw me a wink and, simultaneously, stuck his hand under his armpit and squeezed off a long, wheezing fart.

Years ago, Gil had been an important official, a psychology professor and a dean at the university. Now he was just an old man, dying with uncommonly good cheer.

In his time, my grandfather, Henry McGlaughlin, had been an important official, too: the president for thirty years of Local 219. At a single word, he was capable of shutting down the Amberson Ironworks, and leaving the skeleton of an aircraft carrier shrouded on a dock for months, like a rich man's summer sloop. Of course, that too had been years ago, and now he was an old man, as well— but dying more slowly than his friend, and with no cheer to speak of.

I was fifteen years old and I wanted badly to please my grandfather, but I was a clumsy, unhappy boy, and I put little stock in the concept of trust, and none at all in faith. In the last few months my world had come to feel like a suit that I put on backward. Dr. Vic had offered me his opinion that this was all a phase—"a life passage," he called it—and that when I emerged, I would be a man. I asked Dr. Vic when he expected to emerge from his life passage. It took him a minute, but then he slapped his knee and said that was a good one.

Papa thrust the paper clip back to Gil. "Here, Gilbert. Stick this in your mouth."

When my grandfather turned back to me, his eyes were suddenly watery with feeling. "We're in this together, George," he said. "That's the thing."

This was a way of saying that we were a union of two, and in a union, you stood up for the next guy and you never broke ranks and you faced down the bosses and the finks and the goon squads with a solid front. "We're all in this together"; it was the essential promise that an organizer made to the workingmen who risked the livelihood of their families in an action. If another guy's family was hungry, you gave them half of what you had. If another guy came up short on his rent, you turned out your pockets. If another guy needed a hand, you reached out.

Here, in this place, Papa needed my help to confront a fink, a young fascist and vandal named Steven Sugar. And I needed somewhere to go, a safe place.

"Together," he repeated, and clasped his hands to show what the word meant.

I knew this was a practiced gesture, a piece of his old soapbox rally, but I couldn't doubt it.

If another guy needed a hand, you reached out.

So I went back to the garage, padded my crotch with a pair of athletic socks, pulled the Richard Nixon mask over my face, and stuck a southwester on my head. Then I ran back and forth in the sun for an hour while my grandfather tried to shoot me full of holes.

Separated by a distance of a hundred feet or so, Papa blasted at me from his position on the patio while I scrambled in and out of the stand of trees at the edge of the backyard. As the paintballs whizzed through the air above and around me, they tattered the leaves and burst against the trees with sharp, wet smacks. He yelled at me to stop moving so fast and play the part right, but I pretended not to hear. I only ran faster, spooked by the champagne pop of the rifle, cedar chips crunching beneath my feet, ozone hanging in the air, paint-stained branches slapping against my back. I ran until I was drenched through and seeing black spots out of Richard Nixon's eyeholes.

Then I heard Papa curse. That was enough, he called out. Goddammit that was enough.

I stayed in the trees until he finished unscrewing the automatic rifle from the tripod and tossed it to the ground with a thud. According to the sporting goods salesman this particular weapon, an IL-47, was the top of the line in paintball assault weapons; the IL stood for "Illustrator."

I emerged from the trees with my hands up. "I'm unarmed."

"Don't be a smartass."

Asleep in his lawn chair, Gil sat with his legs spread wide and a wet spot on the front of his pajamas. In the sun, his bald head was the color of skim milk, so pallid it hinted at blue. My grandfather had told me that the cancer was all through him, the way it had been with Nana toward the end. To me, that phrase, "all through him," described an image of the disease as a growth of black vines, twined around Gil's bones, thickening and choking, getting tighter and tighter, until eventually something would snap and that would be it.

After I shrugged off the catcher's equipment and hung Richard Nixon's sweaty face on the fence to dry, I went to Gil and shook him to make sure he was still alive.

He blinked several times, noted with only passing interest the dampness at his crotch, then looked around at the yard. "Looks like somebody got murdered out here. Murdered bad."

The yard did appear truly gruesome, as if someone had been knifed in the neck and then staggered around dramatically for hours, spouting from an endless reservoir of candy apple red arterial blood. There was paint all over the stand of larch trees, the boles and the branches and the leaves; paint on the patch of wild rhubarb and on the back fence; paint on the grass and on the dirt; paint on the igloo-shaped birdhouse, as if a tiny Inuit had exploded; and even on the pool, where an errant paintball had dissolved into a small pink slick.

Gil grunted himself up into his walker and clicked forward for a closer look. He stopped and peered at the scummy surface of the water. The pink slick drifted slowly, gathering anthers.

"You shot the pool, Henry," he said.

"It's my fault. I shouldn't have jumped around so much."

Gil was sanguine. "Don't blame yourself. Maybe the pool had it coming."

Papa squatted down with a groan and began to snatch up the ammunition wrappers littered on the ground. "Never you mind him, George, never you mind him at all. He's just a contrary old man. You can find one most anywhere. They like to sit off to the side, and criticize, and pick, and pester, and make a general nuisance of themselves.

"Back when I was organizing, we had a name for them: we called them Company Grannies, because when there was an action, all they did was stay at home, complaining and clutching their skirts, and when we finally got the bosses to the table, finally got them to sign the contract and give us our share, the Company Grannies would tell us that we should have made a better deal."

He hauled himself up and held on to the shooting tripod while he caught his breath.

It was from my grandfather that I came by my new height and gangly frame, but while he still maintained a couple of inches on me his spine had developed a pronounced hook, which locked him into the permanent stoop of a man who has been kicked in the shin. Papa hung over me with his rheumy brown eyes, batting them against the late light in a way that was almost girlish. My mother believed that losing Nana had broken his heart and scooped him out.

My mother didn't know about the sniper's nest we were assembling in the guest room.

"Of course, I've come to realize that this particular sobriquet was a grave slander against elderly females, most of whom can at least be counted on to make a fine dessert now and then, and who were at one time a useful part of society, but there you are.

"In any event, although this particular specimen will be dead soon, as you get older you should be prepared to a meet a great many more like him."

"That's true enough," said Gil. He held the roach clip up to the light, and daintily picked away a few tiny embers. "But I will guarantee you of one thing: Al Gore, the very man himself, would not approve."

"Do you want to shoot at me some more tomorrow?" I interjected this question hopefully.

Papa patted me on the shoulder. "Don't worry, George. You did your best. You did your part. I just needed to get a feel for the weapon. You just keep doing your part, help keep this old man on his toes, and everything will work out fine."

He gazed off across the paint-spattered lawn, and a thoughtful smile played across his face, as if he were seeing across a great distance to a beautiful vista that was invisible to us. "When the time comes, I'll plug the little son-of-a-bitch."

We dismantled the tripod and packed the rifle and the ammunition to take upstairs.

He ordered Gil to make himself useful and go around the front and stand by the sign to give us some perspective. "And roll up another one of those," he said, making a smoking gesture.

Then, when we were just inside, Papa stopped and turned back. He threw the sliding door open and stuck out his head to say one last thing: "And you leave Al Gore out of this, goddammit. He's suffered enough."

2.

In the guest room I remounted the rifle behind the small window that overlooked the front yard. Through the scope I sighted on Gil. Hunched over his walker, he was blithely rolling a spliff on the hood of my grandfather's Buick. A few feet away on the grass, the 15 × 15-foot sign was positioned at an angle to the street, to confront the drivers who drove north up Dundee Avenue, heading toward the South Portland mall and the I-95 ramp. From the back, the sign was a plain wall of pale blue plastic, but earlier, while I scrubbed off the spray paint, I memorized the contents of the opposite side, which were printed in large bold letters, stark and undeniable:

> Albert Gore Jr. won the 2000 election by 537,179 votes, but lost the presidency by 1 vote. DISGRACE. The leader of the free world is now a man who went AWOL from his National Guard unit, a huckster of fraudulent securities, a white-knuckle alcoholic, and a gleeful executor of the mentally handicapped. CRIMINAL. Our nation is in the midst of a coup d'état, perpetrated by a right-wing cadre that destroys the environment in the name of prosperity, hoards in the name of fairness, intimidates the voices of its critics in the name of patriotism, and wraps itself in the word of God. FARCE.

And below that there was a solemn ink portrait of Gore, underscored by the legend:

THE REAL PRESIDENT OF THE UNITED STATES.

I drew the curtain and tucked it over the rifle. The end of the barrel still poked from the corner of the open window, but in the shadow of the eaves it would be invisible from the outside, even if someone were looking.

The effort of carrying all of the gear upstairs had exhausted Papa. He collapsed into a straight-backed chair in the corner of the room and watched in silence as I reassembled the gun. There was a jar of peanuts on the side table. He uncapped it and fished around with one finger. He spoke without looking up. "Well, that should just about do it, I think. Yes, sir, indeed. That should do it. Your grandfather is now a full-fledged lunatic."

"What's that make me?" I asked.

"My henchman," he said. "How's Gilbert coming along?"

I bent down and looked through the Illustrator's scope. Gil was still picking through his battered peppermint tin of buds. "He's working on it."

Papa sighed. In the blue gloom, his face was tired and sunken. He crunched a peanut.

This was the room where, a few months earlier, my grandmother had lain in hospice.

A series of mostly black-and-white 5 × 9 photographs in plain frames crossed the walls in a band: Martin Luther King Jr., FDR, JFK, Walter Reuther, Mother Jones, Cesar Chavez, Joseph Hillstrom, and others, all of them dead, most of them martyred. During one visit my mother described the decorating motif as "Vintage Progressive." Emma wondered out loud if they might do something to brighten up the place. To this Papa replied very smartly that as far as he was concerned, the room couldn't be much brighter: the walls were "covered with stars." Unable to speak, Nana signaled her concordance with this declaration by raising one small wrinkled fist, like the black sprinters in the 1968 Olympics. To this, my parent threw up her hands. If I ever wondered why she got pregnant at eighteen, Emma said, there was all the answer I needed.

It was a few weeks later that I trotted upstairs with the newspaper to read my grandmother the latest travesty—the Bush Administration had pulled the country from the Kyoto Protocol—and discovered her staring at the photograph of Joseph Hillstrom, with that expression of recoil frozen on her face, as if Nana's last living act had been to take a sip of curdled milk.

Now, it was July, the summer of 2001, and my grandfather was alone, save for the company of his discontent, which was ample. I understood; I had problems of my own.

In the framed photograph above Papa's head, even Woody Guthrie seemed to have an idea of the direction things were heading. Woody was seated on a guitar case, his clothes white with dust, his jaw spattered with a sickly growth of beard and a ragged straw hat perched way back on his crown. On his face Woody wore the resigned grin of a man expecting to be punched and eager just to get it over with.

"Well? What do you think? Have I lost it?" Papa rubbed a palm over his twitching eye and blinked at the floor.

I examined my fingernails. "No," I said.

He glanced up, cock-eyed, still twitching.

"Maybe," I said.

"I don't know either, George." He pushed himself to his feet and his knees went through a series of rhythmic cracks, like a figure on the castanets. "But what about him, though—do you think he's crazy?"

Of course, by *him,* Papa meant Steven Sugar, his ex-Sunday paperboy, who I knew better as the commander of my high school's two-soldier chapter of the ROTC. The history of their dispute dated back to June, when my grandfather's Sunday *New York Times* began to arrive without the Travel section.

When Papa called to point out this discrepancy, the paperboy immediately barked that he would come over to discuss the problem "face to face, sir." Roughly ten minutes later Steven Sugar appeared on my grandfather's porch and dispensed a half-dozen severe cracks with the decorative brass knocker before Papa could get the door open.

A big round boy with a black brush cut and full freckled cheeks, Steven Sugar had a cuddly quality that was in no way offset by his full camouflage uniform. He listened to Papa's complaint at ramrod attention, his slight paunch jutting forward, jaw tipped up. In spite of this posture, however, my grandfather later said that he detected a smirking certainty about the boy, a glimmer of amusement in his eyes. It was a glimmer that my grandfather associated with petty-minded civil servants—state troopers, town selectman, postal clerks.

"I can assure you that I check each and every copy thoroughly, Mr. McGlaughlin," said Steven Sugar.

"Nonetheless," said the retired president of Local 219 to the ROTC Captain of Amberson County–Joshua Chamberlain Academy, "My Sunday *New York Times* lacks a Travel section."

"You must have lost it, sir," said Steven Sugar, then added helpfully, "old people lose things all the time."

This exchange instigated Papa's first complaint against the delivery service. In July, when the Style section started to disappear, too, and the Travel section had still failed to be reinserted, he lodged a second complaint. It was this protest which led, summarily, to the decision of the delivery service to remove Steven Sugar from his route; and then, to that now *ex*-paperboy's reappearance on Henry McGlaughlin's porch.

"Listen here, young man," said Papa, yanking the door open before Steven Sugar could slam the knocker again. "Your service was unsatisfactory. I voiced my dissatisfaction. You have apparently been fired. This was not my intention. My intention was to receive the entire Sunday *New York Times*, which I paid for. This is where my involvement in the matter ends. Your employment is wholly beyond my sphere of responsibility."

Steven Sugar's large face reddened.

Seeing how upset the boy was, Papa tried to soften the blow with some advice. "Well, do you have tenure? If there's some sort of tenure system for paperboys, then you might have some recourse."

"Recourse? Recourse?" The paperboy pulled off his camouflage hat and slapped it against his thigh.

At the bottom of the steps, his lieutenant, the only other member of our high school's ROTC, stood with their bicycles. A lanky, frail boy named Tolson—who, like me, would be a sophomore at Joshua Chamberlain Academy in the fall, while Sugar would be a senior— glared and squeezed the brake handles.

"Yes, recourse. That is, some means of appealing your termination."

"Fuck you," Steven Sugar told my grandfather, and flipped him off with both fingers. "You can go fuck yourself right in the ass with your recourse."

The paperboy climbed onto his bicycle and, with his lieutenant, made a couple of circles on the lawn, both of them flying double birds. Then they took off, Tolson ripping a divot with his back wheel, and Steven Sugar howling, "This isn't over, you shitheel!"

That was the part everyone laughed about. "Shitheel," said Gil, clearly delighted. "That's one I haven't heard in a while."

"It's old school," I said.

Gil cackled, waving smoke.

"Hey, Old School." My grandfather snapped his fingers for the bowl they were sharing. "Pass that along."

It happened that this incident nearly coincided with the delivery of my grandfather's billboard. He had composed the text some time after Nana died, and ordered it professionally made by a union printer in Providence.

"Take a good long look, George," Papa said to me when I came over to see the sign. He wore a big smile on his face as he tapped the text with a finger. "This is what democracy looks like." He moved his finger to the drawing of Al Gore. "And this: this is what a president looks like."

The first attack took place a week after that. Spray-painted across Al Gore's face, in glaring pink, the words: **GET OVER IT SHITHEEL! YOU LOST!**

From the get-go, there was only one suspect. "Get over it? Get over it?" my grandfather asked rhetorically, as the two of us rubbed at the paint with soapy sponges. "Who does this little terrorist think he is, George Will?"

Then, no sooner had the sign been cleaned than it was vandalized for a second time, and on this occasion Papa had stumbled out of bed to investigate a clatter outside. They were gone before he could make a positive identification, but down the street, he thought he saw a pair of diminishing forms on bicycles. There were also two other pieces of evidence: first, a second act of vandalism against the billboard—**LOVE IT OR LEAVE IT SHITHEEL!**—and perhaps more ominously, a hunter's flare that he discovered still smoldering in the hedge alongside the house.

Papa stomped out the flare, then went inside and called Gil. They had watched satellite television and smoked buds until first light, at which time Henry McGlaughlin went into action.

Summarily, he placed phone calls to Mr. and Mrs. Rodney Sugar of 113 Elkington Drive, then to the Amberson Township Police, and, finally, for good measure, the ACLU.

Papa offered no introduction to the Sugars, but went right to the crux: "Your son has impinged on my free speech, and I want to know what you plan to do about it."

"Pardon?" asked the groggy female voice on the other end of the line.

"My free speech has been impinged. Violated. Trod upon. My First Amendment right. By your son."

There was a moment of silence before Mrs. Sugar gathered her wits. "Free speech? At five-twenty in the morning? Are you serious? Well shit on you, you crazy old coot."

She hung up, but before lunch the Sugars' lawyer messengered over a response. *Mr. McGlaughlin*, the attorney wrote, *we are aware of, and sympathetic to, your recent loss . . . However, if this harassment continues, on behalf of my clients we are prepared to apply for a restraining order . . .*

The investigating police sergeant gave the area around the sign a cursory inspection, and grimly scratched his goatee with his unopened notebook. "Okay, chief," said the officer, "It does appear that we have a case of vandalism on our hands."

"Yes, my former paperboy—"

"I know, I know. But there's no proof. The parents say you've got the wrong man, and you're ready for the bughouse to boot. Now, that's not for me to say, but"—the officer paused, and made a point of sniffing the air—"are you aware that cannabis is illegal in the state of Maine, Mr. McGlaughlin?"

My grandfather took a deep breath and looked up at the sky. "Are you aware, Officer Corcoran, of a document called the United States Constitution? It has a list of amendments—laws, that is—the first of which gives me the right to free speech."

The officer flipped his notebook open, squinted at a blank page, and flipped the notebook shut again. "If that's how you want to play it, chief, that's fine with me." He put his hands on his hips and shook his head at the ground. He licked the mustache of his goatee with the tip of his tongue. "Let's face it, a sign like this, I bet it pisses a lot of people off.

"Tell you the truth, it kind of pisses me off. It's unpatriotic as hell if you ask me. Now look, I believe in free speech as much as the next guy, but not so far as this sort of garbage goes. What do you think about that, chief?"

"I think," said Papa, "that you have a very nice goatee, Officer."

The ACLU lawyer came third. Papa told her the whole story, and she listened, asking a few questions, but mostly staying quiet. When he finished, she apologized. "There's no angle, Mr. M."

"What about my free speech? How's that for an angle? You know, I gave money to you jokers when it meant something. I gave when Hoover was in office."

"Your free speech isn't being violated by an entity here, sir, just by a paperboy. Look, if your paperboy were being funded by an interest group, or backed by the KKK or something, I'd have this thing on the front page of *USA Today* tomorrow." Papa heard the hiss of compressed air as the ACLU lawyer opened a soda. "Besides, and I'm hardly being facetious here, but down in D.C. we've got Ashcroft probably planning to compile a database of everyone who's ever had fun before. If we let this guy out of our sight for a minute, he'll start having people scourged for picking their wedge on the Sabbath. Really, sir, and with all due respect to the good and honorable work you've done, when it comes to brass balls, Old Mary Hoover couldn't have budged the pair that Ashcroft is hauling around. Take my word, as an American citizen in the year 2001, a dink paperboy is not the worst problem you've got."

Of course, by this time, my grandfather's Sunday *New York Times* had become something else entirely. Which brought us up to the present day, and the third attack, the one that had convinced my grandfather to settle matters himself.

I could not recall ever having spoken to Steven Sugar, or even having heard his voice, although he was a familiar sight in the halls: a chunky kid two grades ahead of me, who clomped from class to class in his combat boots and baggy desert-toned fatigues, usually followed a few steps behind by the lieutenant, Tolson.

Still, before all of this—before **GET OVER IT SHITHEEL! YOU LOST!**

before **LOVE IT OR LEAVE IT SHITHEEL!** and, before **COMMUNIST SHITHEEL!** were scarred in blazing pink across my grandfather's billboard and Al Gore's face—I didn't know if I ever spared Steven Sugar so much as a single conscious thought.

Now I imagined him punching through the dark suburbs on his bicycle, the summer night rushing through his brush cut, the newspaper satchel packed with spray cans clattering against his hip, a vessel of absolute calm and purpose, locked and loaded, a true believer and an armed combatant. The vision amazed me, and a part of me envied him, this budding fascist who had fucked up my grandfather's Sunday *New York Times* and written right across his First Amendment rights. I could only marvel at his confidence, at his criminal's justification. I did not understand Steven Sugar's motives, but I sensed his satisfaction, like a dark mass on a radar screen, like an iceberg, and grand like an iceberg, too.

I pictured Steven Sugar, hunched under the tent of his blankets, as he crinkled through the purloined newspapers by flashlight. He turned over the last unsullied islands of the Mediterranean, the white beaches and the ancient piles of stone, and he licked his lips over column inches of the weddings of well-to-do young women in Manhattan, with Ivy League degrees and careers in handbag design.

What did it mean to him? Did he imagine laying waste to these beautiful landscapes, and rolling tanks through rustic villages? Did he fantasize of ripping these bright new wives from their honeymoons and their husbands? Or, maybe, he hated our little Maine town, and longed more than anything just to travel far away, to start again, and make his life in another country altogether. Was it possible that Steven Sugar read the wedding announcements for research, for that time ten years from now when he would be a surgeon (or a hedge fund tycoon), and it would be time to marry his own twenty-six-year-old producer of a children's television show (or director of marketing at a glossy magazine), his own pretty, pale-eyed Hannah (or Caroline)? Maybe it didn't mean anything to him. Maybe Steven Sugar stole from my grandfather's newspaper for the simplest reason—just because he could.

Just because he could. The idea raised the skin on my forearms and caused me to breathe through my mouth.

My grandfather placed an expectant hand on my shoulder, and repeated his question. "Well, what is it? What do you really think, George? Is he crazy, or he is angry?"

"No," I said. "I don't think Steven Sugar's crazy. I think he's just angry."

Papa squeezed my shoulder and walked across the room to the window. "Then that makes us even, because I may be crazy, but I surely am angry, too." The old man bent over the rifle and peered into the scope. "And I've come to realize that the only way to talk to these monsters is to speak in a language they understand."

3.

The difficulty of communication was, in fact, the source of my own personal distress. I wasn't getting along with my mother, and I didn't care to get along with Dr. Vic. Of late, I suffered not so much from a feeling that my voice wasn't being heard, as from a sense that I was speaking an entirely different language. Or perhaps, I thought, to their ears my voice was soundless, on the wrong frequency, like a dog whistle, and they only waited for the moment that my lips stopped moving to smile, and shake their heads, and explain what it was that I failed to understand.

We had moved into Dr. Vic's place that winter, a sprawling new three-story that sat right on the shore of Lake Keynes. From the window of my attic loft I had an obstructed panorama of the lake, which spanned a couple of miles across, toward pine-covered foot-hills and farther away, to a bald mountainside where tourists came to ski in December. This vantage point also offered a clear view of the deck, and the landing where Dr. Vic tied up his putt-putt and his kayak.

Earlier that summer they were engaged, and since the weather warmed up, my mother and her lover had kept a nightly ritual of dancing on the landing at the end of the deck. They took a portable stereo out with them, along with a stack of CDs, a couple of mugs, and a can of insect repellant, and sometimes stayed for hours, slow dancing until the early morning. Their object was to find their "wedding song," the perfect song for their first dance as a married couple.

The sounds of Dr. Vic's music collection drifted up in a tinny echo, and if I wanted I could watch them from my window. Instead, I sat beneath the sill, back against the wall, and hated myself for even wondering what song they would pick, for surreptitiously playing along with their stupid game. Between songs I caught snatches of their conversations, their laughter, the clink of their toasts.

Frequently, Dr. Vic's taste sent my mother into paroxysms of laughter, and I would hear her rolling around on the deck, overcome by it, as if he were the funniest guy in the world. The sound dropped through me like a heavy object released from a great height, and never seemed to hit bottom.

One night I heard her scream with delight at the discovery of a Don Johnson CD. It was like finding his porn stash, she whooped. My mother laughed and beat her bare feet on the deck.

"Come on," said Dr. Vic. "You liked him, too, you know you did. You know you never missed an episode."

This was porn, she howled, this was emotional porn. *Crockett Sings Just for You*! My mother began to weep as she laughed.

"Wait a second, wait a second. 'Heartbeat' is good. Seriously, you've got to admit that 'Heartbeat' is a pretty good song." Now Dr. Vic was snickering, too.

A few moments passed before my mother could speak again. She thought she'd fallen for a respectable country doctor, Emma gasped, but in actuality, she had fallen for a nine-year-old girl from 1984, and oh, my God, was it wrong that she loved him anyway? Because she did. She loved him, loved him, loved him.

Their kisses were inaudible, but I was old enough to know that was what came next. Sometimes they listened to CDs until the night turned gray, and after I fell asleep Dr. Vic's middle-aged music, the Wynton Marsalis and the Phil Collins and the terrible seventies pop

which all seemed to bear edible names—Bread and Juice Newton
and Humble Pie—infiltrated my subconscious and provided the
soundtrack for my dreams. I chased after them in these dreams, my
mother and her fiancé, as they strolled arm in arm along crowded
sidewalks and through parks and malls. I ran beside them and
jumped around and screamed for my mother to listen to me, to
fucking turn that shit off and listen to me, because I had something
to say, something very important to say. At most, Dr. Vic might
shush me, or my mother might give him a look of apology, but they
never stopped, and in the morning there were tears of frustration
crusted beneath my eyes. I was embarrassed by the childish ob-
viousness of these dreams, and the way that I could feel them
gathering inside of me even when I was awake, each angry ob-
servation floating up like a little black balloon, until night came
again and my sky jostled with them.

It seemed that I was letting go of those balloon strings all day long:
every time I saw him rub her shoulders while she sat reading a book;
every time I saw her standing outside with him in a cold drizzle,
holding the umbrella while he walked his dogs; every time we drove
somewhere and Dr. Vic told me to go ahead and take the front, and I
knew that it was something that they discussed in private and decided
to give me.

To them, I was just the jealous kid of a single mother, with no
understanding of sex or intimacy, or the difference between a lover's
love and a child's love, and why an adult needed both. To me, this
was a slanderous lie. Dr. Vic was the exception. We had lived all over
and my mother had dated all sorts of different men, and there was
never a problem before.

In Blue Hill, there had been Paul, the raccoon-eyed owner of a
pottery studio for tourists, who helped me fire and paint a cookie jar
in the shape of a Jerry Bear for Emma's birthday. When my mother
worked at the University of Maine, she dated a German graduate
student named Jupps, who would let me watch anything I wanted on
television, and laugh uproariously, no matter if the show was about
ski slope accidents, or the big bang. The first year we moved home to
Yarmouth, before Nana got sick and before my mother took the job

at the local branch of Planned Parenthood and met Dr. Vic, she went out with Dale, the editor of the local weekly, the *Amberson Common*. Dale and I used to play a game where I tried to guess the classifieds that he made up, things like,

Wanted:
SWM seeks cheeseburger, Coke, respect

CAN YOU PITCH?
Lefthander wntd. Must be bipedal, animate. Respondents should report immed to Fenway Park, Boston, MA.

After they broke up, Dale posted me a classified that said,

Old White Dude:
OWD can provide referncs, illeg firewrks, home remdies, etc. Cool kid always welc.

I liked them all—even Jupps, who reeked of mouthwash and sometimes unnerved me with his maniacal laughter. That was because these men simply accepted my presence, and let me determine the level of our interaction. They had, so to speak, paid their dues.

The evening after my grandfather used me for target practice, I offered to take Dr. Vic's two yapping little Pekinese—"the Laddies," he insisted on calling them—for a walk while dinner was on the patio grill. This was something I had been doing a lot lately, to Dr. Vic's obvious pleasure. "Even after the longest winter, there is a thaw," I overheard him whisper to my mother.

But my mother knew me better. Now, sitting nearby on a lawn chair, she indicated her suspicion with a deep breath.

"Don't put up with any guff from those rascals, okay?" said my mother's fiancé. He chuckled and sipped his glass of white wine. His clip-on sunglasses were slightly askew.

"Nice shades, Doc," I said.

"Thank ya very much," he said, like Elvis.

I turned from him to sneer at my mother. She shrugged, tapped her finger against the zipper of her shorts. I rolled my eyes at her. She tapped the zipper of her shorts again. I looked downward—then jerked up my fly and started into the house.

"You know, Emma, I think that our young George here, may just have stumbled upon one of the great secrets of manhood here," said Dr. Vic, and I didn't have to see the huge, open-faced smile that he was giving to my mother to know it was there. "Back in my single days, I took the Laddies from pillar to post and back again. It might seem a little devious, but a regular guy has to make his breaks where he can, and not everybody can play guitar. For a regular guy, a dog is the next best thing to being a musician. You might even say that the Laddies are 'The Bomb.'" He emphasized this statement with index finger quotation marks. "You might even say that they're 'The Shit.'"

This was typical of Dr. Vic, to make a big, cheesy production out of everything, even the names of his dogs. Every time he spoke, his wide doughy face opening up in a way that reminded me of the singing clams in Disney's *Alice in Wonderland*, I felt a little part of myself die from shame. In fact, I believed that Dr. Vic must be the most embarrassing person in the world.

To begin with, there were the little absurdist poems that he wrote about how much he loved my mother, and what he would do if she were suddenly transformed into something other than herself, something inanimate usually, like a toaster or a grape—

The Woman I Love Is A Grape (For The Purposes Of This Poem)
By Victor Lipscomb
If she were a grape and I was still an ape
I'd wait for days and try to think of some way
Not to eat her, to reanimate her
But if I had to, I'd be glad to

Because Emma is so sweet.

For our enjoyment, he taped these poems to the fridge, like a first-grader would his watercolors.

Then there was his music, of course, the awful songs Dr. Vic always listened to in his car and in his study, stuff like "Seasons in the Sun" and "Dreamweaver"; songs that were so damned impossible to stop singing to yourself they were like dippy little Post-it Notes pasted to the inside of your skull, and until the glue dried up and the note fell off, there was nothing you could do to defend yourself against the insipid, endless trickling of the Dreamweaver's synthesizer, or to keep from chanting, helplessly, over and over again, "We had joy, we had fun, we had seasons in the sun."

And Dr. Vic talked to his crossword puzzles; every time he found the answer "Yoko," or "Ono," he cried out, "There she is again!" like he was in a bingo parlor; and when he poured wine for my mother, he stood with a dish towel over his wrist and twirled the end of an invisible mustache while he waited for her to nod; and in restaurants, Dr. Vic liked to hand his credit card to the cashier and make an introduction, "Peter: Paul, Paul: Peter"; and finally—and I thought, most tellingly of all—there were the utility pants he wore, which drooped from the weight of all the hard candies and dog treats that he stuffed in the tiny pockets, so that much of the time he walked around with one hand holding up his belt, like a goddamned clown.

There was a horrifying optimism in everything he did, which struck me as completely false, even as I knew that he could not be more sincere—that he was, really, incapable of insincerity. Everything about him—his clomping steps, his bright, solid-colored L.L. Bean shirts, the deflated tube of a belly that hung over his belt—testified to this irrefutable fact.

Dr. Vic could be wounded, but he could not be discouraged. When he told me that all of this was "a life passage," I could see in his eyes that he was actually imagining some abstract tunnel in his own mind, with a bright light at the end, and the sound of chirping birds and jingling ice cream trucks.

Perhaps there was nothing more at the heart of my dislike for my mother's fiancé than simple incredulity. I was the son of a single mother. I had lived in neighborhoods where ice cream trucks didn't go. It seemed to me that good will could only carry a person so far, and after that, you were on your own.

How this tenet translated into my current sabotage campaign was not completely clear even to me, but I knew this was not the time for hesitation, or half measures.

In the pantry freezer I retrieved the small plastic bag hidden under a mound of ice behind a stack of swordfish steaks. I slipped on an oven mitt and herded the Laddies into the front yard and down to the meadow that lay a few hundred yards west of the house. Well trained by weeks of practice, the two Pekinese bolted forward in full play mode. They dashed ahead and then dashed back to implore me to hurry up. Their entire hind ends wagged with enthusiasm.

"Okay, okay," I said, and pulled one of the frozen turds out of the bag and hurled it across the field. The Laddies tore after the soaring brown lump, disappearing in a wake of trembling blue bonnets.

The notion that there was anything cruel about teaching my prospective stepfather's dogs to fetch their own feces, or that there was something more than a little demented about the trouble that I had gone to—sneaking outside after dark to pick up these pieces of crap and then freezing them so that they could be thrown—did occur to me at a few odd moments. Luckily, I was usually able to slough off such attacks of conscience. If this was a war—and it was—would a real soldier—like Steven Sugar—be able to worry about a couple of crap-eating toy dogs who weren't even smart enough to have their own names? Somewhere along the line, probably in a Vietnam movie, I had picked up the term "collateral damage," and it seemed to apply quite nicely to the situation at hand.

I even had a line I wanted to use on Dr. Vic, and I imagined myself saying it like Gil, with a wink and a smirk, punctuated by a big, jolly armpit fart. "Seems to me that there's nothing worse than a shit-eating dog," I would wryly observe, and then wait a moment before adding, "except maybe two shit-eating dogs."

After a few tosses the frozen turds inevitably began to soften, and I quickly worked through the bag, chucking the shit into the high grass until my shoulder started to click. The dogs were relentless, though, tumbling off in pursuit and returning with wild foaming grins, the hard black biscuits clamped in their jaws.

Somewhere around the twentieth throw, one of them limped back, dropped a turd, and collapsed at my feet. The dog gave a few strangled retches and panted heavily. Its eyes slid anxiously back and forth; the dog coughed, and seemed to pant harder.

Sensing his brother's weakness, the other Laddie darted in and snatched up the crap, then bolted into the grass to hoard his prize.

The sick Pekinese flopped onto its side. I knelt down, feeling my stomach give a twist. "Shit poisoning," I thought to myself, unsure if such a condition even existed.

I laid a hand on the animal's flank, and he lurched up. He looked up from beneath his mop tassel bangs and grinned. The dog licked my palm. I let him for a moment before realizing where his tongue had been. I slapped his snout. The dog jerked away and yipped in protest.

"Jesus, okay," I said. "Okay, I'm sorry."

Leading them inside, I reminded the dogs that I didn't feel sorry for them. "You don't even know any better," I said.

My mother watched me grab a handful of dog bones from the cookie jar. The Laddies started crunching happily. She blew a strand of dark hair from her eye and nodded questioningly at the oven mitt still on my hand. I shrugged and crumpled it back in its drawer.

I'm thirty-three years old and I can damn well do what I please, my mother wrote.

As a form of nonviolent protest I had stopped speaking to her. Not deigning to explain the nature of my demonstration, or even that it was a demonstration, I simply started carrying around a yellow legal pad for those occasions when communication was unavoidable. Maddeningly, my mother had responded by refusing to speak to me as well, and purchased her own yellow legal pad. Now, instead of yelling at each other, we argued by shoving our legal pads back and forth across Dr. Vic's dinner table.

This particular argument started with the oven mitt. What had I been doing with it, my mother wanted to know, and why did it smell so funny? My evasions quickly led to the inevitable destination of all our arguments these days, to the real heart of the matter. That is: Why are you doing this to me? Have you looked at the man sitting across the table? That foolish-looking man over there? The roly-poly one with the American flag tie thrown over his shoulder? You're going to marry him? That guy? Him?

How can you be so stupid? How could anyone be so stupid?

I've done a lot of stupid things in my life, George Claiborne, not the least of which was giving birth to a child at the age of nineteen. However, that particular error in judgment has turned out to be the greatest joy of my life, in spite of your current behavior. A lot of people called me stupid when I kept you. Stupid and I have a pretty fair track record.

I knew I was vulnerable on the matter of my conception, so I responded by jotting down a favorite stanza from one of Dr. Vic's poems:

> *If she were a toaster, I'd make a toaster-coaster*
> *If she were a toaster, I'd be a toaster-boaster*

As she wrote, my mother pressed down so hard the pen made a whining sound. *What does any of this have to do with him? He's never done a thing to you. Although it would be hard to blame him if he did.*

I hated the way she underlined things. *You're a blackleg.*

You're a little shit, and furthermore, you don't have the first idea what that word means. You're just reaching for the nearest pejorative, George. This isn't the legend of one of your grandfather's strikes. This is the story of a little boy who still has a hell of a lot of growing up to do.

At the end of the table Dr. Vic sawed morosely at a chicken breast. He dabbed at his damp face with his patriotic tie. "I feel like I should get a notebook," he said, but no one answered.

While she awaited a response, my mother maintained a posture of nunlike serenity, hands folded, long black hair tucked neatly behind her ears. Her first streak of gray had appeared that spring; a fine, silvery tributary of her part that I hoped was a biological reaction to her agonized conscience, although to this stage she had conceded nothing. A few mornings, in the bathrooms of those crummy apartments in Orono and Blue Hill and Waterville, after a night of drinking with her friends or her lover, I held that hair back while she vomited.

My grandparents had taught me about sides, about the line that separated one side from the other side, and the impossibility of straddling that line. You were either in, or you were out. Until Dr. Vic came along, the men in my mother's life had always gone about trying to get on *our* side. But when it came to Dr. Vic, my mother told me that some things were not open to negotiation. All the years of moving from one town to another while she made her hiccuping way toward a bachelor's degree, all the years of crummy apartments with three fuzzy channels and hose showers and cat hair in the corners, all of it had been an alliance of convenience. Now I saw that the two of them, Emma and Dr. Vic, were on their own side, and I was on the other, and there was a very real line separating us. Now she looked at me like that, with her hands clasped and her back straight, like a study hall proctor.

". . . And I've come to realize that the only way to talk to these monsters is to speak in a language they understand." That was the way Papa had put it.

I wanted to throw gravy in her face.

He let Nana die, I wrote and sent my notebook skidding across the table.

Later that night, she knocked on my door, and when I opened it, just stood there. Her cheeks were stained with tear tracks, and her eyes seemed to be directed at a point somewhere over my shoulder.

"Well?" I asked.

Her hand flew up, and I heard the report of the slap before I felt it. The sound seemed to expand, to fill the entire house, to carry across the lake and into the wooded hills, like a gunshot. I didn't even take a step back; I was too startled.

My mother's expression never changed. Her gaze still focused on that place behind me. Emma reached into her pocket and threw a balled up note rattling across the floor. Very softly, she closed the door.

When I was alone the memory of her tear streaks gave me solace, even as I forced myself to cry a little. The note said, *Someday, you will be ashamed of the way you acted tonight.*

I was further comforted by the slamming of doors downstairs, and the echoes of my mother yelling, and of her lover—my late grandmother's oncologist and my prospective stepfather, Victor Lipscomb, M.D., Ph.D.—trying to calm her. His deep voice pleaded up through the heating vents: "Emma, honey," and, "Come on," and, "We just have to keep working at this." Nor was I unhappy to register, as I drifted to sleep, the quiet of a night without music.

I awoke from a nightmare at dawn, gasping and rubbing the sheets against my chest, attempting to wipe off the words that Steven Sugar had spray-painted on my body.

In the nightmare I was tied to a tree, and the Richard Nixon mask was on my face, making it hard to breathe. From the shadows, a figure emerged; Steven Sugar was dressed in his army fatigues and his eyes were my mother's eyes, dark and unforgiving. He held a spray can.

As I wriggled and cried for help, he patiently filled in the letters, bending the words around my torso in cheap red paint. **GET OVER IT SHITHEEL! YOU LOST!**

4.

Stationed in the guest room, my grandfather and I kept watch through the next afternoon, and waited for Steven Sugar to make his move. The lights were off to keep the room cool, and the main source of illumination came from outside, through the curtains. The filtered light spilled across the room in a bright orange column. Papa sat in the chair alongside the rifle and tripod, and flicked back the curtain every minute or so to see if anything was moving on the C-curve segment of the street that was visible from the window.

For the most part, we sat in silence. I had simply showed up and plopped down on the guest room bed. Papa said, "Howdy," without glancing from his window. In the attic I had discovered a box of my mother's brittle old Choose Your Own Adventure paperbacks— where you moved through the story according to your own strategic decisions—and I absently paged through one entitled *The Alien's Tomb*. Out of the corner of my eye, I kept an eye on Papa; light fell across his forehead, and made him look young. I wondered if he was thinking about my grandmother.

If you trust the dead alien, and follow him through the doorway into the Forever Country, turn to page 12. If you retrace your footsteps to the nearest Time Pod, turn to page 34.

"You should be out with your friends." He lifted the corner of the curtain, grimaced at the street, and dropped it back down.

"I haven't got any," I said. "Not really."

He sucked on a peanut, then slowly ground it up. "I hold this claim in dubious regard."

"We moved too much." My mother and I had lived in six towns so far during my school-age years, which in adolescent terms made me a kind of Okie. It wasn't that I didn't get along with people, or nod to friendly acquaintances in the halls at school. Rather, I thought, very rationally, that growing up was embarrassing enough without trying to gain an invitation to the party. Maybe I was more lonely than I let on; maybe after two years in the Amberson school system it was time to accept that my boyhood fantasy of staying put in one place had finally become a reality. Then again, I found it hard to accept Dr. Vic as a part of any dream come true.

If you stay with the jackass and his shit-snarfing dogs, turn to page 11. If you ramble on to another town, turn to page 45.

"A boy ought to have friends, George."

"I'm fifteen."

"Pardon me. A teenager ought to have friends, George."

"I get along with people."

"Well," he said.

"Well," I said.

He pulled back the curtain, looked, let go of it. My grandfather cast a sideward glance in my direction. I raised my eyebrows at him and brushed at the collar of my T-shirt. He snorted, flicked the peanut crumbs from his button-down.

"You're afraid, aren't you? It's a risk, isn't it? To try and break the ice?"

"Sure." I wasn't about to deny it.

Papa rocked back and patted his knees and nodded, as if that just about made everything obvious. "Well, you're a goddamned freak, aren't you?"

This statement hung in the air between us for a minute. My grandfather stared at me with perfect assurance; I was too baffled to be hurt.

"Thanks a lot," I said, finally. "That helps. That really helps a lot."

"I mean, kids are curious. They love freaks."

"Jesus, Papa. This is great. Do you think you might be able to give me a kick in the nuts, too?"

"No, no," he said, and drew his foot up over his knee. He patted his slipper. "Your toe. Show your toe. It's a conversation starter. It's interesting."

I slumped back on the bed.

"Let me see it," he said. "Come on."

"See this," I said, and showed him my middle finger.

The old man cackled, then turned his attention to the watch.

So, I read the rest of *The Alien's Tomb,* and following a series of wrong turns and misadventures, discovered that the best I could do was to get back to the place where I had started.

At some point, I nodded off, and woke up to see Joseph Hillstrom staring back at me. The man in the black-and-white photograph was hatchet-faced, and his eyes held a spooky clarity, almost like a blind man's eyes. It was a gaze that seemed not so much to look into the camera, as beyond the camera. I rolled away from him.

Beside the window, Papa was still in his chair, and slightly slumped, so that now the sunlight fell on his hair, and revealed the pink scalp beneath.

I turned onto my back and blinked at the ceiling, letting myself come all the way up.

It was Nana who had told me the story of Hillstrom, the song-writer and organizer, convicted on circumstantial evidence and executed in Utah in 1915 for killing two men in a robbery. My grandmother said that on the night of the killing, a witness claimed to have seen Joe throw a pistol far into a field, although the weapon was never recovered. Furthermore, the police knew that one of the dead men managed to fire off a shot; and when they came to see Joe, they discovered he was bedridden with a bullet wound. Joe said he was shot defending a woman, but would not reveal her name, for it was a question of honor. On the eve of his execution, Hillstrom had been lucid and fearless enough to write to a friend, *Don't Mourn! Organize!*

And he was the last thing Nana had ever seen. I could feel sweat on my forearms. I didn't know why I was suddenly uneasy. I rolled back to look at the photograph of the dead man again.

"Old Joe is a kind of saint to the Movement, Georgie," Nana had said to me, and in the next moment, crossed her eyes to break the mood of seriousness created by a story concerning murder and execution and martyrdom. I was about seven years old at the time. "Not, mind you, that the gentleman in Rome with the silly hat and the special red telephone up to God is liable to recognize him any time soon."

I forced myself to hold the eyes in the photograph, and after a moment the uneasy feeling passed. I supposed that was how a saint should look: calm and guiltless, and made of steel that no pagan bonfire could ever melt. I supposed that was what Nana had seen.

"Gore would have rolled back NAFTA."

Papa announced this apropos of nothing.

I sat up.

My grandfather still sat as before, slumped, the light falling on his white hair. He had been awake all along.

"That's Gil's new line. NAFTA this, NAFTA that." He gave the curtain an irritable snap. His good humor seemed to have passed. "And if it's not one *N* word, it's another." He cleared his throat, and made a disgusted pronouncement: "*Nader.*

"Al Gore did more for working people last night, while he slept in his bed, than Ralph Nader has done in his whole life. That old man likes to needle me, George, and he knows how to do it."

"What's NAFTA?" I asked.

"A mistake," said Papa, and seemed to fumble for something more, before settling on "A well-intentioned mistake. A flawed document of collective bargaining. A compromise. *A com-pro-mise.* Something that son-of-a-bitch Nader wouldn't know the first thing about." Papa pulled up the corner of the curtain. "I get damned weary of all the blue cars," he said.

On my evening ride back from my grandparents' house I felt a wiggle in my rear tire, and pulled over to check it—a flat. Choosing between calling Dr. Vic to pick me up, and swinging by the clinic to get a lift to the gas station from my mother, I opted for Emma. I coasted the half mile to the professional park that housed the Planned Parenthood clinic and a number of other doctors' offices.

What I hadn't anticipated, however, was that the GFAs had attacked again.

My mother was out front, working with a bottle of Goo Gone and a putty scraper to scour off a fake picture of a mauled infant that had been plastered to the glass doors. This infant appeared not so much to have been aborted as microwaved, and then dipped in red candle wax. For that matter, the infant appeared not to be an infant so much as a doll.

I braked at the curb, and she shook her head at me. Tendrils of hair stuck to her cheeks and forehead.

"You're just in time, George," said Charlie Birdsong, the clinic's head security guard, who sat on an upside down paint bucket with his shirt off, perusing an issue of *Elle Girl*. "The GFAs have been busy with their Photoshop program again, and this time they used a buttload of Krazy Glue. And that's with special emphasis on the Krazy, doc."

Echoing this sentiment, my mother sighed wearily and knocked her skull a few times against the papered glass doors.

GFA was shorthand for God's Favorite Assholes, the name my mother had awarded to the group of Evangelical Christians who maintained an isolated community in the scrubby hills north of Amberson. Every once in a while I'd see one around town, at the supermarket or Sam's Club: the female GFAs tended to be bright eyed, and almost squirrel-like in the way they would challenge your gaze and at the same time rush past you with a giant cube of generic toilet paper; the typical male GFA was more dour in his bearing, lank haired, and often outfitted in the kind of T-shirts you could buy for a dollar at gas stations, featuring air-brushed illustrations of wolves or caribou. These good Christians eked out their livelihood largely by selling buckets of fishing worms to tourists, and otherwise mostly kept to themselves.

The exception to their isolation, unfortunately, was my mother's clinic. Until recently, they had limited themselves to staging conventional—if exuberant—pickets in front of the building, blasting Christian rock music from the back of their rusted blue minivan and using a megaphone to address the pregnant women who were rushed across the parking lot in a protective wing of volunteers. "Leave your whoremaster and come unto the Lord!" one particular GFA harpy was infamous for howling as she stomped back and forth on the roof of the minivan.

Recently, however, the GFAs had apparently discovered the power of Photoshop and taken to creating enormous posters of tattered fetuses—like the one now plastered to the glass doors of the clinic—and applying them with industrial epoxy during random, late-night guerrilla attacks. Vandalism, it seemed, was on the rise all over town.

(After the first assault on Papa's billboard, my mother had pointed out that the vandalism fit the GFA's pattern. "No," said my grandfather after a moment's thought. "It's the damn paperboy. Those kooky wormdiggers are on a mission from God. They're above politics."

There was no reason to believe that the GFAs were coached by Steven Sugar—or vice versa—but if the two ever did get together, there was no telling what kind of damage they might do.)

What's NAFTA? I asked my mother. After fifteen minutes of pouring over *Elle Girl* with Charlie my mind had started to wander.

She stepped back from the glass and took the legal pad from me. *Seriously?* My mother plucked one of my shirtsleeves to dry her sweaty hands.

I yanked away, and tapped the question impatiently with my finger: *What's NAFTA?*

My mother blew a damp bang out of her eyes and checked her watch. Her face was flushed with exertion and the poster hung in tenacious ribbons from the glass. Emma shook her head. *Ask Charlie. I want to finish dealing with the slaughtered unborn here in time to get home for the news.*

"Charlie, what's NAFTA?"

A sallow-faced, affectless Native American man, Charlie was as unimposing as any armed person could possibly be; along with his habit of whiling away his time at the security gate by reading the women's magazines from the lobby, the price sticker—$241.99—was still stuck to the bottom of the butt of his pistol.

Without looking up from *Elle Girl*, Charlie said, "NAFTA. Okay. I used to work at a shoe factory. Full health benefits, eighteen-fifty an hour, vacation, and a parking space based on seniority.

"Now, some poor destitute prick in Guatemala is working in my old company's new factory for, like, a buck an hour. Meanwhile, now I work here, get accused of murder by white people, ten dollars an hour, and have to pull weekends in the bedding department at Filene's to make ends meet. Plenty of parking spaces, too, but I had to sell my car. Now I ride the bus."

"What about the union?" I asked.

Charlie spat a laugh. "What about the union? Clinton was a Democrat, wasn't he?"

I contemplated this for a few moments, as my mother's scraper made a sound like a shovel blade being dragged across a rock.

Charlie flipped a page, sighed. "I'm telling you, it really sucks to be a fat girl."

My mother dropped me at the Citgo, and I spent a couple of minutes at the air station, pumping my tire up. Through the scarred window I could see a glass cooler filled with Styrofoam tubs of GFA fishing worms. Each label was adorned with a small hand-drawn gold cross and the promise that these were FAT WORMS! NONE FATTER!

A car honked and I turned around to see Gil and Mrs. Desjardins in their Land Rover. They waved me over. I rolled my bike over to the driver's side—Gil's side—and he lowered his window.

"Afternoon, stud," said Mrs. Desjardins, leaning over and blowing a kiss.

"It's evening, Lana."

"Evening, stud." Mrs. Desjardins smiled at me. Her lipstick was a radioactive green. She was dressed in a glittering cocktail gown.

"How's it going, kid?" Gil was wearing his silky black pajamas.

"Fine," I said. "I'm kind of wrestling with this whole NAFTA thing, though."

He took this in stride. "Okay, run in the gas station, fetch me a Coke Slurpee, some Twizzlers, a jar of petroleum jelly, and some Aleve." Gil snapped a twenty-dollar bill from his pocket. "Then you can keep the change and I'll tell you all you need to know about NAFTA."

The clerk gave me a skeptical look and rang up the purchases. "How old are you, kid?" he asked. The clerk was a Goth-type in his early twenties, with rings in each of his nostrils and a fork tattooed on his Adam's apple.

"Excuse me?"

"Forget it." He shoved the things in a paper bag and told me to scram.

In the lot I passed the bag through the window to Gil and he handed it off to his wife. "Any trouble with Count Dracula in there?"

"No," I said, not wanting to get into it.

"Right, then," said Gil, "NAFTA."

I nodded.

"Between you and me?"

"Sure," I said.

"I'll just close my ears, then," said Mrs. Desjardins.

"All you need to know about NAFTA, my boy, is this: it was inevitable. Your grandfather is going to tell you that it was a compromise. I'm telling you that it was erosion." There was a merry crinkle around Gil's eyes. It occurred to me that in a few months, or a year, I would probably be looking down on his face as he lay cushioned in velvet, hands folded on his chest. "The lobbyists had been chiseling away for fifty years. The center, politically speaking, would not hold, George. Democrats, Republicans, it doesn't matter. The money needs more money."

I nodded.

"You understand?"

"Not really."

Gil chuckled, and fingered at the top button of his black pajamas. "Look, it's a shell game. The politicians said it was about 'Free Trade.' Bullshit. It was about 'Cheap Labor.' Just like every other manner of deregulation in this country, NAFTA was just another way of pumping up corporate profits under the auspices of the 'American Way.' Gore went along with it, just like all the rest of them. Every single one of them—corporate flunkies, hypocrites— with their hands out and their eyes closed. That's the System. Gore, Bush, they're both part of it, they both run on the same track. Stick a quarter in their backs, and they'll race all day.

"And, as much as Henry disparages him, it so happens that there was, in fact, only one candidate who didn't belong to the system." He winked at me. "And that was Big Ralph."

"Big Ralph," repeated Mrs. Desjardins with a little trill, "oh, dear me."

One of my earliest memories was of my grandmother setting the needle down on a scratchy Phil Ochs 78, and his guitar strumming a melody, at once flat and deep, as if he were playing at the bottom of a hole and singing up to us:

I dreamed I saw Joe Hill last night
Alive as you and me
Says I, "But Joe you're ten years dead."
"I never died," says he.
"I never died," says he.

This memory carried strong associations with the no-bake cookies she used to make and *The New Testament Bible* that we used for my reading lessons. On the title page of that thin blue book, I remembered the minuscule parenthetical that Nana added in her cramped cursive:

THE NEW COVENANT
COMMONLY CALLED
THE NEW TESTAMENT
OF OUR LORD AND SAVIOR
JESUS CHRIST (ᴅ-ʙᴇᴛʜʟᴇʜᴇᴍ)

"It doesn't matter if you believe in God, Georgie my love," Nana said to me once as she rubbed a wet washcloth over my chocolate-stained chin. (She was the only one who could ever call me Georgie and hope to live.) "But it's imperative that you understand Jesus was a real person. It's imperative that you realize that he was exactly the sort of man that these so-called Christians today would have pilloried for being an agitator and a Communist.

"They killed him because he was a mouthy liberal."

In her final weeks, my grandmother made no last-minute conversion or requests for spiritual assistance, although once, after Dr. Vic administered a heavy dose of morphine, she commented on the tintype of Jesus on the wall, the one that was nestled between the black-and-whites of Emma Goldberg and Joseph Hillstrom. Papa had been sitting alongside the bed, holding her hand. "When they dope me up, the Jesus gets so small, Henry. I keep expecting him to disappear altogether."

My grandfather cleared his throat.

"Then we'd have a white space right in the middle of everything. What would we do then, Henry?"

Papa gave a relieved smile, as if he'd already considered such a scenario, that Jesus might someday dwindle away to nothing, and leave the wall gaping. "Gore. How would you like that, Geraldine? We could put up a nice one of Al Gore."

The old woman's eyes cleared then, and for a moment she was the woman who had played catch with me in the yard when I was small, winding up and stinging it into the pocket of my mitt; the woman who cried, "Is that my devil-toed grandchild?" when I answered the telephone; the woman who sat at my grandfather's right hand, and demanded that the flunkies from the corporate office give the workers their fair share, or else their board of directors might as well just pull up a few lawn chairs and watch the pigeons crap on the dry-docked skeleton of their aircraft carrier until it turned completely white.

Nana squeezed Papa's hand, and at same time, met my eyes with a knowing, mirthful gaze. "Do you think this mean Al Gore died for our sins, darling?"

And that was how a photograph of Al Gore had come to take Jesus' coveted position to the left of Joseph Hillstrom, and the Son of God had been relegated to a spot above the light switch.

The next day, as I took my turn in the rifle seat and Papa stretched out on the bed, I contemplated the odd juxtaposition of the clean-cut politician in his navy blue suit, and the hatchet-faced convict in the high collar.

If you think that Al Gore would have rolled back NAFTA, turn to page 32. If you think that Joseph Hillstrom could eat Al Gore's gizzard with a smile on his face, turn to page 44.

I looked away, flipped up the edge of the orange curtain. Except for a single squirrel, painstakingly dismantling an acorn in the shade of the hedge, nothing moved. A shiny blue pickup came around the bend, and disappeared a dozen yards later around the edge of my grandparents' roof. I dropped the curtain. From the bed, Papa's breath came shallow.

"Papa," I said.

He didn't answer. He was asleep. Maybe it was better that way. There was something I wanted to ask, just say out loud, just to try on. His hands were folded in his lap.

"Doesn't it seem like—Joseph Hillstrom—with the gun, and with the bullet wound, and the mystery woman thing—doesn't it seem like—"

"—No." His voice was clear and hard; it was like a voice a behind my ear, and I jumped a little in my seat.

"No?"

"Suspicion is not proof, George. Suspicion is never proof. 'Suspicion' is how they see things the way they want to see them. It's an excuse for cracking down. Bosses use it, cops use it. Presidents use it. And it counts for nothing." His hands lay still on his belt buckle and his eyes remained closed.

Then what about Steven Sugar? What have you got him besides suspicion? I wrote on my legal pad. If my summer of correspondence had taught me anything, it was that it was easier to be a smartass when you didn't have to use your mouth.

I turned over the corner of the curtain to see an aqua-colored sports car round the corner. "You're right about the blue cars," I said, tore off the sheet, and crumpled it up in my pocket.

Late that afternoon, we switched positions, and I drowsed off on the bed. I jerked awake at the champagne pop of the rifle, and the sound of Papa cursing, "Goddammit!"

We rushed downstairs, and out to the lawn.

The squirrel lay twitching in the grass, in a pool of red paint. The paintball had hit him in the head; his neck appeared terribly twisted, corkscrewed almost. The animal's limbs fluttered and swam in the paint, as if it were trying to dig itself out of something, sand or mud, but just kept sinking.

Papa ran a hand through his hair. "I saw him out of the corner of my eye, George. It was—reflex."

The squirrel stopped moving and a little while later I dug a grave in the backyard with my grandmother's trowel. Gil crutched over with his peppermint tin. He rolled a joint, but my grandfather took a pass. "I feel like shit, Gil. A squirrel, for God's sake."

"Back in Nam, I believe this is what they called 'collateral damage.'"

"Yup," I said. I knew all about it.

"Oh, shit," said Papa. "Shit, shit, shit."

Gil fired up the spliff. In the cooling twilight, the dirty burn of the cannabis mixed with the deep green scent of the full summer trees, and produced a carnival smell, sweaty and sweet at the same time.

My grandfather tamped the turned ground with the toe of his shoe. He shook his head. He had been shaking his head almost continuously since we found the paint-spattered body.

"But it's not as though you shot the president, Henry. It is just a squirrel," said Gil.

"It's a travesty is what it is," said Papa. He went inside, and slammed the sliding door shut.

Gil raised an eyebrow at me. He leaned on his walker and extended the smoldering joint. "Toke?"

I shook my head. I was curious, and not overly self-aware, but drugs never seemed worth it. "When people in my family get high, they get arrested. Or pregnant at eighteen."

"Or they kill squirrels," said Gil, and winked at me as he helped himself to a long, hard draw on the spliff.

When I left to go home, Papa was in the bathroom, blowing his nose very hard and running the faucet.

5.

The following morning, we reconnoitered in Papa's Buick. Gil drove the Skylark in slow loops through the dozen blocks of their north Amberson neighborhood while I sat in the front and watched to make sure he didn't drowse off. Papa sat in the rear with the rifle under a blanket at his feet. My grandfather hoped that we might catch Steven Sugar unawares, and beat him at his own game.

We undertook these missions in the afternoons, when the well-kept row houses were either empty for the workday, or curtained against the heat. A few sprinklers swepts back and forth, and on the lawn of one local eccentric, a rank of glitzy whirligigs detected a faint wind, but the majority of movement was limited to the heat snakes that curled up from the macadam.

"Henry, you realize that we've transformed into disaffected young black men? Armed gang members who cruise the streets for their enemies? The parallel is unavoidable." Gil made this remark as he steered us past the whirligig house.

It had been over a week since Steven Sugar spray-painted **COMMUNIST SHITHEEL!** across Al Gore's face in hot pink, the longest interval between attacks so far. July had melted into August. As the miniature windmills stirred, they spilled colored speckles across the road.

"I'm not complaining, mind you," said Gil, "I actually kind of like being a disaffected young black man." He gave me a bloodshot sidelong wink.

Papa took a peanut from the can in his lap and popped it in his mouth. My grandfather wore the kind of sunglasses that are given out at an optometrist's office to protect a patient's dilated eyes: a pair of filmy orange squares.

Gil's eyes fluttered and his head nodded. The Skylark drifted left. I shook his shoulder, and he snapped up straight. "You know, Henry, like in the rap music. Compton and South Central. Long Beach."

"Like a drive-by," I said.

"Old school," said Gil.

"It's not the same," my grandfather said, finally unable to contain himself.

"It's not?"

"We're not out to kill the little shit. That's the difference. We're sending a message."

"The methodology's the same. It's a hit, Henry."

"No, it is not." Papa stomped his foot several times in the backseat well. "It is not."

We drove past a postage stamp of a park, a tetherball with no ball, a slide, a few benches, and trees. A tabby cat lay on its belly in the grass, waiting for a pigeon to get careless.

"Back when I was organizing," Papa began, and I had to stare down at my shoes to conceal a smile. This opening gambit was one of my mother's favorite pieces of shorthand, our family's equivalent of the "When I was a boy, I had to walk to school . . ." speech.

If I complained about the too soft spray of the showerhead in our latest apartment my mother was wont to say, *Back when I was organizing*, and sounding her best and gruffest Papa imitation, *we considered ourselves lucky indeed if, on occasion, the company goon squads deigned to release us from our cages to bathe in a rainstorm.*

The grin was still curling the corners of my mouth when I glanced up and caught sight of Papa in the rearview mirror. For an instant, a trick of refraction briefly caused the skin of his cheap sunglasses to warp translucent; and I saw that my grandfather's eyes were locked on me. I quickly cast my gaze away. We took a right onto a new street, like the other streets, houses and grass and pavement.

He continued: "We never lost a fight. Because we knew it was a fight. When some scab crossed the line, he was kicking another guy's kid right in the face, tearing the clothes right off another man's wife, burning down his house. That's a goddamn fight." He stomped his foot again, and this time his optometrist's sunglasses slid off his nose and down into the well.

For a few seconds he scrabbled around for them. Then there was a crinkle of plastic and a grunt of triumph. Papa sat up, and I looked in the rearview mirror to see that the sunglasses had been restored, but the thin orange lenses were dented now, as if someone had clocked him. He sat breathing hard for several seconds.

When my grandfather spoke again, he sounded oddly sedated. "I'll give you an example," he said, and then he told us about Tom Hellweg.

My grandfather, Henry McGlaughlin, grew up with Tom Hellweg in Bangor, a city in the northern part of the state. They had lived on the same street, and once broke their legs together. This was in a sledding accident on Drummond Street Hill when they were both thirteen, only a couple of years younger than I was now. The steepest road in town, Drummond scaled all the way up from the bank of the Penobscot River to the residential hills where the long-departed lumber barons of the nineteenth century built their mansions with fortunes made on the backs of unorganized sawyers and lumberjacks.

It was in one of these Victorians—which like many of the great manors of the previous century had by that time been carved into a baroque and unheatable boardinghouse—that a half century after the last log spun down the Penobscot, the two boys came to know each other.

They made an obvious pair, Tom and Henry, if for no other reason than because of their fathers, or rather, their lack of fathers. Tom lost his in the mud of Amiens, and knew nothing of the man but the single gaiter that had been shipped home and sat in the place of honor on the mantelpiece, right beneath the crucifix. Henry's father wasn't dead, but Old Renny McGlaughlin had been in a threshing accident, and spent his days on a stool in the Whig & Courier, silently sipping black beer, with his stump propped on the neighboring stool so folks knew to stay away.

Tom and Henry walked to school together; they played ball together and fished together and made lists of the things they would buy with the money they made robbing banks together; they used a pulley system to send notes back and forth between Tom's second-floor window and Henry's first-floor window; and after they filled the gaiter on the mantelpiece with daffodils and cattails, when Mrs. Hellweg came home, the two boys were marched out into the yard together, and ordered to break off each other's switches.

In other words, they were the kind of boys—the kind of friends— who looked out at the great, ice-sheathed roller coaster of Drummond Street Hill one Sunday morning in February, and both saw that it wasn't road at all, but an enormous, shiny black tongue, *na-na-nah-nah-ing* at them, like a bully.

They lugged their two-man toboggan out into the freezing rain and along the sidewalk until they came to the crest of the hill. A half inch of black ice coated the road, and the cutbacks and swoops glittered all the way down to Valley Avenue.

For a minute, they sat in the chute, their hands on the cold ground beside the runners, taking in the massive drop. It was a mile to the bottom, maybe two miles, maybe ten. At the foot of the hill, a hundred yards beyond the road's end, the Penobscot River poured between the snowy banks, streaming dark and bobbing with slabs of ice.

"You know, this is how my dad really lost his leg," said Henry, and slapped the blade of one of the toboggan's runners.

Tom turned to look at him.

"Cut him clean off at the knee."

Tom bit his lip. He scratched his forehead.

Henry cackled.

"You bastard," said Tom, and kicked off.

Henry clutched Tom around the waist, expecting the rush of speed that carried them the first few yards, but not the takeoff that ripped the toboggan clean from its rails. His mouth opened in a scream and he was thrown forward. His teeth sank into the back of Tom's head. The dark green on the pine trees streaked across the slate gray of the sky and he tasted his friend's hair and his sweat and his blood. Wind shot through his clothes; his jacket ballooned with air; he flew.

At the bottom, in a snowbank more than a hundred feet beyond the crossing of Drummond and Valley, they came to rest in a pile of tinder. Tom's right leg had twisted with Henry's left; blood speckled the snow; the icy drizzle fell on their bare heads, their caps torn away or maybe disintegrated.

"We were a mile from home, and it was below zero, and we both had the same fracture, a clean break at the shin, and did it hurt? It goddamn hurt." Addressing me in the rearview mirror, Papa opened his mouth and pointed at a discolored incisor. "And this, too. I lost the tooth, and he had it sticking in the back of his head. You think that hurt a little?"

And the first thing Tom said was, "Do you think we can put the toboggan back together again? It won't be this good for long."

To which Henry said, "I don't think we can put it back together again, but I bet we can borrow one."

And the two boys leaned against each other, sharing legs, Henry's right and Tom's left, taking turns, one foot after another to get home.

"That's how far and deep I went back with that son-of-a-bitch Tom Hellweg."

So far and deep that, twenty years after Tom Hellweg's family moved to New Hampshire and the last time Henry saw him, when the former appeared on the latter's doorstep one morning and asked for a job, Henry never even paused. "For Christ's sake, Tom, put your hat back on. We're going to be late for work."

A full-time position in the painting shop was assigned to Tom Hellweg before the day was out, and by the time the quitting bell rang, a group of men on their days off had already moved his wife and three children into an apartment house.

The matter of his friend's felony record—eight months upstate for running a bait-and-switch telephone scam hustling Quebecois migrants into wiring emergency money to their gravely sick *mères* back home in the province—a felony being a strict prohibitive in the strongest union in Maine, was no prohibitive at all to Henry McGlaughlin. Henry believed in second chances, and Tom Hellweg was a man who had once propped him up, and borne his weight as if it were his own.

That the Tom he knew had matured into a gaunt, raccoon-eyed malingerer capable of bilking people so poor they made their shoes out of potatoes was something Henry refused to consider. Neither did he permit himself to disapprove of his old friend for, besides being the slowest worker in his shop, ritualistically painting the word **CUNT** into every plate and board that came before his brush, and then filling in from there. The only thing that mattered was that the work got done, and after all, someone had to be the slowest. Henry also chose to overlook Tom's drinking, and his habit of sitting apart from other men at lunchtime; and although it was a struggle, he even kept it to himself when someone told him that the Hellweg children collected handfuls of cigarette butts out of street gutters and brought them home for their father. Some men drank; some men liked to eat alone; and some men had their own ideas about raising their children.

And Tom was his friend, goddamn it. That was something you never forgot. That was the essence of decency.

"That was what the union was about," said Papa.

Gil cleared his throat.

My grandfather cut him off before he could start. "Not a word, you. Just keep driving."

A few months passed, however, and a situation arose regarding his old friend that Henry could not ignore. Henry received a report that Tom, on two occasions, both well after midnight, had blithely asked other workers to give him a lift from a local bar to the pipefitting shop on the Ironworks campus, because he wanted to see "how they had things set up." Tom said he was thinking of putting together a workshop himself, at home, you see, and he just wondered how they had things arranged.

These reports matched up with another set of reports, from the morning foreman of the pipefitting shop, who found tools scattered around along with signs that someone had been welding after hours.

"What's that sound like to you, Gerry?" Henry asked his wife. He didn't look up from the table.

"Cross-training," said Geraldine McGlaughlin, and went to retrieve the bottle from the cabinet. She poured two straight.

This came at a time when Local 219, like every other union in the country, found itself in a battle to find some kind of higher ground in the wake of the Taft-Hartley debacle. After fifty years of struggle and progress, the Taft-Hartley Act had served notice to the entire movement that the cripple was buried in Hyde Park and the men who inherited the family monopolies were back in charge—and they had the veto-proof Congress to prove it. In the name of free trade, Taft-Hartley's deregulations had kicked the Communists out of the movement, limited the unions' power to strike, and above all else, pinched off the increasing influence of organized labor over middle management positions.

It was one thing for the commoners to organize, Taft-Hartley seemed to say, but it was quite another for such things to get out into the greater community, where men wore ties and worked at desks. That wouldn't do at all.

And it was this last point that should have resulted in Local 219's complete unawareness of the midnight shop work, because this group of low-level white-collar workers most certainly included all of the foremen of the Amberson Ironworks, the on-site representatives who filed the reports to New York. Except—

—Except that upon the passage of Taft-Hartley, Henry McGlaughlin had, much more quickly than most, gauged the new lay of the land, and taken preemptive action. That is to say, in the best interest of his constituents, Henry immediately began giving a select group of Ironworks' foremen a monthly token of Local 219's appreciation—a very modest bribe. Along with this cash subsidy, in 1952, it may still have meant something to these managers that Henry was a fellow like them, who lived in a house like theirs, and not in some apartment in New York City with twelve-foot windows overlooking Central Park, and a bathroom with one of those gold-plated sinks to wash your ass.

Or, as Gerry put it when she visited the wives of these managers every third Monday afternoon to present the crisp ten-dollar bill that promised their husband's loyalty, "You know we're all in the same boat, honey."

Nonetheless, as Local 219 flouted the direction of the Taft-Hartley wind, and demanded new safety regulations and full benefits for a dozen part-time hires, Henry McGlaughlin had lately been much concerned; the *Lewiston Sun-Times* reported that several unidentified sources promised that a lockout was inevitable.

"We [company officials] don't like it [Local 219]," says one anonymous source. "Those people [the workers] have been given an inflated sense of self-importance. It's bad for them [the workers], and it's bad for business. We're not running a socialist enterprise here. We plan to re-establish the chain of command. We need workers who want to work, do their jobs. What we don't need are whiners, reds, and other undesirables that the unions typically carry along and suckle."

All of which leant Tom Hellweg's unauthorized after-hour's visits to the pipefitting shop a particularly suspicious appearance. It was a well-known scheme among downsizing companies to cross-train workers, to teach them how to do more than one skilled task, so that in the case of a sudden layoff production would not be affected. The problem, of course, was that while production would not be affected, the men who lost their jobs and the families of those men would most certainly be affected.

After a second glass with his wife, this one with a bit of ice, Henry McGlaughlin went off to find his old friend, Tom Hellweg. He went off to ask Tom—formerly the boy with whom he tamed the black roller coaster of Drummond Street Hill, the boy who bore Henry's weight as if it were his own—just what was going on.

Or, as Henry McGlaughlin put it then, "What the fuck are you up to here, Tommy?"

Tom stood at his station in the painting shop. He stared at Henry from beneath drooping eyelids, a crocodile stare, the one that says that the crocodile would eat you, if only the meal weren't so paltry as to make the effort redundant. Tom spat a tiny cigarette butt out onto the floor, probably one that his children had picked from a gutter so that he could get another three drags out of it.

"Well, speak up, Tommy," Henry said. "I'm asking you a question."

Tom turned back to the section of metal plating that he was spraying with red industrial paint, and carefully spelled the word "**HENRY**." Over the top of this word, he then wrote the word "**CUNT**."

"No," said Tom. "I'm asking you a question, Mr. McGlaughlin: just what the fuck do you think you are doing?"

Then his old friend plucked another grimy butt from his pocket. Tom lit it, turned his back on his union representative, and returned to work.

*   *   *

From that point, the plot unraveled with the craven simplicity that was considered standard business practice among the upstanding board members in New York and D.C., whose knowledge of the Amberson Ironworks extended only as far as the third column of numbers on a monthly profit sheet.

A cursory investigation revealed that a stranger, a gentleman from Boston who carried his cigarettes in an ivory case, had in recent weeks spread around a great many free drinks in the local pubs. Among the stranger's drinking partners had been several members of Local 219—including Tom Hellweg.

Acting on this tip, Gerry called the Portland hotel where the stranger with the ivory cigarette case was said to be staying. She spoke in a deep baritone, and started to badger the desk clerk before he could even say hello: "This is Mr. Fink, Chief Officer of the East Coast Branch of the Pinkerton Detective Agency, and I need to speak to my man immediately. I don't know what name he's using, you can never be too careful when you're dealing with the sort of riffraff we deal with in this business, but he's been charging the room to a company account, and I really must speak to him right away."

The jolted desk clerk quickly rifled through his ledger. "Do you mean Edgar Hallsworthy in room sixteen? Oh, but wait a minute: he's charging his room to an account belonging to St. Cloud Detective Agency—"

"—That's right," Mr. Fink cut him off. "That's exactly right. He's from the St. Cloud arm of our operation. Now put me straight through to Hallsworthy."

A moment later, the clerk connected him to room sixteen, and a man with a Brahmin accent answered. Gerry asked if he had sent down four shirts to the laundry. The cheerful Brahmin-voiced man said, "Wrong room, sweets. I don't go around trusting my linen to just any old chink, you know." She apologized, and rung off.

"So?" asked Henry.

Gerry shook her head and went to refill the glasses, but the bottle was empty.

Henry put his foremen on alert, and by the end of the week

received another series of corroborating reports: all of their shops were opened in the night, as well, tools and equipment disturbed.

The president of Local 219 added the sum of all these figures, and concluded that the company was preparing for a strike by buying off a skeleton crew of cross-trained workers who could keep the Ironworks going during a lockout.

"We've got blacklegs, honey," said Gerry.

"So we offered a quarter pension to the traitors who turned themselves in, and in exchange for another quarter pension, the rats all ratted on each other. Every man except that son-of-a-bitch Tom Hellweg. They all fingered him, but he wouldn't admit anything."

Gil had piloted the Skylark all the way around the neighborhood again, back to the house with the whirligigs on the lawn. It was almost noon. Papa's voice slipped to a monotone, and I sensed that he was reading the story from a set of long-prepared notes. I risked a glance in the rearview mirror and saw that he now sat deep in the corner of the backseat, as if his narrow body were slowly being sucked into the crevice of the cushions.

"So, he got nothing, and that was that. But Tom wanted to rub our faces in it. He hung around, sent his children and his wife out begging. The woman used to knock on our door almost every night and ask for another chance—and we gave her nothing. All winter they stayed, until the kids, there was hardly anything left of them— you could look out the window and see the wind push them up the street. And we gave them nothing. And when Tom himself finally came around, we gave him nothing. And he cried. And that didn't matter, either, because when Tom Hellweg cried no one could even hear it. Because that could have been our wives and our children. Because that was a goddamned fight.

"And that's how it is now, that's my point, with these so-called Christians who are running our government. They want everything for themselves, and piss on the rest of the world. We're not even humans to them. Well, they're not even humans to me, not anymore. Tom showed me that, way back then, but I guess I didn't learn the lesson well enough."

The wheels droned over concrete. Gil smiled broadly at the road.

Papa groaned, and dropped his head against the seatback. He gave the well one last, half-hearted stomp. "You know, I almost feel like that little son-of-a-bitch spray-painted me. It's a microcosm of the whole sorry state of the nation. We all saw what happened down in Florida: a bunch of fat little fraternity boys didn't want the votes counted, so they banged on the doors until they stopped. A brave little bunch of trust fund patriots, barging in to stop the vote. They bullied the country away from us. We can't let ourselves be bullied anymore. I won't be bullied anymore."

We waited for more, but my grandfather was done talking.

6.

Papa was asleep by the time we turned onto Dundee Avenue. Gil stopped the car at a red light a couple of hundred yards from a strip mall. It was a C-shaped structure, holding an office for the local branch of the DMV, a Laundromat, a sporting goods store, along with several empty storefronts, windows plastered with For Lease signs tanned the color of parchment by the long summer.

In front of the sporting goods store, a couple of shirtless teenagers were running an American flag up a leaning pole. One kid—blade thin and ghastly pale—sat on the shoulders of another, who was bigger, tall and thick around the middle. The smaller kid dragged on the halyard, but it was caught, the line knotted somehow in the toggle, and the flag stuck at half-mast. He stopped pulling and paused, catching his breath. As he rested, the thin kid sort of slouched over the back of the big kid's head, like a monkey. They both wore baggy camouflage dungarees.

A moment passed before I realized: Tolson and Sugar.

"Papa—" I started, but Gil put a hand on my arm.

He pressed a finger to his lips. "Shhh."

As we pulled away from the light, I saw Tolson, the thin kid, jerk up straight and pat Steven Sugar on the head. Sugar wheeled around and took a step, as if he meant to chase us. Then he stopped short. He peered after us, and although the distance hooded his eyes, I could feel them boring into me. Steven Sugar seemed larger than I remembered him from the previous school year, lengthened somehow, drawn upward like the flag.

Perched on the back of his partner's shoulders, Tolson made a rifle from his naked arms and sighted us.

We swung into the bend and they were gone. They knew. They knew my grandfather. They knew us. Knew me. The realization was like a baby's hand, suddenly squeezing my stomach with tiny fingers.

The Skylark dipped over the hill and the mall disappeared.

"I don't want to shoot anybody today, George," said Gil, under his breath. "This stuff is crazy. Your grandfather's not thinking clearly. He thinks people are out to get him. He needs to relax. Forget about the Sunday *New York Times* and forget about Al Gore. None of it's worth it. Like the old Jew said, 'We're all just pawns in their game.'"

He pulled the car into the driveway. Papa mumbled in his sleep. I got out and fetched Gil's walker from the trunk, then held his bony elbow as he doddered to his feet.

"All this stress over politics? Over a politician? Over Al Gore? Does that make sense to you, George?"

In the high noon light his bald head and his round, smooth face appeared as if they were carved from wax.

I shrugged.

Gil settled into his walker with a grunt of satisfaction. "Of course it doesn't. For heaven's sake—and I'd appreciate it if we kept this between us—but a man of your grandfather's beliefs should be saying good riddance to Gore. Four years of Bush and maybe people will have suffered enough to elect a man of real principle. Someone with a few more inches in the crotch department if you get my drift."

He saw me scratch my head. Gil said, "Now, now. I didn't say the *N* word, George, don't worry. I didn't say Nader."

"You just did," I pointed out.

Gil put a finger to his nostril and winked.

When I started to see him to the sidewalk, he waved me off. "Go on and help your grandfather, George. I'll be fine. I just want to go home and smoke a joint and take a nap. And maybe if I'm feeling ambitious, I'll try to screw my wife, but that's it."

He scraped forward a couple of feet and stopped. His back was to me. "See anybody?" he asked.

I spun around, expecting to see Sugar right behind me, Tolson on his shoulders, scowling like a gargoyle. The street was empty of traffic and the driveway of the house across the street unoccupied. The day was hot and still, broken only by the distant wails from the public pool. Inside the Buick, Papa snorted in his sleep.

I exhaled. "No."

"Good." Gil started to fumble with something I couldn't see.

"Gil? Are you okay?"

He answered with a deep, hitching sigh. There was a trickle as he began to urinate onto the driveway. A yellow rivulet made its way along a crack in the pavement.

I stood, slightly unnerved, not sure where to put my eyes. Any car that came along . . .

Gil seemed to read my thoughts. "At my age, George, when you get the feeling, you can't mess around. You have to whip it out."

"Yeah," I said, and reminded myself that he was dying. When you were dying, you could do anything you wanted, I guessed.

In the car, Papa slept on. I opened the door to wake him. He sat with his head back, mouth wide open, so that his breath came in a wet rasp. His left hand trembled in his lap while his right rested peacefully on the butt of the IL-47. Maybe he was dreaming sweetly of my grandmother; maybe he was dreaming of Steven Sugar, of the surprise that would be on the kid's face when a paintball stung the back of his naked ear, the red paint stippling his hair like real blood; or maybe Papa was just dreaming of old friends.

I thought of how Gil saw the world, rotten straight through, and until people were ready to start over again, a joint and a nap were about the best you could get. My grandfather, on the other hand, saw life as a war, and if you didn't martial your forces, if you didn't shoot first, they might start just by taking the Travel section of your Sunday *New York Times*, or spray-painting your property, or making you wear a yellow star, but in the end, they would take everything, then hand you a shovel.

It seemed to me that the old men were both correct in their own way, that their points of view were parallel islands of inviolable truth. My feet, spread very wide, were planted on each. I knew that no resistance could achieve what I wanted; but I also knew that except for resistance, I had nothing at all.

I put a hand on my grandfather's shoulder and shook him until he opened his eyes.

Afterward, I killed an hour or so at the library crinkling through a summer of Sundays. I perused the Travel sections and the Style sections of the Sunday *New York Times*. I wanted to understand why Steven Sugar had needed to take them. Sunlight fell through the bank of leaded windows by the reading table, warming my left ear and gilding the colored front pages.

Here were far lands and beautiful sights; here were the new ways people were living and here were the announcements of marriage. I followed the lines with my finger and studied the photographs of vistas and smiling faces, but the sunlight distracted me. Outside, seated on a bench, a girl with red hair and a blue peasant blouse was alternately reading a paperback and using her fingertip to apply layer upon layer of lip gloss. One of her bra straps hung loose around her white shoulder. I could make out the shine of dampness at her throat.

My attention wandered between the newspaper and the girl, scanning the columns and tracking her finger as it lapped around and around her mouth. Later, I would find myself able to remember only two articles, both—unsurprisingly—with a sexual content: the first, a travel piece about Rhodes, and the second, a report on the culture of elderly swingers.

The travel article was by a professor who had visited the island of Rhodes after each of his four divorces. The professor wrote that he felt an interminable sadness in the city, in the great abandoned keeps and twisty avenues of the Old Town. The Crusaders had built this place and been vanquished without a fight. So, in his sadness, he took comfort in the failures of other committed men. The professor liked to imagine that the last Knights of St. John had somehow been transformed into the swarms of stray cats who haunted the cornices, licked ice cream off the cobblestones, and baked themselves on the rock walls above the beach, in view of the nude sunbathers. If the Army of God could resign itself to such simple gratifications, the professor wrote, he believed he could love again.

In the Style section I was enthralled—and not a little mortified—by a report on the challenges, and the dangers, faced by aging swingers. Viagra didn't work for everyone, and for some it worked too well: men threw out their backs; one woman, her skull cracked against a headboard, suffered a concussion and a lingering case of vertigo. "I'm not sure if I'm sexually aroused or just obstinate," a retired stockbroker was quoted saying at one senior orgy. He was described as being seated on a piano bench, wearing only black socks and garters. "No matter what, though," said the man. "It's nice to be among your peers. No one here is going to be doing it standing up, that's for sure."

But I found myself drowsing between paragraphs, and stole glances at the red-haired girl on the grass, both of us distracted by her mouth. I rested my head down on the union of a theater director and a bank vice-president, and traced a lazy fingertip along the cool ridge of a leaded window.

The clap of the hand against glass snapped me straight. The legs of my chair scraped back with a shriek of protest. Steven Sugar, cheeks flushed and eyes wide, stood on the other side of the window. Pressed flush against the glass, his meaty hand was inches from my face.

He leaned forward until his nose touched the glass. I could see the scraggly black hairs poking from his chin and the tornados of freckles under his eyes.

"Can you hear me?" he asked, his voice deadened but clear.

Yes, I mouthed.

"Speak up," said Sugar.

"Yes," I said.

"I've seen you driving around with the geezers. Old Man McGlaughlin, he's your grandfather, ain't he?"

"Uh-huh," I said.

"Tell him I didn't take his newspapers."

"Okay," I said.

Steven Sugar flared his nostrils, nodded to himself. He took a step back, still glaring at me.

Then, suddenly, he jumped forward, smearing his face up against the glass and knocking off his square-billed camouflage hat. "Tell your grandfather I will burn down his motherfucking house if he doesn't leave me alone."

Tolson, the lieutenant, appeared over Sugar's shoulder. He sneered and rapped a knuckle on the window. "Maybe we'll burn down your house, bitch."

"I will make him my own private Vietnam," said Steven Sugar. "You got that, kid? I will make you all my very own private fucking Vietnam."

I said I had it.

"Hey, bitch. Bitch, you've got black all over you," said Tolson and patted his cheek.

They turned and walked to where their bikes leaned against a tree. Sugar spun around, shot a thick finger at me, and then climbed on his bike. They rode across the park to the street and disappeared into traffic.

In the bathroom I splashed water on my face, and scrubbed the newspaper ink off my cheek.

I paused on the front steps of the library, blinking at the high, late-afternoon sun. My skin prickled at the sudden change in heat and humidity from the cool, dry confines of the library. I still wasn't quite awake. The encounter with Steven Sugar and his lieutenant had a fuzzy, dreamlike quality in my mind, although I knew it had been real.

I put a hand over my eyes and scanned the park to see if they were waiting for me. I remembered asking Papa what I was, and how he had said I was his "henchman." In Mafia movies, when there was a gangland war, the dons often sent each other's dead henchman back and forth like letters. I imagined Tolson sitting on Sugar's shoulders and running my corpse up the flagpole in front of the sporting goods store.

The park was empty, though; even the red-haired girl with the lips was gone.

"Hey, you! Hey, sexy!"

The voice came from behind me and I took an involuntary step forward, the sole of my sneaker slipping on the slick marble. I teetered for a moment, about to fall face first. She grabbed my shoulder and I threw out my hand. I caught hold of something small and spongy and cloth covered, and steadied myself.

The red-haired girl cleared her throat, laughed.

I removed my hand from where it clutched her breast. Heat spilled across my face.

"You surprised me," I said. "I reached out."

"Yes, you did," she said.

For something to say, I blinked several times at the space over her right shoulder.

"I'm Myrna Carp," said the red-haired girl and stuck her hand out. "And you must be George." She was eighteen or nineteen, I figured.

We shook. She had damp little hands.

"George," she said again, and shook her head and giggled. I halfway expected her to whip out a stick, throw it, and tell me to fetch. I probably would have.

Myrna had a crooked way of smiling, like she was one up on you before you even talked. Of course, Myrna Carp was one up on me; she already knew my name.

"How—?"

"—I worked for Planned Parenthood second semester. I was your mother's intern. Emma's got a photo of you right on her desk, you know? Of you in your Little League uniform? Number twenty-five? Tri-City Auto Parts? Very sharp, my friend."

"Hey, you know, that photo's a couple of years old," I said.

Myrna leaned back slightly and gave me a look of open appraisal. Then she smiled at me with her funny jagged smile, as if she had determined that I was a charming, but very fake diamond.

"I can see that. You're much taller in real life. And you didn't have sideburns then, right?"

To the best of my knowledge, this was the first time someone had deemed to call the wispy curls at my temples sideburns.

"Anyway, I just recognized you, and, man, George, did you know that your mom is fucking awesome?"

"Yeah," I said, swallowing down the lump in my throat. "Sure."

"Your mom wrote me the most kick-ass recommendation, which is probably the only reason I got into Vassar. She also talked my frigging mother into letting me get on the pill, which is probably the only reason I didn't have to kill anybody senior year of high school.

"Your mom is my dogg." Myrna Carp laughed and ran a hand back through her red hair. "My dogg. Jesus, listen to me, huh?"

Something in my face made her rewind. "Well, I'm sure it's a little different for you. Being as she's your mom and all." There was an expectant pause. The library doors hissed open as a man bustled out with an armload of books, and a gust of air-conditioning washed over me.

"Did I just tell you that your mother helped me get on the pill?"

I nodded.

She put a hand over her face and peeked at me between her fingers. "I've embarrassed you, haven't I?"

"No, no," I said. "No, really."

Myrna cocked her head and squinted at me.

"Really," I said again, a little desperately.

Her gaze relaxed, but still held me, green eyes fading to amber as she leaned forward into the bright patch of sun that lay between us. She reached out and grabbed my shoulders. Then, slowly, she drew me into her chest and embraced me. A moment passed. I hugged back. Myrna sighed. "People should say hello like this," she said, and kissed my forehead.

Myrna broke away, spun and took the stairs in two big steps, and skipped away. "Nice to meet you, George! You're even cuter than in your pictures," she called over her shoulder. "And tell your mother I love her!"

*   *   *

So I'm polydactyl; I have six toes on my right foot. Only about one or two in every thousand people have a condition like mine. It's a genetic tendency, something I have from my father's side of the family. As a toe, it's not much more than a pink nub at the far edge of my foot. My extra toe looks like something that just kind of crawled on, and stuck; the nail is nothing but a dab of gloss. My grandmother used to tease me about it. Nana called it my "devilish toe." Papa liked to say it made me a freak. "It proves you're one of us," he said.

I once asked my mother if I could have it removed. When I put this question forth, I was sitting on the cracked linoleum of the kitchen floor in our apartment in Farmington, clutching a piece of coarse sandpaper.

My mother raised an interrogatory eyebrow.

"I thought I might be able to sand it off," I said. At the time I was only a kid, ten years old.

Of course, Emma said.

Two scrapes, however, had reduced me to tears. The devilish toe was tiny, but it was really attached, no doubt about that.

She sat down across from me Indian style, and put her hands on my knees. Then, she asked me why, and I told her the obvious thing, because of my father. "I don't want any part of him."

The last few days had been hard. Somehow or other, my father had obtained our phone number. "Who is this?" he had asked when I answered the first time. "Is that you, George? Is that you? It's your dad, it's your old man." A moment passed. The only sound I could manage to produce was a humming noise. My father started to laugh, and then he broke into wrenching sobs. "Say something, George. Can't you fucking say something to your old man? Or are you too fucking good?"

Since then, we had just been letting the telephone ring. Sometimes it rang for twenty minutes. The jingles hit me like screaming voices. I had wet myself having a nightmare about a man with a glistening black telephone for a head. The man with the telephone head had scrabbled up the stone blocks of a well, like some awful spider, and I couldn't seem to back away.

"I hate it," I said and slapped my foot, slapped the sad lump of my extra toe that was already raw and sore.

Emma nodded. Her face wore the peaceful expression of a cemetery angel—mournful, but carved with the assurance that no further harm can come.

Suppose, she said, that a birth defect is like a work-related injury.

"Like when Papa's dad lost his leg in the thresher?"

My mother rolled her eyes at me. Yes, she said, but without the blood and guts, my beautiful little psychopath.

Now, she went on, you got an extra toe on the job. So you turned to your Workers Comp, because you were organized and had benefits and so forth.

"Naturally," I said. By age ten I was well versed in such necessities.

But your injury is different, George, because you didn't lose anything. She stressed this point, staring hard. You gained something. You have something more. You're not handicapped at all.

"Well then, how am I getting Comp?" I asked.

My mother took a deep breath. There's a special clause in the life contract for workers who are born with extra toes, she said. Comp applies to them even though the extra toe isn't detrimental.

"That sounds like featherbedding," I said. "My union is going to be under investigation if it isn't careful."

She looked at me.

"Okay," I said. "But it's just a toe. A toe can't do shit."

It's a gift, Emma said, it's a gift. And Workers Comp insured you while you learned to utilize that gift, and afterward the union found you another job. Some task your special gift is uniquely suited for.

And watch your language, she added.

I touched my toe. It was barely anything; it was half of a chunky french fry; it could not possibly have a function.

"What task?"

She shrugged. We're still in the rehabilitation stage, she said. I'm your Workers Comp, by the way, Emma added. Roughly speaking, that's what mothers provide for kids. They rehabilitate them for life.

I studied my toe. It was nothing.

You'll see, she said. It'll come in handy.

Then my mother said, I love you. Then she said, And he loves you. He does love you.

The phone started to ring, and we sat on the floor of the kitchen for a while longer without saying anything.

At the time of my conception in the spring of 1985, Ty Claiborne held a good union job, as a movie theater projectionist at the Amberson Pavilion Two. This was how Emma McGlaughlin, the daughter of the local union heads, Henry and Geraldine McGlaughlin, happened to meet him. It was her first summer job, and Ty Claiborne—tall and broad and possessed of the crinkled, soulful gaze of a much older man—was her first real crush. He carried his pack of Lucky Strikes rolled up in the sleeve of his black T-shirt and wore huge sunglasses, like a state trooper. I wish he'd pull me over, Emma told her friends.

If, however, a week into the summer, the Northeastern Projectionists Union had not gone on strike, maybe things would never have gone beyond a crush stage—but the theater chain told the union to take it or leave it, and the projectionists walked in June. So it was in the spirit of unity that Emma promptly quit her summer job, and whipped up a big batch of pot brownies to lift the spirits of her fellow workers.

Ten years older, Ty drove a car that was almost new, rented his own apartment, had painstakingly collected every album Bob Dylan had ever recorded—*on vinyl*. Ty Claiborne could also put away a whole mess of pot brownies. In her teenage bedroom, Emma's poster of River Phoenix rubbed shoulders with a magazine clipping of Woody Guthrie posing with his "This Machine Kills Fascists" guitar; she never had a chance. Ty seemed like the perfect combination of both, a dreamboat and a union man.

What Ty Claiborne did not seem like was a man with a drinking problem. Nor did he seem like a man with a cocaine addiction, or a man who would very soon be forced to sell his complete collection of Dylan records to support that addiction. He did not seem like a man on the verge of his third strike with the Northeastern Projectionists Union, or a man three months in arrears on his rent, or a man who would lift cash from his seventeen-year-old girlfriend's Minnie Mouse leatherette purse. Perhaps above all other things, Ty Claiborne did not seem like the sort of man who would use a condom that he found in the sleeve of a thrift store copy of *Another Side of Bob Dylan* (a condom with an expiration date clearly printed on the back, 3/1/66), and who would still use said condom after carrying it around in his tool pouch for weeks, along with the ring of screwdrivers and pins that he used for projector maintenance. He was, however, all of these things—and so, of course, it was lucky for me that my mother didn't know.

But in the fifteen years since, we had both learned plenty about my father. For instance, there were lessons about bankruptcy, about creditors, about rehab, and about the cost of collect calls between the hours of three and five A.M. Once, in the parking lot outside our apartment in Blue Hill, we learned that laid-back Paul Bagley— hippie potter, borderline narcoleptic, and Green Party stalwart, Paul Bagley—was capable of disarming a strung-out junkie ex-husband wielding a Swiss Army knife, and then of beating the wretch unconscious with a snow shovel. We learned about restraining orders.

Meanwhile, my father discovered that he could maintain his fix by stealing cars, but one night in Lewiston he learned that it was a bad idea to pass out while idling in a stolen BMW in the drive-through line at Arby's. After that my mother and I learned that when someone sent you a letter from a maximum security prison, the envelope was sliced open by an administration official and perused for obscenity, threats, incrimination, or anything else that might be interesting, before it was taped shut and sent along for delivery.

And somewhere along the line, I became self-educated in the indispensable mechanism of pure wishfulness, and I began to fantasize of a Real Father, a superhero, unavoidably delayed by matters related to the security of the universe. This was the kind of father I needed, because only the planets and the stars were important enough to forgive for putting us through all this.

*　　*　　*

Now, as I rode home with Myrna Carp's college girl lips still printed on my forehead, the old despair tickled at the back of my neck. It had never really left, I knew. That feeling was as much a part of me as my extra toe; it was attached.

I told myself that college was full of beautiful girls, beautiful girls who had not shared their reproductive concerns with my mother. At a place like Vassar College—wherever that was, and whatever it was—I bet they practically fell down out of the sky, like rain. I bet at Vassar College you needed to wear an army helmet to deflect all the gorgeous, precipitating girls, and the birth control pills pinging down like hail. I told myself that she had liked me.

Unconvinced, I pedaled down Route 12 with a hard-on and a feeling of general gloom. I imagined Myrna Carp falling nude through the sky, and landing, with a squeal of joy and a pillowy bounce of her breasts, onto the broad shoulders of Steven Sugar. "Let's raise the flag, babe," said Steven. "Oh, let's!" cried Myrna.

Then, at dinner, I almost choked on a lump of mashed potato. I started coughing and needed to drink half a glass of water to get it all down.

"You okay?" Dr. Vic asked.

"Did you ever sell a Bob Dylan record?" I hacked a fragment of potato into my napkin.

Dr. Vic scratched his head. "Pardon?"

My mother lowered her forehead to the table and sighed.

I repeated the question.

Dr. Vic said he was sure he hadn't. "I don't know as if I was ever hip enough for Bob Dylan, you know?"

"Yes," I said, relieved. "We can see that."

7.

Dr. Vic cleared his place at the table and announced he was going down to the dock. He didn't ask my mother if she wanted to come.

Shutting the sliding glass door with painstaking care, Dr. Vic slouched outside, his footfalls creaking heavily on the planks.

She remained in her seat, doodling on her legal pad. She drew a cartoon of Bob Dylan, with the incredible sixties Afro, the opaque sunglasses, the jagged nose and the dubious eyebrows, and slid it over to me.

I gave her a thumbs-up. Then I penciled a light saber into Dylan's hand. I gave him a speech bubble: *LUKE, I AM YOUR FATHER.*

Her sudden, tinkling laugh stung my eyes. *Do you want to assist me in a secret mission?*

Yes, I wrote back.

Meet me in the car. She stood up, patted my shoulder, and left to gather her things. I wiped my eyes.

Before we left, my mother loaded the trunk, and when she climbed in, I saw that she had changed into a navy tracksuit. She handed me my black windbreaker, and I put it on. This seemed promising.

We pulled onto Route 12 and passed through the quiet of Amberson at nine o'clock on a Tuesday night.

In the old brick-faced downtown—where the buildings stood together in a stately arrangement that always reminded me of the well-worn but carefully polished and soberly colored Oxford shoes that lined the bottom of Papa's wardrobe—there were signs of the recent economic downturn. The shoe store had a HUGE SALE, the art supply store had an EVERYTHING MUST GO SALE, and according to a Jimi Hendrix poster taped in the window, the head shop was SORRY: CLOSED FOREVER HONKIES! (The statement bloomed from the corner of Jimi's mouth in a psychedelic word bubble.) At the Amberson Pavilion Two, a film called *Rat Race*, about people willing to undergo any humiliation in order to win a fortune (performed by actors who were apparently willing to take any part), played on both screens. The pawnshop seemed to be doing okay.

It occurred to me that for days, my life had been narrowed to a window not much larger than the circle at the end of the IL-47's scope. Papa should get out more, I thought to myself, before everything in town goes out of business.

Some skaters were pushing themselves around the modest town square. They wore long, jingling wallet chains, and low-hanging carpenters jeans, and wove their boards in drunken circles around the WWI monument of a huddled squad of battle-weary doughboys. Parked at the curb a couple of cops sat in their cruiser and kept watch, probably listening to the Red Sox as they finished up a disaster against New York, or just started on one with Oakland.

My eyes naturally drifted upward, to a second-floor office in the squat, ten-story building that overlooked the square.

It was from this office that Dale Crispin, my mother's last ex-boyfriend, wrote, edited, and published the local weekly, the *Amberson Common*. When they were dating, I spent a number of happy hours playing cribbage in that office, and listening in wonder and admiration at the musical vulgarity of Dale's speech.

"The shoe, my young friend," I remembered him saying to me as he counted a clutch double-run to pull himself within range of the finish line, "is now on the other dick."

But in the next hand, when he mud-holed, and I won with a flush double-run, Dale threw up his hands and pronounced, "Great Scott! The shoe returneth dickward! Of all the piss-ass luck!"

Dale swept up the cards and started to shuffle. He sprayed them back and forth between his hands and directed a keen look from under the bill of his tattered Red Sox cap. Along with his twenty-year-old cap, Dale's salt-and-pepper beard seemed to exist in a permanent state of two-days' growth, which endowed him with something of the ultra-cool, imperturbable bearing of a war correspondent. Of all Emma's boyfriends, Dale had been my favorite.

"Now. Two questions haunt me, my friend:

"First, can this streak of piss-ass luck be broken with just the simple intervention of a juju priest, or am I going to need a living sacrifice? Second, do you believe that your mother would ever consent to marry someone so far below her son's station, cribbage-wise?"

This second question hung in the air.

I felt heat rise up my neck. "What—?" I asked, and the word lay on my tongue like a mouthful of spoiled food.

"I'm just throwing things out here," said Dale.

I shrugged, flicked the head of the Ross Perot bobblehead on Dale's desk. Ross nodded like an idiot. Say something, I yelled inside myself, still not sure what precisely was going on.

"What's—a juju priest?" I asked.

"Nice dodge, kiddo." Dale produced a wry grin and stuck his hat on my head. "Deal the cards, O Purveyor of Stinging Yellow Destiny."

My mother wrote something, and then passed me her legal pad and a pen flashlight.

We were waiting parked behind a Dumpster at the rear of the parking lot adjacent to the Planned Parenthood office. She had shut off the lights and the engine. From our vantage point, we could watch the area directly in front of the clinic through a vertical gap between the Dumpster and the corner of the building. So far there was nothing to see. A pair of arc lights illuminated the entrance to the lot, highlighting the chiggers that circled over the dry grass of the diamond-shaped traffic island.

I took the legal pad and the flashlight to read: *I'm going to need you to do some driving.*

I nodded at her—affirmative. Over the years, we had lived in six different apartments, a duplex, a triplex, and for a few weeks one summer in Rockland, a fourteen-foot boat where I slept in the cabin and my mother slept in an inflatable tent on deck. From the time I was tall enough to reach the pedals I was trained to sit in the double-parked car while she unloaded boxes, and to move it if another vehicle needed to pull away from the curb.

This is about the GFAs, isn't it? This was the time of night that they made their strikes. *What are we going to do?*

My mother grinned like a pirate. *You'll like it.*

I tried to return a grin of my own. I rolled down the window, caught a pungent whiff of Dumpster, and rolled it back up.

The parking lot was windless. The cloud of chiggers stretched and undulated above the grass of the traffic island. I could feel the itch of them along my spine.

My mother scratched a new message on the pad.

What are you thinking about?

This required a more complex answer than I supposed my mother might have expected—or maybe not. I was thinking about how nice it was for the two of us to be alone, doing something together that Dr. Vic didn't know about; and I was thinking of how lame and childish it was to feel that way, like a kid feels about his mother, not like a young man who would be old enough to apply for his driver's license in five months.

I was also thinking about Dale, missing him, missing the times we played cribbage in his office. This, too, was deeply, inarguably lame. After all, it wasn't like he had been a superhero or something. Dale Crispin ran a two-bit newspaper that was so cheap you wouldn't dare to wrap fish in it. Still, I felt a little sick to remember how he asked me that question and how for some reason I couldn't find an answer.

I looked at her; she looked back.

Sometimes it stunned me, stunned me like being shaken awake, to realize her youth. The face I saw now was not very different from the face that my father saw roughly sixteen years ago, maybe even as they sat in a dark car like this one. The possibility didn't strike me as incestuous. Rather, it seemed almost holy, like a magic snapshot, like some moment out of time.

What are you thinking about?

To her question, I responded with one of my own: *Why didn't you marry Dale?*

Headlights swung across the windshield, and I glanced up to see the familiar, rusted blue minivan turn into the parking lot. My mother squeezed my arm, gently popped open the driver's side door, and slipped out into the night.

The minivan flicked off its lights and ground to a clattering halt in front of the curb. The side door wrenched open and three GFAs piled out. There were two men carrying rolled paper cylinders, and a woman with a brush and a bucket. I recognized the woman, decked out in her familiar baseball cap with a glittery cross instead of a city insignia or a mascot. She was the GFA who stood on top of the van and yelled at the patients to "leave your whoremaster and return unto the lord." (When my mother had told Dale of this singular entreaty, and of the woman's crucifix ball cap, Dale had sent us the following classified:

Now Batting:
For the Jerusalem Jesuses No. 69, at Desgnatd Whremaster, 1 Crzy Btch.)

In the mirror, I saw my mother pop the trunk. She removed something, and eased the trunk closed with only a faint click.

(Emma's stealth amazed and half frightened me. Only a mother could be so soundless. I made a silent resolution never to jerk off again without first checking the hall and jamming a chair under the doorknob.)

The GFAs disappeared around the edge of my view. I heard one of them drop something and curse. They were at the front doors, the point of their previous assaults.

My mother moved at a crouch around the side of the Dumpster, bracing herself against the blistered steel flank for balance. I saw her take a deep breath and poke her head around the corner, then just as quickly pull it back. She turned and gave me a thumbs-up. Something dangled at her side.

Now she eased out, standing up straight. My breath caught—and my mother strode directly across the lot, as calmly as if it were broad daylight, and three possibly dangerous, and certainly felonious, worm-digging religious fanatics were not around the corner. Clenched at her side was a small plastic bag that I recognized. It was the very same plastic bag into which I had been dutifully depositing the Laddies' shit for the last few mornings, and tucking away in the usual place beneath the steaks in the freezer.

Perhaps it goes without saying, but there are few instances in a young man's life when his mother is more awesome than when he watches her sneak to the minivan of anti-choice fanatics with a bag of frozen dogshit.

A dozen steps carried Emma to the back of the vehicle. She grasped the handles of the double rear doors, and I saw her jaw tighten as she slowly pulled the latch and opened. My mother swiveled around and threw me a quick wave. Then she climbed into the back of the minivan and closed the door behind herself.

The next minute turned into a second minute, and then a third. They're going to come back, I thought to myself, hearing the words like a song. (*They're go-ing to co-me ba-ack. Hur-ry the FU-UCK uh-up, ple-ase, Mom.*) By the start of the third minute, I realized that they didn't have to come back, because one of God's Favorite Assholes had stayed behind to sit in the van in case they needed to make a quick getaway, and he was probably at this very instant stabbing my mother to death with the same trowel he used to dig fishing worms.

Just then one of the rear doors swung open, and my mother slipped down to the pavement. But instead of running, she paused to shut the door, releasing pressure on the latch by infinitesimal increments, until finally she leaned into it with her shoulder. The door fastened, and Emma let go.

She turned and faced me across the parking lot.

She exhaled. She blew kisses. She bowed.

That was my mother.

It would be more than two months before God's Favorite Assholes discovered the bag of dogshit that my mother stashed beneath a floor panel, and sealed tight with some of the epoxy they brought along to plaster their poster to the front doors of the clinic. Through August and September the humidity would work to warm the shit, and eventually to melt it, and swirling the feces up with the anchovies that my mother tossed into the bag for extra spice. The smell would start out faint—an odor that could be excused by sweaty running shoes— and grow into a more pungent, more textured stink that suggested engine trouble, before finally exploding into a rotting, gutty stench that would seem to be explained only by the presence of a dead animal, or maybe a dead person. When one of the GFAs finally did pry up the floor panel, a cloud of insects burst up into her face, and she passed out, overwhelmed by the sight of something even more horrific than doll parts splashed in blood.

She climbed into the passenger seat, and I switched the car into neutral. I guided us back along the side of the building, and around to the opposite face of the clinic, where a twelve-foot chain-link fence bordered the slope down to the interstate.

We hugged, and I felt she was soaked through, and shivering. For fifteen minutes or so we just sat there, intermittently snickering in the dark.

Her cell phone vibrated and she answered. It was Charlie Bird-song; she'd had him stationed on the lookout in case anything went wrong.

Charlie reported that the GFAs were gone. Mom offered to give him a ride, but he wanted to stay and finish reading *Glamour*, then go to work on the new dead baby poster. My mother told Charlie not to stay up all night doing it, just to try and scrape the gooey head part of the fetus off. "Affirmative," I heard Charlie say. "It's definitely the gooey head that puts people off the most."

Emma let me pilot us out to the main road. We didn't talk. She rolled down the windows and the car filled up with sweet night smells, oak and wet lawns.

At a stop sign, I put the car into park. My mother had picked up the legal pad.

Why didn't you marry Dale?

She looked at me, a crease in her forehead. Emma licked her lips, as if she were about to speak.

I tapped the dashboard and shook my head. No talking. Not yet.

She jotted on the pad and held it up for me. *It's funny you should bring that up. We actually just got invited to Dale's wedding. And how much would Dale have loved this little escapade, by the way?*

I briefly gazed out the window. Outside, and running perpendicular to our parked car, a bus blurred past, the lit console and rows of darkened windows, maybe just arriving, maybe just leaving.

My mother wrote more: *He's marrying Gail Dahl, the art teacher from the high school. You had her last year, right? Mrs. Dahl? I guess she'll be Mrs. Crispin now, huh?*

I reached out and put my finger on the original question. I didn't know what I wanted to hear, but it suddenly seemed tremendously important.

In the harsh light of the roadside stanchions my mother no longer appeared so young. The streak of silver hair shone like it was polished. She grimaced, tapped the pen against her chin. She wrote, *I didn't think we were ready.*

I stared at the words. I took the pen. I underlined one word: *we*. She nodded at me.

I climbed out of the car and started to walk home.

But Emma refused to leave me; it was well past midnight and, after all, she was my mother. The car ground along just ahead of me, clinging to the shoulder, while I walked behind the trunk. I watched her headlights bob in the eaves of the roadside trees and wished to disappear, to wink out like an ember. I wished for her last glimpse of me to be in the rearview mirror, and for the rest of her life to be spent wondering what happened, what made me burn away. A dozen or so mosquitoes took up orbit around my head, but I refused to get back in the car.

Before we turned onto Route 12 and the final stretch to the house, I walked over to the all-night Citgo to seek a respite from the mosquitoes. My mother parked out front.

I bought an orange soda and the Goth cashier with the fork tattooed on his Adam's apple rang me up. "Dammit. Janet." With his purple-ringed eyes, he stared at me in stoned expectation.

"What?" I asked. "I just want a soda."

"I thought you rolled with the sex geezers?" He scratched his fork. "They don't take you to the movies, little hombre?"

"A soda," I said. I slapped a dollar on the counter.

"Dammit," he said, and took the dollar. "Janet."

I pushed out into the night and Emma wheeled around, taking the point down Route 12. By the time we reached the driveway, my feet ached, and my bare calves pulsed with bites. When she left the car, my mother didn't spare a backward glance, just clicked the electronic alarm, and walked inside. The only reason I didn't end the protest there and then, and start screaming at her, was that I was too tired.

A few minutes later, my body found its way into bed. I was asleep even before they started to fight.

8.

The next morning Dr. Vic stopped me when I called the Laddies to come for a walk. "I already took them out, George," he said. He was at the table, hunched over his morning crossword. "Come to think of it, I guess that's the way we might as well run it for the time being. It's good for me, taking them out. I need the exercise."

"Whatever you want, Doc." I pulled my house keys off the hook by the door.

"There's that damn woman again," he said, under his breath, jotting *Yoko* or *Ono* into his puzzle. Dr. Vic tossed down his pencil and his crossword book, and stood up with a screech of chair legs. "Let me give you a ride over to your grandfather's. We need to talk."

"I don't talk to strange men," I said.

On Route 12, the BMW pulled onto the shoulder and up beside me. He slowed down and unrolled the window. "Are you sure you don't want a ride?"

"I don't accept—"

Dr. Vic swung the BMW back into the road, turning up a spray of gravel.

But when I reached the house on Dundee Avenue, I found Dr. Vic already there; he was on the front lawn, helping Papa add a beard to Al Gore. Dr. Vic acted as though nothing had happened, just gave me a "howdy," and went on talking with Papa. My grandfather stood on a milk crate, using a Magic Marker to meticulously dab in the former vice-president's much discussed new whiskers. Some pundits had wondered if it was a statement of some kind, further evidence of the man's unbearable liberal pretension.

"They can't even let the man groom himself in peace," said Papa. "So he's not shaving. He's probably depressed. He's got a right to be. It's not enough they stole the election, now they're after the man's dignity, too."

Dr. Vic stayed on the ground and kept a hand on the other man's belt to make sure he didn't fall. "So let me get this straight, before the little bugger started vandalizing your sign, he stole your Travel section?"

I sat down on the hood of the Buick and crossed my arms.

"That was the start of it."

Dr. Vic shook his head. "What kind of a kid wants the Travel section of the Sunday *New York Times*? It's all stories about places you'll never go or, even worse, places you've been to, but that the article ends up making you feel guilty about because you missed all the really great stuff that stupid tourists don't know about."

Papa paused to extract a crumpled magazine page from his pocket and consult a picture of the former vice-president with his new beard. "He looks dignified, I think."

"I'll tell you, though, Henry, if you look on the bright side, at least the kid saved you the trouble of throwing it out."

"He took the Style section, too," said Papa. His voice contained an edge. He was shading in around Gore's cheeks, filling out the last few inches of gristle.

"Well," said Dr. Vic, "I suppose I can see how that might rile a man."

After Papa finished, he braced himself on Dr. Vic's shoulder and stepped off the crate. He gave a tiny groan when his shoes hit the grass and his weight came down. Dr. Vic asked him if he was okay. "Fine," said Papa, and shrugged off the other man's hand.

We all walked out into the street and surveyed the billboard:

Albert Gore Jr. won the 2000 election by 537,179 votes, but lost the presidency by 1 vote. DISGRACE. The leader of the free world is now a man who went AWOL from his National Guard unit, a huckster of fraudulent securities, a white-knuckle alcoholic, and a gleeful executor of the mentally handicapped. CRIMINAL. Our nation is in the midst of a coup d'état, perpetrated by a right-wing cadre that destroys the environment in the name of prosperity, hoards in the name of fairness, intimidates the voices of its critics in the name of patriotism, and wraps itself in the word of God. FARCE.

And below that the adjusted portrait of Gore, underscored by the legend:

THE REAL PRESIDENT OF THE UNITED STATES.

Below the text, Gore, and his beard, fixed south.

Papa held up the crumpled magazine page with the up-to-date picture of Gore, and we all looked back and forth between the two. The rendering was, I thought, quite accurate:

The former vice-president's facial hair appeared soft, almost tentative, hinting at curls if it were allowed to grow long enough. It was a beard that belonged to a much younger man, and it gave Al Gore's expression a morose quality, as if he were staring at the road for a ride that was late in coming, or more likely, never coming at all.

"You got him," said Dr. Vic.

Papa folded up the magazine page, and went over to the billboard. He took a rag out of his pocket and gave a quick polish to the union bug in the corner that marked it as the work of the printer in Providence.

"Even better," said Dr. Vic.

"Ayuh," said Papa. He rummaged in another pocket for a handful of peanuts, and started to crunch.

"Say, you should take it easy with those things, Henry. Not too many and not too fast, as they say."

"I don't want to hold you any longer, Dr. Lipscomb." Papa walked over to the BMW parked at the curb. I hopped off the hood of the car and followed him. "Be sure and tell Emma I said hello."

My grandfather gave me a wry glance, and added, "Or write it to her. Or do whatever it is you people do to communicate with one another these days."

"Will do," said Dr. Vic.

Papa held the door of the BMW open for his prospective son-in-law.

If he felt rushed, Dr. Vic didn't show it. After he shook my grandfather's hand and climbed into the car, he took his time feeling around for the keys. "And you'll give my best to Gil?"

"Very well, Dr. Lipscomb."

Dr. Vic didn't look up as he patted his breast pocket. "Who's his doctor, anyway? And how's he feeling? Emma told me that it was her impression that it was—pretty serious."

"I don't know. You'd have to ask Gilbert. But I guess he's hanging in there the best he can."

"Of course he is," said Dr. Vic. "Of course he is."

Bending his tall, lean frame at the waist, my grandfather reached through the car window, and poked the car keys. They jingled from the visor. The fob was a plastic cartoon Pekingese, wearing shades and riding a surfboard. "There."

"Ah." Dr. Vic snapped his fingers. He stuck the key in the ignition. He gave Papa a big smile and sat with his hand still on the head of the key. "I've got to ask: you feeling okay, Henry? You seem—I don't know. A tad frazzled."

The old man sighed. He jammed a hand in his trouser pocket and grabbed more peanuts. A few nuts popped out and went rolling crazily across the pavement.

"I'm fine," said Papa, and tossed back the peanuts. He started to chomp, talking between bites and breaths. "Mind you, our country is being run by a man who would just as soon wipe his ass with the Constitution as read it—and my First Amendment right is being trampled on by a member of the local chapter of the Hitler Youth— and everyone around here just walks around like they're deaf, dumb, and blind." He swept out his arms to indicate the scope of the catastrophe. A peanut fragment wobbled at the corner of his mouth. "Other than all that, Dr. Lipscomb, everything is fine. Everything is super."

Calm, and still holding the older man's gaze, Dr. Vic nodded. "And you lost your wife, Henry."

"That's right," said Papa. "I did lose my wife."

"Have you ever considered seeing a grief counselor?"

"Did you vote for Bush?"

"No."

"Did you consider it?"

"Yes."

My grandfather nodded. "No."

Dr. Vic raised an eyebrow.

"No, I never considered it. Going to a counselor. For my grief."

"I know a good one," said Dr. Vic.

They smiled at each other for a few seconds, the kind of squinting smiles that men use when they aren't really happy.

Dr. Vic turned the key and the engine awoke in a whoosh of high air-conditioning. "I'm going to have to insist that you start calling me Vic."

"Very well," said Papa. "Vic." He gave the BMW a rap on the roof.

Dr. Vic pressed the automatic window button and said, "I'm picking you up at four, George." He gave me a tight grin from behind the glass and backed up his car.

When the BMW disappeared around the curve in the road, Papa put his hand on my shoulder. It closed like a claw; I could feel him shaking. "I need to sit down."

We crouched down together. He hung on to my shoulder, lowering his rear, and then dropping the last couple of inches with a groan. I sat down beside him.

The pavement was warm from the sun. He breathed and clasped his hands in his lap. I reached out, flicked away the peanut at the corner of his mouth. He nodded, rocking a little, his breath hitching. Seconds passed, minutes. A car drove by, another car, a truck, cars and trucks.

I thought my grandfather might be about to cry. I had no idea what I would do if that happened.

"I've never sat in the driveway before," I said.

"I guess it's one of those places you don't usually sit."

His voice was tired, but controlled. Papa scanned around, taking in the lawn, the sign, the diminishing, ground-level viewpoint of the tall white house. "Well. Now you can check it off the List."

"The List?"

"The old Things-I-Did-Before-I-Died List."

"You, too," I said.

"Me, too," he said. A thoughtful, faraway expression came over his face. "You know who I bet has a hell of a list?"

"Who?"

Papa gestured in the direction of the Desjardins' house. "Gilbert."

"Really?"

"He's a hedonist."

"What's that?" I asked.

My grandfather grinned. "Better you don't know." He started to laugh—and then abruptly, his eyes grew wet and he stopped. He coughed several times and rubbed at his eyes. "Don't look," he said, and I closed my eyes while he blew his nose on the pavement.

When we were inside, making our way up the stairs, he leaned on me again, digging into my shoulder with his fingers. At the landing we stopped to rest. I could feel the vibration of his breath in my chest.

The previous autumn my freshman biology teacher, Mr. Capers, a spindly and excitable graduate student on loan from USM, had achieved some minor renown for raising a tarantula named Boris in the class aquarium. We marveled with repulsion at the creature's hairy, scuttling hunger, the way it devoured dead bugs and ravaged the papery fly corpses. Six classes worth of feedings, however, caused Boris to swell to the size of a fist, and he went belly-up over Christmas break. For the edification of future biology students, Mr. Capers, instead of disposing with the spider's body, installed Boris in a block of Lucite to use as a paperweight. But there must have been a breach in the paperweight's seal. Moisture soon appeared on the surface of the Lucite and one day, Boris's legs broke off. After that, the tarantula's body fell completely to pieces and rattled from one side to the other when you turned the paperweight over. Mr. Capers, soured by a full year of dealing with adolescents, began to patrol the class while holding the Lucite block of loose tarantula parts, and, if he saw a kid who wasn't paying attention, he would shake it aggressively at them.

The hard little tips of Papa's fingers brought up the memory of the tarantula in the Lucite block, all broken into pieces, the legs like matchsticks.

"Maybe you should see the doctor," I said.

"Just a little spell," Papa said. He let go of my shoulder, straightened, and walked the rest of the way without stopping.

I trailed him into the guest room. He sat in the chair by the orange-curtained window. "You know, sitting here, sometimes I feel like that bastard Oswald." One of his hands flopped in his lap. He squeezed it. "Don't worry. It was just a little spell, George."

For the first time, it occurred to me that if he wanted to, Steven Sugar could kill my grandfather, really kill him. If he had a grip on Papa, Steven Sugar could break the old man. I could see him doing it, could see him snapping my grandfather over one knee. I remembered how when Mr. Capers's Lucite paperweight was tilted, all the parts of the tarantula would pile up on one side like a mess of tiny blackened kindling.

I decided to tell Papa what happened at the library.

When I was done, he gave a grunt of satisfaction. "We're getting to him," he said.

I asked if we should call the police.

"'My own private Vietnam'? He said that?" Papa peeled back the orange curtain and peered out at the sign. "Well, well, who's the sore loser now?"

"What about the police?" I asked again.

"What about them?" Papa held up his hand and flexed it a couple of times. Everything seemed to be under control.

"He said he would burn down your house."

My grandfather laughed. "I've heard that one before." He shot a finger pistol at the photograph of Joseph Hillstrom. "Isn't that what they always say, Joe?"

*   *   *

A few minutes later, he was asleep, one hand on the IL-47. I draped a blanket over him. Papa's hand stayed certain on the oiled wood of the grip.

When I went downstairs, I found Gil watching television and building a garbage joint from the buds in the ashtray. "Pull up a rock, lad. You know what time it is?"

I looked at the clock on the wall. "Noon?"

Gil crumbled a cinder into his paper. "Nope. It's Bare Ass O'Clock."

That was all the invitation I needed. I took a seat in Papa's armchair.

Gil had let himself in to see his favorite channel, an obscure cable station at the end of the dial that showed almost nothing besides an import about the lifestyles of naked Europeans, called *Bare Over There*.

In the months after Nana died and Gil's cancer was diagnosed, I often joined the two old men while they smoked up and vegetated for marathon sessions of *Bare Over There*. The three of us had been virtually hypnotized by astonishing wonders like the story of a pastry shop in a suburb of Zagreb where the topless waitresses served breast-shaped pastries, or the segment on the popular and contro-versial Latvian garage band who performed wearing nothing except Lincoln beards, and then fellated each other at the end of each show while simultaneously playing a (remarkably credible) cover of "Won't Get Fooled Again." We had seen other episodes about naked Spanish farmers who were tanned to the color of photo negatives, a naked mayor in Finland who married other naked people, and a benevolent cult of do-gooding nudists who rode the tram in Vaduz, offering to help old people carry heavy things. All over the world it seemed, people were living and working unrestricted by garments.

This afternoon's first episode concerned a nude circus troupe traveling through Spain.

"George?" Gil held up the glowing garbage joint. He stuck his hand under his arm and squeezed off a juicy fart. He winked at me. "When you get to college, you'll be glad that you did."

The mention of college put me in mind of pretty, pliant-breasted,

red-haired Myrna Carp of Vassar College, and how the pill had
saved her from having to kill anyone, how she planted that kiss on
my forehead. At Vassar College, I supposed, weed was common-
place. I also considered how much it would piss off my mother. Weed
was where it always started, and where Ty had started, too.

"What the fuck," I said.

"That's the spirit," said Gil.

He watched me draw a couple of hacking inhalations before
plucking the spliff from between my fingers. "Take a toke," said
Gil, giggling, "but don't choke."

I nursed a stone hard-on through the raven-haired looserope
walker's gymnastics, then grew nauseated by the performance of the
clown, a spidery-limbed creature whose balls were painted red, and
whose best trick was to pull miniature dildos from the hair of women
seated at ringside. On the couch, Gil watched through a pall of smoke.

I started to feel nervous, sweaty; I was aware of the hair on my
forearms and the old man's croaking laughs seemed to resound
within my head.

"Just about makes you want to drop everything, run away and join
the circus, doesn't it?" The smoke seemed to cling to Gil's skull, the
way fog hovered over a marsh in a scary movie.

"No," I said. "The clown is fucked up."

"You think he looks like Nader? The clown, I mean."

"What?"

"Ralph Nader," said Gil. "Try and picture the man with no clothes
on."

"I don't want to," I said. Ralph Nader was the furthest thing from
my mind. "Ever." Now my face felt tired. On the television the clown
was involved in a comical chase with a lion that was dressed in a lion-
sized pair of panties.

"I think there's a real resemblance," said Gil.

I nodded off for a couple of minutes, woke up for a second when
Gil shut off the television and walked out, then fell completely asleep.
I had a dream about my mother. We were at the table again, passing
our notebooks back and forth, as if we were having a conversation,
but our pens were charged with invisible ink. We cackled like mad

people. We threw paper everywhere. I went to a rally in front of my grandfather's house. Ralph Nader was on the stage, at the podium. He began to speak, his voice grave, his face graver, his skin hanging loose and masklike. "My Fellow Americans . . . I have gathered you here because our democracy has devolved into a single party system operated at the behest of a few monstrous corporations." He paused for effect. "I brought you here because my balls are painted red." I dreamt about riding my bike. I wove through miles and miles of road jammed with station wagon taxis.

My head ached and the clock said it was almost four. I went to the kitchen to find something to eat. The refrigerator, however, contained only V8 and condiments. In the cabinets I found several half-eaten jars of peanuts, and a few packets of bouillon.

Through the window over the sink, I could see the pool. Gil lay asleep, drifting nude on a purple inflatable recliner. A dictionary was open on his crotch, but the dark head of his penis poked, molelike, out from under the shelter of the pages.

"Jesus Christ," I said out loud, and hurried to be on my way.

9.

At the foot of Dundee Avenue I parked my bike behind a hedge and finished off a jar of peanuts. When I saw Dr. Vic's BMW drive past and around the curve, I remounted and started home the long way, looping around town to the south. Near the town line, without giving it much thought, I took a further detour, and swung into the development where Dale lived.

All of the houses here had been cranked out of the same mold, nondescript ramblers painted either white or sky blue, spaced out along a series of sweeping lanes that I supposed were meant to make the development seem less prefabricated and more like a village, but which instead gave the neighborhood a disorienting, House of Mirrors quality. It had been a while, and I got lost. Around every bend, I immediately recognized every house, only to realize a moment later that it was all slightly different—or maybe it wasn't, and I'd just come around in a circle. I remembered staying up late one night and watching a remake of *The Invasion of the Body Snatchers*. It was only later that I started to puzzle over the ramifications of the story; what happened when we were all gone, when we were all Pod People? I mean, what came next? I guessed maybe the Pod People would try to live like us, but not exactly know how, and they would end up building developments like this one where Dale lived, everything exactly the same, because that was what they thought it was like to be human.

When I finally did find Dale's house it was because of the black cat silhouette in the garage door window. I had been with him when he taped it up a couple of Halloweens ago.

The plastic kiddie pool in the front yard was new, though. As hot as it had been lately, I figured that Mrs. Dahl's kids must have loved to splash around in it. The driveway was empty.

I bet they played catch out here, Dale and the kids, the way we used to. That was last summer. When we played catch Dale opened up the front windows and jacked up the sound on the television so we could hear the ballgame at the same time. Cooking lunch, my mother liked to wheel the grill out into the driveway and watch us.

I fished a SpongeBob SquarePants figure out of the pool and twisted the legs off. I tossed the pieces in the grass, and immediately felt sorry. I went back, picked up the legs and the grinning sponge-shaped body. The toy's florid torso looked like a sad wreck to me, sadder still for the expression of happiness on the face, but I guessed some kid probably loved it.

I jammed the legs into their slots and made it a whole again. I set the toy on the rim of the kiddie pool so it looked like it was sort of hanging out, sunbathing or something.

Maybe Dale bought the kid the toy. Maybe he wrote the kid classifieds about it:

New Life: Sea Creature Sought
Sea crture needed fr wndrful new life. Must be lovble, squishy, bzzre. Excllnt kid, othr toys, hot mom, req.

Going home now felt like some kind of defeat, like admitting something—what I didn't know. I biked to the airport.

I sat at the fence in the shade of a wind-stripped oak tree, and watched the commuter planes and private jets land. On approach, they descended from the south, always skimming over the interstate at the same place, seeming to follow an invisible corridor, and sliding down the runway as easily as an arm pulling through a sleeve.

These planes were filled with summer people, vacationers from Connecticut and New York, heading to Kennebunkport and Cape Elizabeth for the weekend, to fish and Jet Ski and drop soda cans on the ground. For a week or ten days they would drink and piss in the lakes and buy grotesquely overpriced antiques and eat lobster until their plastic bibs were streaked with butter and flecks of white meat, before finally piling back onto another plane, aching and sunburned and eager to get back to civilization.

When we lived in Blue Hill my mother's ex-boyfriend Paul Bagley had supported his pottery studio by teaching tourists—and more often than not their bored, cunning children—how to mold and fire their own souvenir coffee cups and knickknacks. By nature, Paul was an almost supernaturally mellow man, whose own artistic creations typically represented a tiny man in a posture of repose, or else a bulbous fish of some kind, sporting a great, sorrowful mustache. That is to say, his sculpture was like himself: inoffensive, prone to very long naps, a little sad, and heavily whiskered. In the bi-yearly mayoral elections Paul dutifully stood for the Green Party, in 1994 garnering a mere twelve votes—which didn't include himself, because he forgot to vote.

But even Paul—soporific and uncritical Paul, who had seen the Grateful Dead two hundred and thirty-one times and swore that every single show was uniquely great—openly loathed the summer people who gave him his living. "Every year they show up and wreck the place," he said to me one night as I helped him sweep up. "They mess up my kilns and they mess up my supplies. Their kids mess up my john. I mean, put up the seat, right? Is that so hard? You put up the seat, right, George?

"Of course you do, but with these people, it's a whole different deal. After they're through, it's like it must have been after Altamont, like after some Downeast Altamont, except in my studio, you know. Broken shit all over the place."

"Do they even pay?" I asked.

"Sure, they pay," said Paul. He stooped to dig at a chunk of sneaker-printed saltwater taffy. "They always pay. That's the worst part. They think they can pay for anything. They think everything's got a cash value."

I watched a Learjet touch down in a whine of rubber and steam. When it pulled around to the terminal, a family of five crowded out. They were all heavyset and dressed in bright shorts and Hawaiian shirts. The son of the family, his torso like a stack of ice cream scoops under his flapping yellow shirt, jerked along a cocker spaniel on a leash and chugged from a two-liter bottle of soda. The spaniel yapped and squirted piss on the tarmac. Hurrying behind the family came the pilots of the jet, each of them bearing one side of an enormous steamer trunk, their ties snapping up in the breeze and whipping their faces.

A few moments after they disappeared into the terminal, the pilots jogged back out to the plane to retrieve the rest of the luggage.

The heavyset family was clearly rich, which meant they were probably conservatives—probably Republicans—which meant that in some deep and essential way, they either didn't care about anyone but themselves, or else believed that common decency was a risk they couldn't afford.

When the summer people went home to their high-rises, and their children returned to their private schools, I envisioned their daily lives as models for selfishness: I saw their route to work, and knew they drove miles out of their way simply to avoid the section of the city where black people shot each other. (That I had in my entire life known perhaps three African-Americans did not, of course, limit my judgement.) I could see the summer people as they went to church in their Mercedes, and I eavesdropped on their silent prayers and heard as they begged Jesus for lower taxes. (That I had, only a few days earlier, lain in bed and asked God not only to help me find evidence that Dr. Vic had committed a murder, but also to bring me a new fishing rod, seemed irrelevant.) I watched as they nodded at the priest's pronouncement that abortion was a mortal sin, and I waited to see no one stand up and ask, "Then what do we do with all the extra children? Who pays?" (Although I was one of these extra children, the kind that my mother could easily have aborted, I felt no debt to the Christians. After all, I wasn't extra now.)

Perhaps this kind of thinking wasn't so different from the way some people took comfort in the belief that affirmative action was the reason they couldn't find a job, and welfare was the reason they couldn't afford to take their children to the dentist. It threw up a great, thick sheet of tinted glass, and from behind it, I could make faces at passersby, and scream dirty words, and feel safe.

The reason I could see into the lives of the summer people so clearly was the same reason that my grandfather could see what a great president Al Gore would have been: because it had to be true.

I couldn't worry about exceptions. It was what they represented as a whole, the way they did what they wanted, and didn't bother with what anyone else thought, let alone how they voted. I may have been only fifteen years old, and only four years down the trail from a wholehearted belief in Santa Claus, but I could see that this wasn't about Al Gore. I could see that Albert Gore Jr., and a man like Henry McGlaughlin—who knew the words of the "Internationale" and relished them so well that he referred to it as a "hymn," and wanted it to be sung at his grave—were not exactly ideological soul mates.

It wasn't Al Gore that Steven Sugar wrote dirty words all over; it was my grandfather's identity, it was his home.

A home sometimes fell into disrepair: the paint peeled, the porch rotted, doorways grew crooked. People who lived in the place died. And, yet, this place was still home, and still held the memories of home, like a dusty jar, sealed tight with last winter's preserves. For my grandfather, there was no time to build a new one.

"So what's your excuse?"

For a moment my voice shocked me into silence. I stood with my fingers laced through the fence, staring at the parked Learjet. The runways were clear, the sky empty, the pine trees at the edge of the field tipped with brown.

"Fuck you," I told myself.

The family of pear-shaped, brightly clothed summer people emerged from the terminal with their luggage train. The fat boy yanked his dog's leash; the dog humped the leg of a porter.

They loaded the trunk of the first taxi at the curb, one of the local fleet of battered station wagons, and piled inside. The door of the taxi slammed shut with a creak of metal and a whine of rust. The cab belched away from the cement island. I slipped behind a tree, and scooted close to the bole, not wanting to be seen.

A few minutes later, Dr. Vic's BMW came around the parking loop. He honked and released the trunk. I waited for a couple of minutes, but he just sat in the front seat, tapping his fingers lightly on the wheel and looking straight ahead.

"I don't accept rides from strange men," I said.

"George, get in the damn car, would you? It's air-conditioned."

I tossed my bike in the trunk and climbed inside.

"Hey, you want a peppermint?" Dr. Vic shifted over to dig around in his pocket. He pulled out a broken dog biscuit, gave a grunt and felt around some more before producing a hard candy. Dr. Vic held it out; his grimace was sympathetic.

I stared at the mint.

"So be it." He unwrapped the peppermint and tossed it in his mouth.

We slid away from the curb.

"How did you know to come find me at the airport?" I asked.

Dr. Vic shrugged. "I figured you might have gone to see—" but he was wrong.

"You're wrong," I told him.

10.

The woods around the house were growing dusky by the time we returned to the house by the lake, but there still remained a couple of hours of good light. Dr. Vic told me there was something he wanted to show me. "There's something I want to show you, too," I said.

"Okay, that's super," he said, so eager that I almost felt sorry for him.

He told me to give him a second, and when he returned from the house he was accompanied by his Pekinese. At this sight, the minuscule insect of sympathy that had just hatched within my heart and was only beginning to take its first tentative steps, gave a brief spasm, and wilted to a husk.

Dr. Vic started for the woods, the dogs bolting out in front of him. I climbed onto my bike and pedaled behind.

He turned at the squeak of my gears. Dr. Vic clicked his tongue and gave his bald spot a dubious scratch. This was the absolute extent of his temper. "I thought we were going to walk."

"I prefer to ride," I said.

"All righty," said Dr. Vic.

We moved away from the house along the footpath that looped around Lake Keynes, passing under the spruce eaves and between the white stilts of birch trees. Around us the ground cover was lush with bursts of fern and checkerberry. The Laddies strained and whined and pitched their weight against Dr. Vic's double leash, like frantic little mops. I rode standing up, stoically grinding out the hard-packed bumps in the path. Odd chips of light, flashing off the lake, shot through the gaps in the foliage. There was a faint scent of char.

"They don't know they're small, do they?" Dr. Vic staggered after them, swiveling awkwardly to smile at me.

"They don't know anything," I said.

"Maybe so," said Dr. Vic, as always, ambushed by my dislike.

After about a half mile the footpath broke and we followed the split to the right, away from the lake and toward the hills.

"How's your granddad?" Dr. Vic talked to me now without looking back.

"He's all right."

"Sounds like this Sugar kid is a real little punk."

"Papa says he's just your basic, garden-variety fascist."

"Maybe so."

We walked a bit farther.

"What are you two fellas up to over there every day, George?" Dr. Vic held back a branch and looked straight at me. A small frown played across his mouth.

"Nothing," I said, and slipped by, then pulled up and waited for him to go ahead again. He let the long black branch snap back. "Horseshit," said Dr. Vic.

"What do you mean?"

"You're up to something."

"Whatever." Again, I caught a whiff of the burnt smell, like old charcoal.

"And I don't suppose you'll care to shed any more light than your mother did, about what you and she were doing last night?"

"You suppose right."

"Listen, George. I agree with everything he put on that sign. Al Gore got a stiff one in the backdoor, and not so much as the courtesy of a wraparound." He coughed. "I'd appreciate it if you didn't tell your mother I put it just that way, but you know what I mean."

"Sure," I said. "I won't tell her that you think Al Gore got fucked up the ass."

Dr. Vic exhaled.

After a few seconds, though, he went on: "Still, at the same time, it's not like they put Adolf Hitler in the White House. Look, Bush might not be the worst thing that's ever happened. He seems like a decent enough guy. I mean, he's a lot of things, but he's not, like your granddad would say, 'a garden-variety fascist.' He's just a good old boy. The country'll survive."

Dr. Vic stopped to pick up the Laddies. They squawked and slobbered with pleasure. In the manner of a commuter with a rolled up newspaper, he neatly stuck one sausage-shaped dog under each arm, and ported them as he squatted to climb under a low, heavy branch. I dismounted and left my bike propped against a tree.

"So whatever it is you two are up to, you better have some sense about it. And it better not be dangerous."

I crawled under the branch. "Or what?"

There was a muddy dip in the path. The Laddies immediately scrambled into the mud and began to wrestle and yip. Dr. Vic pointed to a mossy log in the brush. He took one end and I took the other. We set it across the dip and strolled across. He poked the dogs with a branch; they raced ahead, knowing the way, whipping through the underbrush.

"Well?" I asked. "Or what?"

"Does your grandfather blame me for Gerry dying, too?"

They had barely been able to squeeze Nana's full name onto her headstone: *Geraldine Sarah Niven McGlaughlin*. Her epitaph had read: *Wife, Mother, Worker, "Don't Mourn! Organize!" 1928–2000.*

"No, he doesn't. I don't blame you, either. That's just something I told Mom to make her feel bad."

He tramped a few more yards before responding. "I'm glad. I like your grandfather. I like you, George." I heard the telltale click of his tongue. "I don't think you're a mean kid, either, but that's a nasty thing to say, even if you didn't mean it. Nasty to me, and to your mother. You can't do that."

"I can do anything I want," I said.

We made the last quarter mile in silence and emerged from the trees into a clearing that held the desiccated hulk of an old Studebaker truck. The ground beneath the vehicle had sunk, as if the Studebaker were gradually burying itself. A sapling grew up through the empty trunk and all that remained of the seats were the metal frames. Nearby, a pile of blackened stones and charred sticks marked a recent campfire.

"Neat, huh?"

"Sure," I said. "Neat."

The big man sat down on the Studebaker's running board and patted the space beside him. Pretending not to notice, I strolled over to the campfire and kicked a stone. I stuck my hand under my arm and squeezed off a few indiscreet pops, the way Gil had taught me.

Dr. Vic nodded. Dark patterns of sweat had formed at his armpits and at the crease of his belly, and again, I nearly found it possible to sympathize with him. He was a big man, soft and awkward, gone gray and losing what there was of that, his life held hostage by a fifteen-year-old boy. I guessed he was weary of it. Maybe I was, too.

"I came across this truck one time a couple of years ago. I was just wandering, you know? And, here's this amazing artifact, in what's really a very unlikely place. It really struck me, George, and I've given a lot of thought about how it got here.

"You see, the thing that stumped me is that the fire road's a mile away. So whoever drove through the woods had a rough go of it. Which means the truck must have been in pretty good shape."

The dogs lay down in a heap at his feet, panting happily. He rubbed their heads. "From that point, George, I can conceive of only three possible scenarios:

"First, that it was a bootlegger's truck. Some old gangster jack-knifed it right off the road, came barreling through here, dumped the wheels, the hooch, and headed for the hills."

The ghost of a rawboned country bootlegger, overalls and rubber boots and a pencil-thin mustache, ran through the underbrush in my mind, holding down his straw boater with one hand, and gripping a sawed-off shotgun in the other. He cast a desperate glance over his shoulder, and disappeared into a stand of white pine.

"You like that one, huh?" Dr. Vic grinned at me.

I shrugged, but couldn't restrain a little grin of my own.

"Okay, right. Now in my second scenario I have a guy—a husband, a father—and he lost it, totally lost it. Got completely fed up with everything, and said, 'Forget it all. My job, my wife, my kids, I don't give a good goddamn about anything, anymore. Forget the whole thing.' This guy, he drove the car real deep in here so no one would find it. Then, he walked out to the road, stuck a thumb, and never looked back."

In my mind I heard the dull, painful thud of a patent leather shoe striking a long-vanished hubcap, as the man who just didn't care anymore gave his life one last kick. He limped away, his foot dragging like a snake.

"But"—Dr. Vic held up his hand—"neither of those scenarios completely satisfies me, George, and I'll tell you why. In the first place, a bootlegger—a criminal—might hide his truck out here, but I don't think he'd ditch it. Too greedy.

"And in the second place, a man who'd leave his family, quit on all his responsibilities, I don't think that kind of son-of-a-bitch would even consider ditching his vehicle. Why would he? A guy like that hasn't got a conscience, so how could he be ashamed enough to try and conceal what he'd done? No, I'm nearly positive that our man would just take the truck and drive like hell, try and get himself a head start on screwing up some more folks' lives."

"Okay," I said. I squatted beside the dead campfire and absently picked out a singed paper canister, the wrapper for a firework or a flare. I saw the gangster and the runaway husband hunched around another campfire, this one tucked away somewhere deep in the hills. It was a starless night and the shadows of the flames played wildly across the jagged face of the ravine. Each man held a smoldering a sausage on a stick and regarded the other with a wolfish sneer.

"Which leads me to a third scenario, and this one is where I prefer to lay down my chips. You with me here, George?"

Dr. Vic's wide, soft face was serious now. It occurred to me that this must be the same tone he used when he told a person they were terminal, that the black vines growing in their body could not be weeded out by surgery, or burned away by chemotherapy. I glanced at him and nodded, ready for the diagnosis.

"What I've come to think happened is that the guy who owned this truck was maybe a bit of a loner to start, and that, maybe as time passed, something started to wear him down—I don't know what, bad business, bad love, bad luck. I don't know, something. But whatever it was, inside the guy, he was terrified, and at some stage, when a part of his life changed, he was overwhelmed. What had always scared him most was right up in his face. And suddenly, the guy decided that he couldn't trust anyone anymore. So he withdrew more and more. He hid. He got tough.

"And you know what?"

I crumbled the paper canister between my palms and let the ash trickle through my fingers.

"No," I said.

"It didn't matter. People could still see the guy.

"So, the loner decided he needed a place to go, and he found this spot in the woods, and it was his secret. But there was no shelter, right? Which brings me to how I first imagined this guy: I thought to myself, 'What if someone brought the truck out here piece by piece?' Hundreds, thousands of parts. From the smallest screws to the mirrors and the tires and the engine. Then, he reassembled the whole damn thing out here in the middle of the woods.

"What an amazing effort, right? But at the same time, what an absolutely perverse and pointless act. The truck is useless out here. Out here it's no better than a cave.

"And so I tried to conceive of the kind of person who would feel so bad about themselves that they could waste so much energy, just in order not to have to try and get along with a new way of doing things. So, that's how I got my loner, and that's how I think the truck came to be here. He brought it out, one sad little piece at a time."

There was a sustained silence, and I realized that Dr. Vic intended this to be the end of the story.

"What happened then?" I asked.

He shrugged. "I don't know. Maybe he sat there until he died. Maybe he went home."

"Don't you think people would have noticed that his truck was disappearing? Especially once the guy started carrying away the engine and the doors and stuff."

"Sure," said Dr. Vic, "I bet they noticed."

"Wouldn't they have done something?"

"They probably tried, but if someone wants to dismantle their own property, who's to stop them?"

Dr. Vic stood up and took a deep breath. "Getting late," he said.

"So you're saying that I'd rather tear everything apart than adjust? Is that what you think, Dr. Vic? Well, maybe some things get taken

apart for a reason: because they don't fucking work. Like us, Dr. Vic.
You and I. We don't fucking work." My voice cracked at the end, but
I didn't. I stared him down.

"You're entitled to think whatever you like, George." He gave the
rust door of the Studebaker a sharp knock. He held up his knuckles
and blew away the red dust. "All I was talking about was how once
upon a time, some odd body up and decided to waste a perfectly
good vehicle."

At dinner, Dr. Vic remembered that I had wanted to show him
something, too. "What was it?" he asked.

My mother and I were both eating according to the rules of the
engagement, not speaking but with our notebooks at the ready beside
our plates, like third utensils.

This, I wrote, and drew an → pointing back at myself. I slid the
notebook over to him.

He read it, and looked at me.

I slowly raised my middle finger.

Dr. Vic's eyebrow lifted. There was a moment of silence—un-
broken by the clinking of silver or the ticking of clock hands—
complete silence. Then, a great, toothy smile broke across the big
man's face. He rose halfway and leaned over the table with his own
hand outstretched and flying the proud bird of his meaty middle
digit, letting it hang there only a couple of inches in front of my nose.
I flinched slightly, leaned away. Dr. Vic stayed half bent over the
table, smiling with all those teeth, letting his finger hang there for
several seconds.

My mother made a small noise, like a punctured inner tube. She
stood up and left the room. Dr. Vic slid back down into his chair. He
tucked himself into the table and began to eat. I sat there and tried to
find things to look at—the windows facing out onto the water, the
Eakins print of men sculling through light and shadow—but my eyes
kept returning to Dr. Vic. He continued to eat, working blankly and
patiently with his knife, pausing to add salt and pepper, thoroughly
chewing each bite. When his plate was cleared, he half rose again,
and I flinched back again; but he ignored me and reached for the

serving bowl, helping himself to seconds. I jerked from my chair and went upstairs.

A while later, Papa phoned. He wanted to speak to my mother. "You might want to keep your head down tonight," he said before I handed him over.

My mother talked to him in the kitchen using the cordless phone. I pressed my ear to the door and made out a few scraps of conversation; to begin with, my grandfather had some kind of hunch. My mother thought he was being nosy; she tried to change the subject; she asked what he and I had been doing every day of the summer. Papa's hunch kept popping up, though; my mother started to sound irritated. Finally, she hung up, pointedly foregoing the usual "I love you."

After that I heard drawers being whammed open and shut. She emerged from the kitchen, glanced at me, frowned, and went outside. I saw she was carrying a little plastic-covered booklet.

Through glass doors I could see Dr. Vic sitting on the patio and drinking a beer, the floodlights illuminating the mites circling his head. He glanced up from his crossword to find my mother marching at him. She was holding out the little booklet—a checkbook—carrying it gingerly between her thumb and forefinger, like something filthy.

I didn't have to strain to hear the conversation now; my mother's yells cut clearly through the glass, and Dr. Vic's embarrassed protest seemed all the more shamefaced for the deep bass of his voice. "Hold on, hold on. You've got this all wrong. He wasn't my first choice, Emma. I was just covering my bases with some of the guys at the hospital who were involved in the fundraising. And I gave just as much to Gore. I canceled myself out."

A nauseated feeling came over me and I didn't want to hear anymore. I locked myself in the bathroom. Perched on the toilet, I told myself this was it, what I wanted all along. I was vindicated; the truth about Dr. Vic had finally come out. It wasn't evidence of a murder, but something almost as bad—proof that Dr. Vic donated money to George W. Bush's campaign.

From inside the bathroom their voices sounded tiny and detached, but somehow that brought the argument closer, as if it were happening inside my own mind, and being fought between warring personalities. "And what the fuck are you doing sifting through my checkbook, I'd like to know?" asked Dr. Vic, finally gathering steam.

The matter of Dr. Vic having surreptitiously donated two hundred dollars to the presidential campaign of George W. Bush turned out to be only the starting-off point, for this raised questions about their entire relationship. My mother wanted to know if Dr. Vic had been leading her along from the very beginning, pretending to support her career at Planned Parenthood; and whether he was lying when he said he believed in a woman's right to choose. What about contraception? Did he realize that in the eyes of the man in the White House, the man he gave money to, that his fiancée was bound to burn in hell for the mortal sin of teaching teenagers how to use condoms? Did it concern a big-money Republican donor like himself that—and so on, and so forth, and even when I retreated to my bedroom, their voices chased me up through the windows and the floors, and with my head buried in a pillow, I begged them to stop.

I fell asleep for an hour and two, and woke to find the house quiet. My mother had slipped a note under the door. *I always told you that you could succeed at whatever you wanted. What you're doing now, what your grandfather is helping you to do—to Victor and me—is no exception. I wish I could be proud of you again. I don't know if your grandfather put you up to it, but it doesn't matter. I raised you better. I'm so ashamed of you both.*

The silence was only an intermission, however, and they started up again almost as soon as I finished reading. At the same time, the Laddies yelped and hurled themselves against the chain-link fence of the kennel, like rioting lunatics. My mother and Dr. Vic took their argument out to the dock now, where so recently they had drunk wine and danced and kissed and laughed about all the funny things you learned about someone when you fell in love with them. Their voices were now indiscernible, just sounds, Dr. Vic rumbling in protest, and my mother snapping back, every word like a whip being cracked. The barking and the yelling mixed with a series of splashes, but by then I couldn't even bear to raise up and see if they were drowning each other.

11.

I dreamt that I was stranded at the side of the road. The moon hung in the air like a porthole in the night, like an entrance to the day.

I started walking. A Studebaker taxi pulled past me, then ground up onto the shoulder. It kept on going, just staying in front of me, but I was tired of being left behind. I hurled a rock off the back window. The taxi crunched to a stop.

Myrna Carp pushed open the door and told me to come on. From the Bob Dylan album she was holding, she suggestively extracted a record-sized condom.

"I thought you were on the pill," I said.

"Just get in the damn taxi," she said.

I did.

12.

The cackle of a loon roused me at dawn. I went to look out the window.

The night sky had paled to a woolly gray, but the lake was still black, so the silver circles floating in the shallows by the dock were sharply defined. There were roughly three dozen of these flashing objects, drifting on the placid water like tiny, baffled UFOs.

I cracked the window to let in some air. I wiped my eyes with my fists and took a few deep breaths to clear away the last of the dreaming.

The silver circles were still there when I looked again, slowly rotating on the surface of the lake. The first ray of the sun shot over the hills on the southern end of the lake and burst across the circles in a single snap, like a giant flashbulb going off.

They were compact discs, I realized, all those silver circles. There was something mesmerizing in the sight, the way the little pieces of plastic filled with light. It didn't seem strange, only sad and pretty.

I worked it out, then, that there was only one person in our house who had a vast enough music collection to account for so many discs. From there it followed that when the argument proceeded onto the deck, the splashing I heard must have been the sound of my mother throwing her fiancé's maudlin CD collection into Lake Keynes.

This was a very humorous development, I decided, a final come-uppance for everything that made Dr. Vic, Dr. Vic. "It's a wonder the lake didn't spit them back," I pronounced, because the moment of victory was not the time for the hero to drop his cavalier attitude. Oddly enough, however, I found it impossible to produce the correct grin of satisfaction.

I reminded myself of the situation: there was a line, and it was our line, and you had to be very careful about what kind of person you let come across. Just as a union acted for mutual benefit, it was founded on mutual trust. It had never until now been more clear to me why I couldn't believe in Dr. Vic's commitment—what made him so different from the men my mother dated before, Paul and Jupps and Dale and the others, who had respected the line, and understood exactly how close they could toe up to it. What made Dr. Vic different was not his big, lumpy, ridiculous body, or his pockets full of dog biscuits and peppermints, or the corny scraps of poetry that he stuck on the fridge. What made him different was the cross-training, the same act that had made Tom Hellweg a blackleg. If he simply wanted to be my mother's husband, maybe that would have been okay, maybe we could have negotiated some kind of settlement. I could be reasonable. Except, Dr. Vic had been cross-training from the beginning: sitting me down to talk about life, taking me for a walk to discuss things—all the time, trying to be the man, the man of the house, the one who explained how things were and how the world worked, the man who gave me rides home.

That first blast of daylight clung to the silver discs and rimmed them with gold sparks. "It's a wonder the lake didn't spit them back," I repeated to myself, because it was just so funny.

*　　*　　*

Before leaving the house I paused at the door of the master bedroom and pressed my ear to the door. Dr. Vic's sound therapy machine was on, a soothing tide, low breakers falling and receding, but behind the gentle rush I could hear talking. The conversation was modulated now, almost hesitant, like a discussion of the weather in a beginners' language class. The argument was apparently over, although I didn't know what that could mean. I waited, scared and nervous and excited, but the soft tones did not lift and the small waves continued to lick at an invisible shore.

When I reached my grandparents', I found the two old men sitting in the living room with the air-conditioning on high, a fresh bowl smoldering, the television on mute, and the radio on the windowsill turned to the local talk station. Gil curled up on the couch in his pajamas, his naked head propped on a pillow. Papa slouched in the armchair, and the bowl rotated back and forth between them.

My grandfather glanced up at me with eyes slit to bloodshot quarters, and nodded. "Grandson," he said. "Comrade." He seemed to be searching for more words, but settled for another nod, and turned back to the television.

"You're just in time, lad," said Gil. "We've got bare-assed Swedes."

The show was muted so that my grandfather could listen to the radio at the same time.

I sat down on the floor. I felt relieved to be away from the house, relieved and safe and somehow more myself. I realized how tired I was then, how fitfully I must have slept while my mother and Dr. Vic yelled through the night. A part of me wanted to blurt out, "How could you?" and demand that my grandfather tell me why he called my mother and started the whole thing. Another part of me scolded this thought; wasn't that exactly what I wanted? Was I about to start doubting him now?

The old men coughed the bowl back and forth, the one dying, the one crazy, but the only people that I could really trust. In this place, I felt no doubt that we were all on the same side.

"Look at all those bare-assed Swedes," said Gil. "They don't have a care in the world, do they?"

A group of middle-aged Swedish exhibitionists were taking a walking tour of the countryside, nude except for their hiking boots and knee-high black socks. Against the backdrop of blue mountains they trod among a grazing flock of Highland cows.

I watched with my legs crossed, slightly horrified, but also enthralled by the supple rumps of the Swedish women, and the dark flashes of their genitalia as they climbed. It seemed a kind of dream to me, to be middle-aged, and Swedish, and naked among livestock.

"Get an eyeful, son. This is why we fought World War II," Gil said, and bestowed me one of his patented dirty winks. The waxy tone of his skin and the depth of his eye sockets only made the gesture dirtier, as if he were dead, but still horny.

"No, we fought World War II to save the planet from tin-pot fascist imperialists who claim divine inspiration for mass murder, and give countries to their friends." My grandfather seemed to say this to himself. He gazed at the screen with a glassy lack of attention.

"Here we go," said Gil. "And just when we were getting to the good part."

But for several minutes my grandfather didn't say anything more, just sat nodding in the armchair, eyes fluttering. The Swedes made a picnic, breasts and cocks drooping helplessly toward the bowls of potato salad and the crocks of meatballs. On the radio the right-wing commentator led his audience through a litany of democratic and liberal crimes, high taxes and activist judges and the ACLU and affirmative action and gay marriage and welfare mothers, all the things that real Americans were sick of tolerating. "I'll tell you what, my friends, I prefer the original welfare," said the man on the radio in a voice like Santa Claus, "It's called work. Get a job, leeches!

"For heaven's sakes, these are people who are not even smart enough to vote right! And to that, my friends, I say: 'Thank God!' "

While some of the Swedes set up a net and played an uncommonly buoyant game of badminton, the commentator gloated about how, only seven months after the fact, the country had accepted the Supreme Court's decision not to allow a recount in Florida. "We got those liberals on the run, pardners!" he cried. There was a canned track of a trumpet playing "Charge!" followed by the sound of whizzing bullets, and then the sniffling of women. "But, seriously, folks, if all these liberals don't like democracy, then why don't they take a hike? That's—"

I switched off the radio. I had caught a movement from the corner of my eye, and rose to reach the windowsill before Papa. Without speaking, my grandfather had stood, and held a Swiss Army knife folded open to the full blade. He was breathing hard, face drawn, and the hair at the back of his head standing up in a white fan of static electricity from the wool-covered armchair.

Gil dropped his peppermint tin into his front pocket and groaned up into his walker. The show was over: the Swedes had arrived at their destination, a mountain pool, and frolicked while the credits rolled. An unappealing repeat about a naked aerobics class in Warsaw was on next.

Papa frowned at the knife, and then at me. There was something wayward in the frown, as if he were not quite sure how the knife came to be in his hand. He carefully closed the blade. "It's not right, Gil. That man did not win. It was a coup and anyone can see it."

"You can't save the world, Henry. You can only give yourself a heart attack," said Gil. He clicked around the couch and toward the door. "It doesn't matter anyway," he added under his breath. "As a wise man once said, 'It's not as if there's any real difference between the Republicans and the Democrats at this stage.'"

Papa closed the knife and set it on a side table. "I think I'm a little ragged, George," he said, and went to the stairs. My grandfather leaned his way along the banister to the landing and out of sight.

Gil made his way to the window and gave me a pat on the shoulder. "You're a good grandson, George." He scraped forward to the door, stopped and twisted around. He nodded with a smile toward my waist. "Just be careful you don't poke someone's eye out with that thing."

I looked down and recognized the tent of my hard-on pressing from my shorts. Heat rushed up my neck. I dropped my hands.

"Don't be embarrassed, son. It's healthy," said the dying man. "If you can't get excited about a bare-assed Swede, what's the point?"

13.

My grandfather lay on his side on the bed in the guest room, blinking at the framed photo of Joseph Hillstrom. I didn't have to ask him what he was thinking about. I lingered in the doorway, uncertain whether to enter.

In the photograph, Joseph Hillstrom's famously cool eyes were as small and undead as always, his lips thin and tense. Whom did the fearless organizer see approaching? It was a question the photograph inevitably raised, and would go on raising for eternity. I thought again of the morning I discovered Nana cold, the ambushed expression on my grandmother's face.

I thought, *Hillstrom did it.* Circumstantial evidence or not, we all know that he killed those men. *Don't Mourn! Organize!* The words were true, but the man was a liar.

"The thing was, Gerry said she couldn't live with it. The company people, they all thought she was so hard, they hated her. She never gave the bastards an inch. Even our people, they never really understood, how it was between us, how a woman could be a part of it." He closed his eyes. "But I was so relieved. I didn't argue, not a whit."

There was a note of finality in this last statement. I sensed the importance of it, but I couldn't follow his line of thought. It occurred to me that my grandfather's line of thought probably now looked like the green dash that raced across life support monitors in television shows, jagging up and plummeting down. Or maybe his thoughts weren't even going in one direction; maybe he was so confused, so sad and so angry, that his thoughts were only flashes, bursts of neon paint: **GET OVER IT SHITHEEL! YOU LOST! . . . LOVE IT OR LEAVE IT SHITHEEL! . . . COMMUNIST SHITHEEL! . . .**

"I don't understand what you're talking about, Papa," I said.

The old man sighed, but didn't open his eyes. He pulled up a corner of the comforter and blew his nose on it with a dry honk. "Couldn't help it," he said, barely above a whisper.

I thought he meant the comforter. "Do you want some tissues?" I asked. I remained hovering in the doorway.

"Gerry, she said, 'We tell them we're all in this together, and Tom Hellweg's old enough to understand that, and his wife's old enough by now to understand what kind of man her husband is, but what about those kids? Where'd they sign on?' Gerry asked me.

"They'd stand outside the gate in the morning, you know, those two kids, and their father had them taught to ask all the men, 'Can you spare a dime today, mister, or do you want to help Mr. Big Shot Henry McGlaughlin starve us some more?' And when everyone was inside, they'd come around to different windows and stare in at people. Just stare in at them while they were trying to work. One metal worker was trimming a girder, happened to glance up, and the little girl was on the other side of the window with her shirt pulled up and her little belly pressed against the glass. The guy, he was so surprised, his hand slipped, and the flame of his blowtorch caught the back of the shirt of the man next to him, and almost burned this other fellow up.

"Someone would chase the kids off and they'd be back the next day. Someone would catch their father on the street and beat the tar out of him, and those two kids would be back the next day, looking in the windows, asking, 'Do you want to help Mr. Big Shot Henry McGlaughlin starve us some more?'

"When Gerry finally said we needed to do something, I was so relieved."

My grandfather opened his eyes, and squinted at Joseph Hillstrom. Joseph Hillstrom returned the gaze with his eternal, thousand-yard stare. I hadn't moved.

"What did you do?" I heard an odd distance in my voice; I realized I was afraid of Papa's answer. I imagined the child pressing up to the smudged window. Her face was empty like a doll's face, and her belly was a little balloon swelled against the glass. I was afraid that my grandparents had them killed; that they had the blackleg and his family executed for stepping across the line.

The purple bags beneath Papa's eyes were the size of butterfly wings. He must hardly have slept for weeks, sitting beside the window until dawn, with his rifle and scope, on the lookout for the vandal Steven Sugar.

"First thing in the morning I called an old hand I knew at the yards in Norfolk, and I asked him if he could clear a spot for a friend of the family who needed a change of scenery. Gerry made the offer, and the son-of-a-bitch Hellweg said he was amenable to the idea, but only on two conditions: First of all, he wasn't partial to traveling coach, since it cramped the leg he'd broken when he was a kid. Second of all, long trips gave him dry mouth.

"So, by that night we had them in a first-class car from Portland to Boston to Norfolk with a case of beer and a bottle of whiskey." My grandfather barked an abrupt laugh and broke into a series of deep, hacking coughs. He put the corner of the comforter up to his mouth and continued hacking for more than a minute. When the coughs passed, he continued in a whisper. "And the next I heard—the last I ever heard—my old friend Tom Hellweg was working as a riveter, pulling a pension and a family health insurance plan, double over-time and five weeks of vacation a year, just like any worker deserves. A living wage and some respect, what Gerry and I spent the better part of our lives fighting to get for our people."

I let out the breath I had been holding.

My grandfather looked down at the wet smear on the comforter. He touched it with the tip of his finger. "You understand that it was a moment of weakness, George," he said. "If Tom had his way, that could have been the daughters of any one of the hundred men at the Works who would have lost their jobs. You understand that, don't you? You understand that compassion will get you nowhere when you're dealing with a man who doesn't even have compassion for his own offspring?"

"Yes," I said, and Papa nodded and then he said a few more things, about the president's shameless pandering, about the unchecked corporations and the systematic dismantling of the Bill of Rights, about the obscenity of "compassionate conservatism" and about a lot of other things that were also true and which made people feel bad to even talk about. But they needed to talk about it, damn it. Staying quiet was the reason we were in so much trouble in the first place, and he, for one, wasn't going to shut up. He wasn't going to be picked on (**GET OVER IT!**), either, and he wasn't going to be intimidated (**LOVE IT OR LEAVE IT!**), and he certainly wasn't about to be libeled (**COMMUNIST!**), not by anyone, boy or man. No, no, no. Not at this late stage.

When he ran down, I tucked another blanket over him, and he shut his eyes and fell asleep. I sat down in the armchair by the window and took aim at the yard, at the blue plastic backing of the billboard, at the empty street. I woke up the same way, hunched over the rifle, the street still void of targets.

It was late afternoon when my grandfather came to. The wind had suddenly kicked up, blowing eddies of dust and cut grass down the street, and shivering the tree branches. The rush of air came in through the open window and rustled the orange curtains. Papa groaned and pulled himself upright.

"Thunderstorm," I said.

Papa rocked back and forth, slapping and rubbing his arms, as if he were cold, although it must have been eighty degrees in the upstairs room, and humid, too. "Gotta wake up, get the juices flowing," he said.

I offered to stay the night. He said that wasn't necessary. His eyelid twitched, and he plucked at it. "If you really wanted to help out an old man, though, I wouldn't protest if you went next door to see if Gil couldn't scare up a few spare herbs." Red blooms appeared on his arms where he slapped them.

"What do you think of Dr. Vic?" I asked. I had never spoken to my grandfather about the situation at home. I assumed that he and my mother had discussed it; but that he wanted to give me space to bring it up on my own.

Papa shrugged. "As a doctor, or as a son-in-law?"

"Both," I said.

"As a doctor, your grandmother liked him. That was what mattered to me. Lipscomb was honest, and to the point, and didn't make any promises he couldn't keep. She was terminal from the get-go and he told her straight. Lipscomb said he'd make her as comfortable as he could, and I believe he did that." Papa rubbed his thighs and clapped his hands. "As a son-in-law, he's a fat man, which is embarrassing in light of his profession. He's also too old for her, which means that it's likely that before all is said and done she'll have to be his nurse. Furthermore, he gave money to that sacrilegious son-of-a-bitch who stole the election, which was at the very least a failure of some kind of nerve, and a goddamned shame in general. And, of course, he's boring, which is a personal disappointment."

He reached out, then, his long, wrinkled finger hovering less than an inch in front of my face. The gesture froze me; I thought he was about to give me the finger, like Dr. Vic the night before; that he was about to accuse me of sulking, of cruelty to animals, of admiring Steven Sugar for his courage, of envying his capacity for destruction, of all these and many other crimes of which I was guilty. An apology filled my mouth. I nearly blurted out, "I'm not really like this. I want to fix this!"

Papa flicked a sleep seed from the corner of my eye. It was a gesture I remembered from when I was very small, when the hair at his temples was black. "But disappointment is no surprise. I've been disappointed on a regular basis since Congress passed the Taft-Hartley. Therefore, knowing what she knows now, if your mother insists on loving the man, then I will resign myself to having a closet Republican for a son-in-law. At least he's not a Yankees fan.

"I spent my life working under a system of collective bargaining. Collective bargaining is a synonym for disappointment. The act of collective bargaining is, essentially, the act of bilging a sinking ship that is beyond the reach of land or rescue. Although it's hopeless, you keep on doing it until you drown."

"Why?" I asked.

"Because only a crazy person lets themselves drown."

He smiled, a wide, strong, yellow smile—so strong and so hard a yellow that it looked like it could have slipped out of his mouth and fallen to the floor and not even chipped. I smelled his bad breath, the marijuana and the peanuts that were the only thing I ever saw him eat anymore.

I smiled back.

The old man reached out for the jar of peanuts on the bedside table, grabbed a handful.

"And while it's my opinion that workers deserve democracy, real democracy, I also believe that in life the best we can hope for is collective bargaining." My grandfather shrugged then, and said, "But I'm sure I don't have to tell you about that, George. If I recall, you've known some disappointment yourself."

Gil's wife ushered me into the Desjardins' house, a dainty brick structure that for me always recalled the story of the big bad wolf. The last piggie had inhabited just such a brick house, and no amount of wolfish huffing and puffing had managed to topple it. In her gingham apron and slippers, stout, middle-aged Mrs. Desjardins went nicely with the fairy tale theme.

"And just in time," she said as she led me into the living room, speaking with the sitcom brightness that was her typical tone. "Gilbert's being incorrigible again."

She was Gil's fourth or fifth wife, my grandmother had mentioned to me once, and like him, a former professor at the University of Southern Maine. "I think she taught literary theory," Nana said, never one to hide her skepticism, "which is bullshit, by the way." Although she was past fifty, Mrs. Desjardins was the sole person I knew who could be described—could *only* be described—as "chipper." At the reception following Nana's funeral she patrolled the living room with a garbage bag, briskly collecting paper plates as soon as they were cleared, and stuffing them away like hazardous medical waste.

I had never understood what Gil saw in her, but I assumed it related to being old and still wanting to have sex and making the best of a limited number of options. I tried not to think about it, though.

For his part, Gil always claimed that their relationship was largely based on Scrabble. I had heard him lecture on the subject several times as the marijuana smoke wavered about his head and Papa looked on with a grimace. "The first time we played, she froze the board, got us all blocked into one corner, and then waited for me to get impatient. And when I finally got flustered and put down *cat*—it was the only thing I could do at that point and I just wanted to expand the board—she drops an *afalque* on the end and makes *catafalque*. Scored one hundred and sixteen points." Gil said that was when he knew. "I had wanted to fuck women all my life, George, but she made me think about the part that would come later, the part that would come when all the fucking was through. It was then that I foresaw I would need a challenging Scrabble competitor."

So when Mrs. Desjardins brought me into the living room I wasn't surprised to find the board was spread out on the table, and Gil hunched over in concentration. Behind him, the bow window gave onto the rapidly darkening afternoon; thunderclouds scuttled over the distant treetops. He was seated in the wheelchair that he used in the house and, oddly, there was a thin band strapped across his forehead, holding a hat or something to the back of his bare skull.

"You have a visitor, Gilbert. The boy's come to see if you might have any drugs that he can run over to his grandfather."

"Hey, Gil," I said.

Gil threw up a hand. "A moment, please, lad." He wore only an undershirt and a pair of blue boxer shorts, leaving his pale-haired, skinny legs and knobby knees exposed.

Mrs. Desjardins rolled her eyes at me. Over her shoulder, on the wall, hung an oversized Helmut Newton print of a towering nude in heels, her face half concealed by a leather bandit's mask, and the rest of her body concealed by nothing whatsoever. The photograph was taken from below and in front of the wrought iron gates of a castle. This angle emphasized the model's blond-haired pubis, and minimized the bartizan in the background, which appeared to grow up from her head like a horn.

"You see the symbolism?" asked Mrs. Desjardins. She had followed the direction of my gaze. Her bright, interested eyes reminded me of a seagull's eyes, the way it looked at a wrapper or a bit of foil lying on the ground—right before stabbing it.

"Yes," I said.

"Of course you do," said Gil. He spoke without removing his attention from his slate of letters. "These days I find that particular image rather discouraging. I'll leave the deduction to you, George."

The frame was slightly off, and Mrs. Desjardins adjusted it with a finger. "It's obvious, but that's the fun. I mean we're not talking about Immanuel Kant."

"You're embarrassing him," said Gil. "And for God's sake, leave Kant out of this."

"What I mean is we're not talking about rocket science. We're talking about the things that everyone does." Mrs. Desjardins gave me a shrug and a roll of the eyes. She mouthed the word "Grumpy."

I had an odd, uncomfortable feeling; a prickle that started in my stomach and moved up through my chest in waves. This was a sensation I associated with the time when I was small and my mother would go on dates. My grandmother, who often babysat on these occasions, could perceive my growing nervousness as the hours passed. "Stop twitching, Georgie darling. You look like someone just sang Irving Berlin over your grave. She'll be home soon." Now, looking back among the towering German nude, Mrs. Desjardins's too curious eyes, and Gil sitting at the table with whatever it was strapped to his head, I had that same sense of vague but insistent worry.

But in the next moment, the feeling dissipated. I realized that I didn't have time to be worried. I suddenly knew that I needed to go home and try to talk to them. I knew that it was time to apply the principles of collective bargaining.

"Papa said he just wanted a couple of buds if you could spare it. He's kind of worn out."

Gil clucked at his letters. "I sympathize. Believe me. It's going around."

This comment elicited a sigh from his wife.

I stood, resisting the urge to jump from foot to foot. I wasn't a bad kid. I wasn't Steven Sugar. I just wanted to make a point, to have my say. It was like the dream in the mall. If everyone would just slow down, slow down and stop and listen, then I could say what I had to say, and—

"The child is waiting, Gilbert," said Mrs. Desjardins.

"Fine," he said. He slid a few letters around his slate.

"Take a look, Dick," said Gil. The old man shifted himself in his wheelchair, pushed up on the armrests, and twisted his body so that the mask of Richard Nixon strapped around the back of his head could see the word on his slate. As always, the disgraced president's expression was arranged in a demented grin, framed by the absurd red bulb of a nose and the wolfish jowls. Gil made a humming noise and nodded his head slightly, which gave the impression that Nixon was thinking it over.

Mrs. Desjardins crossed her arms. "You'll have to excuse him, George. He does this to try and psyche me out," she said. " 'Psyching me out,' he calls it." To my surprise, her sidelong glance appeared to contain a glimmer of real irritation. Then, she sighed and shrugged and chuckled richly. "What a funny old man I have. First, the cancer thing, and now here's Richard Nixon advising him on Scrabble."

With a grunt, Gil dropped back into his chair. "Okay. Dick thinks it's a good idea," he said, and told me to fetch the peppermint tin from the upstairs medicine cabinet. When I came back down, Gil showed me his word: *nascent*. "That's you, kid," he said, and pinched a few dried sprouts onto a cigarette paper.

My grandfather had drifted off again while I was gone, slumped at the window with his mouth agape. With every exhalation a lash of spit unfurled from the tip of his tongue before being abruptly reeled back in the shuddering intake that followed. One of his hands lay clenched in his lap, squeezing a packet of plastic paintballs into plasma. I pulled the packet loose and set the joint on the windowsill.

When I gave his shoulder a shake, the old man sagged to one side, like a stuffed animal that's gone loose with years. There were peanut crumbs on the front of his shirt. He snorted, but didn't awake.

If he wanted to, Steven Sugar could not only vandalize the billboard, he could draw horns and a devilish goatee on Al Gore's portrait, then defecate on the lawn, and go goose-stepping around in a circle with his lieutenant Tolson marching two paces behind, both of them whooping like Indians and shredding the purloined sections of the *New York Times* and flinging the confetti in the air. He could do all that and more, and I doubted my grandfather would so much as stir.

My need to rush home coalesced into a frank realization: in my mind Steven Sugar was suddenly diminished, and I felt diminished by association, as if we had somehow been allied. Here was an old man in a window, desperate to shoot his enemies with a gun that wasn't even a real gun. Steven Sugar wasn't a fascist; he was just an asshole kid. The thought occurred to me with a kind of amazement. This wasn't a fight; this was pointless.

This accomplishes nothing, I thought to myself. Why does Steven Sugar bother? I looked at Papa, slumped over, the thread of drool now leaking over his unshaven chin. Why does *he* bother? It was like taking something apart, just because you could.

"This accomplishes nothing," I said.

As I lifted him straight in the chair, rearranged his hands, and brushed off the crumbs, I repeated these words aloud to my grandfather, but he was beyond hearing.

14.

On the ride back to Dr. Vic's house the sound of approaching thunder alternated with the slamming of windows against the coming storm, and made me feel as though I were being chased, but that I was winning, that I was ahead.

I tried to think of what I needed to say to them. The breadth of the treaty I was prepared to make astonished me. I felt big and strong lunged. I was going to give them a chance. They would want to hug me; I was willing to let them hug me. They would cry; and I was willing to cry, too. These movements were as plain and clear to me as the things I saw at the far end of the rifle's scope, so clear and so plain that a child or a foolish person might attempt to reach around and touch the magnification with their fingers.

The thickening humidity fell over my shoulders like a wool shawl.

Garage doors began to jerk closed as I sped past, as if my wheels were tripping invisible wires.

I was drenched in sweat when I reached the driveway and jumped off my bike running, letting it crash in the grass. At the top of the porch, I looked back and noticed that the windows of Dr. Vic's BMW were down. My legs were pulsing, but I ran over anyway, and rolled them up tight.

As I stepped into the house, my yell caromed through the high, spacious rooms. "Hello? Hello? I'm back!"

I ran down the hall and threw open the door to the living room. "I'm back!" I yelled again, the words crossing my lips even as I saw that there was no one here either, just the drapes lapping in the open window, and a trapped fly buzzing around the suitcases lined up against the wall.

The fly circled and abruptly dropped down onto the handle of the first suitcase in the line, my mother's indestructible old Samsonite. The portmanteau's baby blue facing was dented from all the Greyhound luggage compartments that I had kicked it into, cracked from all the third-floor apartments whose stairs I had used it to sled, and patched so neatly with duct tape that it could almost pass for whimsical.

The careful tape job had always irritated me. I remembered watching as my mother sat on the floor of the apartment we rented in Boothbay, a dreary little box of a place stacked on top of a diner, where the stench of bacon rose up from below, continuously, with the substance of an awful, unceasing fart. Even at age eight, I was astounded by the sight of her crouched on the ochre-colored shag rug, wearing her pajamas and a pair of rhinestone sunglasses, as she went about the meticulous process of trimming off the strands at the end of each piece before laying them down like strips of papier-mâché. Did she actually believe there was any repair she could make to this thrift store luggage that would fool someone into thinking we actually belonged somewhere, that we had a house and a family to whom we were traveling home?

The sight of the suitcases made me uneasy. I told myself that Emma must have been preparing to throw some of our old things away, or maybe she was going to donate it all to the Goodwill store, which is where most of it had come from anyhow. Of course that was it. They were getting married; they must be expecting new luggage. Of course.

The insect jerked into the air again, fluttered hopelessly for a few seconds, and landed down on the last piece of luggage in the line, a black suitcase with a Lufthansa sticker on the side. My mother's ex-boyfriend Jupps Boger had left it behind when he flunked out of his graduate program and went to live in Norway, where his friends ran a hydroponic farm. "I love her, you know? She is a tough one, with the boy and the going to school," Jupps told me the last time I saw him. My mother had been in the airport drugstore, buying him a toothbrush and deodorant. "I am a fuck-up, you know, but less always since I know her." In his zipperless leather jacket with pink piping, my mother's ex-boyfriend hugged his backpack like a little boy and made a confession. "Your mother is very generous, though. Do you think, if I forgot my suitcase, she would bring it to me in Amsterdam?" He attempted a sly grin, but his eyes were wet. "I have completely forgot my suitcase in order only to remember it."

We never did hear from Jupps again, but we took his suitcase along with us everywhere we went, just in case. It was my favorite suitcase, because it was the lightest; the only things it contained were a couple of pairs of medium-sized black briefs, an empty pack of German cigarettes, and a yellowed *International Herald Tribune* from October 22, 1995, with half the crossword completed. We had a moving ritual, my mother and I, of loading everything into the car, and then taking a final walk through the empty rooms of our apartment. When we were certain we didn't leave anything, I would pick up Jupps's suitcase, and say, "Let's ride, Jupps," and my mother would lock the door behind us.

The rising wind slapped the drapes against the sill, and as I stood in the doorway I became aware of my own breathing. I had forgotten what it felt like to look at a line of luggage and know that our whole lives were inside.

Walking through the house, I paused at their bedroom, where my mother's closet had been cleared of everything but a few wire hangers. On the third floor, I found the door open, and the room neat and empty. The walls were naked except for a few holes in the plaster. The smart oak desk for which I had never thanked Dr. Vic was cleared. Fresh white sheets were on the bed; the ragged old quilt of peace symbols that Nana sewed for me was gone, too, packed up with everything else.

I found myself at the window. A bead of rain splashed on the glass, then another. A ripple of dots plinked across the surface of the lake.

The break in the weather, however, appeared to have no effect on Dr. Vic. My mother's fiancé stood at the end of dock, a highball in one hand and a dowel in the other, sipping serenely.

At the sound of my steps on the wood, he turned and squinted through his wet glasses. I stopped at the foot of the dock, but he lifted his dowel in greeting. "Hey, how's it going?"

I didn't know what to do. It wasn't supposed to be like this. I was ready to accept their apology. I was ready to come back to the bargaining table.

The rain had already gathered from a drizzle into a light, steady fall, and the shoulders of Dr. Vic's shirt were now dark.

There was a bench near him at the end of the dock, and I saw a carton of orange juice and a bottle of vodka sitting on it, along with a stack of the compact discs that he had fished out of the water so far. Beneath the bench, the Laddies crouched beside each other with their snouts resting on the planks, like a couple of vagrants huddled under a bridge.

Dr. Vic tossed back the dregs of his screwdriver. He raised the empty highball for me to see. Rain spattered in the glass. The wind was kicking up, sweeping the lake, cutting tiny waves.

"I need more ice!" he yelled.

I didn't understand. I yelled, "I put up the windows of your car, so the seats wouldn't get wet!"

Dr. Vic looked at me without any seeming comprehension.

I made a rolling gesture. "So that seats of your car wouldn't get wet!"

"I need more ice!" He smiled and gave the empty highball a demonstrative shake.

Now I understood, and it scared me a little.

"Where's my mother?"

Dr. Vic cocked his head. His smile widened. "She left me! Hopped on the first choo-choo to Splitsville!" Flourishing the dowel, he gave the empty highball a tap with the handle, the way a magician raps the brim of his top hat with a wand. "Abracadabra!" he hollered. "Stepped the fuck out! And now no ice!"

In the kitchen, I found my mother's note dashed on a piece of lined yellow paper, stuck to the fridge:

George, went to pick up apartment keys from the realtor. Back by six o'clock. Wait.

—Mom

I was too late.

My gaze fell on the poem taped beside the note, one of Dr. Vic's old ones, inspired by the Fourth of July:

If She Were Tea (But She's Not Tea!)
By Victor Lipscomb
The beautiful fireworks blew up the sky
The way a beautiful woman can blow up a lonely guy.
If she were a box of tea
I'd have to keep her with me.
George Washington, see you later!
If loving her makes me a traitor,

I'd rather be a British.

I took a tray of ice cubes from the freezer, found a raincoat, and returned to the dock. Dr. Vic was face down on the wood on his belly, as if he'd been shot in the back. I immediately knew that he had suffered a heart attack. He had had a heart attack and it was my fault. I had screwed up the life of a perfectly inoffensive man, terrorized him for things he couldn't help—for loving my mother, for being a dork—and now he was dead. I killed him.

One of the Laddies emerged from the dock and nudged at Dr. Vic's armpit. He pushed away the dog's nose. The Pekingese gave a whine and trotted away. The dog squatted on the planks and began to shit. Dr. Vic sat up; speared on the end of the dowel was a compact disc. The disc skittered down the dowel and he looked at me with an expression of triumph.

"I got the ice," I said.

"No Jacket Required!" he cried, and shook the compact disc on the stick, like a warrior with a scalp on a lance. "I fucking love this album!"

He was still grinning, glasses streaked with water, when I handed him the tray of ice cubes. "Thanks, George," he said. "I owe you."

The rain was steady now, thrumming off the planks. Dr. Vic sat on the bench and the supports gave a damp creak. He cracked the tray on his knee. I watched him drop a couple of cubes on the deck, and then a couple of more into the tumbler. Soaked through, the heavy material of his orange flannel L.L. Bean work shirt clung to his belly. He splashed in some orange juice and started to pour the vodka. The glass slipped and clattered to the wood. It rolled and bounced swiftly down the planks before flipping off the edge. There was a splash, bubbling. The orange juice on the deck melted away in rain.

Dr. Vic gave a damp snort. His breathing was suddenly thick and emotional.

I glanced away: a good fifteen yards out, I spotted a silver wafer bobbing farther and farther out.

There was a slurping noise, and I turned around to Dr. Vic. He had poured orange juice and vodka into the ice cube tray, and now he was sipping and lapping from the indentations. His eyes blinked at mine over the lip of the tray.

"Have to make do somehow, right?"

"Uh-huh," I said.

"Improvise," he said. "Improvisation."

Dr. Vic sipped his tray, smacked his lips. He smiled at me and gave a sob. I lowered my head to study the dark planks. He breathed, thick and shaky. I could sense the dam about to give way, and the expectation numbed me.

But Dr. Vic started chuckle. The chuckle spilled into a deep laugh, and finally, became a high, wild cackle.

I followed his attention to end of the dock, where the Laddies were hunkered down together, nibbling at a fresh pile of shit.

"You know, George, it seems to me that about the only thing that could be worse than one shit-eating dog, is two shit-eating dogs," said Dr. Vic.

After a few moments, he was able to stop laughing. He cleared his throat and sighed and set his tray down on the bench. His chin trembled.

"George," Dr. Vic said, "I just want you to know that I think you're a super kid. It just didn't work out."

My sneakers carried me down the deck at a run, and I was moving faster when I crossed the lawn, plunging and squishing through the grass, slipping and falling and picking myself up and not even hesitating at the sound of my mother's car pulling up the gravel driveway, not stopping until the sky fell away and a branch stung my forehead, and I was safe in the woods.

15.

For a while, I followed the muddy path with no real idea of where I was headed. I concentrated on the hollow sound of water dripping on the hood of my raincoat. I felt cold and loose-jointed in my clothes. Something about it put me in mind of the Arctic, and the way that hikers sometimes found eighteenth-century explorers frozen on the peaks, perfectly preserved. I pictured my own museum display. "Here is an Ungrateful Child, carbon-dated to the early twenty-first century," a tour guide explained in a nasal tone. "Our studies indicate that this particular specimen ruined his mother's engagement and aided his grandfather in a deranged revenge plot. Very nasty little monster. Died a virgin."

I sat down in wet leaves with my back against a tree. It was near dark and the rain was louder. The ground was cold. I smelled smoke.

They had built a small twig fire in the empty hood of the abandoned Studebaker, and the air almost seemed to itch with the oily smoke from it. The two soldiers sitting in the truck's cab were only faintly visible in the light, but I could see one of them shift to watch me as I approached.

"We had an accident," said Sugar when I came up to the passenger side door. I wasn't afraid.

Beside him, Tolson sat with his head thrown back and his eyes closed. A large purple welt shone on his cheek. What remained of his hair was a scorched mess, and a bloody bald patch lay above his temple. He opened a single eye to look at me, gave two gloomy blinks, and then closed it again.

"Defective flare," said Steven.

"How bad is it?"

"FUBAR," said Tolson. He sounded understandably morose.

"It's not FUBAR," said Steven.

"What's that?"

"He'll be okay after a little R&R."

A gust of rain roared down through the trees, shooting BBs off the roof of the cab. I waved at the damp smoke. Sugar sat as calmly in the front seat as if he were taking a Sunday drive, cruising aimlessly.

"What are you doing now?" I asked.

"Chilling," said Steven.

I nodded. He nodded.

"Wanna come in?" Steven delivered a well-placed heel to the door of the Studebaker and it scrutched open. I said sure and climbed in. They shifted over and Tolson gave a grumble of protest. Steven told him not to be such a pussy. "You just lost some hair, dude."

For a while we didn't talk, just watched the rain rattle the trees. The smoke of the fire billowed from the gaping hood and spilled across the floor of the clearing in tatters. It was dry in the cab, and warm from our shared body heat.

"We've got a bunch of peat logs. We're going to keep it burning all night. Wait out the storm."

"So, you guys hang out here a lot?" I asked.

"Not really," said Steven. "We only set up a camp here recently. When we decided to burn down your house."

I took this in stride. "It's not my house. It's my mother's fiancé's house."

"Well, be that as it may, we were going to raze the fucking thing. Send a message to Old Man McGlaughlin." The bigger boy gave me a frank look. "Your grandfather's attitude has been chapping my ass—big time."

I met the look, shrugged. "Collateral damage, right? That's how it goes. So what happened?"

Steven Sugar grinned. "Tolson fragged himself." He elbowed his partner. "Hey, why don't you try not pointing the flare at your own face next time."

"I'll frag you, you fat prick," said Tolson without opening his eyes.

"Does that mean you're not going to burn down Dr. Vic's house now?" I asked.

"Maybe," said Steven. "The situation is under review." He turned back to the empty windshield. "So what do you do, kid?"

It was the kind of question that wasn't really a question at all, but a challenge. Justify yourself, Steven Sugar was saying, put yourself in the best possible light, impress me. Damp gusts rolled through the trees. Rain pinged dully off the roof.

I thought of my summer: of the hours I spent with Papa, the mission with my mother.

"I'm an activist," I said.

Sugar cast a sidelong glance.

"Activists fight to help people. I want to help people." I used my sleeve to wipe water from my face. "I'm pretty new to it, though."

As night came on, the two boys produced a shopping bag with graham crackers, marshmallows, chocolate, and a single beer. "Don't slobber on the beer," said Steven. We passed it back forth and roasted s'mores until the food was gone and my mouth was rotten and my stomach drum tight.

Steven told me about how he planned to join the army after

graduation. He said he wasn't going in because he was some kind of wannabe asskicker, he just wanted the free ride for technical school. "Not that I'm opposed to kicking some ass, mind you," he said.

I told him I wasn't sure yet, but I was thinking about heading right to college. "Vassar," I said.

Tolson absently plucked blackened tufts of hair from his scalp and cast them in the fire.

We talked until the rain cleared, and the stars came out. Tolson said I shouldn't feel bad about my grandfather. "Mine's crazy, too. He's got that Alzheimer's, and he's, like, obsessed with Sears. Thinks we all work there and nobody is ever waiting on him. He's always like, 'I want some service! I want some service!' Shit bums a guy out." Steven said all his grandparents were dead, but he had a grandaunt. "She's cool. She just listens to the police scanner all day, does a little gardening and whatnot."

A fox strode across the clearing. The creature's eyes glowed green in the dark, and its tail wound in slow circles. We just watched it; no one said anything. The fox disappeared soundlessly into the brush.

We added more peat logs to the fire in the hood. The blaze rumbled higher; sparks wafted into the dark, and died in a blink; the shadows drew long, sober faces across the trees.

"Check this out," I said, and gave Steven a nudge. I removed my shoe, my sock.

Tolson leaned forward to see, too.

I planted my right foot on the ancient dashboard.

"Wow," said Tolson.

"Hey now," said Steven.

"You know what they say about guys with six toes," I said to my new comrades.

I woke at dawn and knew that people were missing me. The other two were still asleep. In the daylight, Tolson's face had a deflated aspect and the coloration of a plum. Steven's snores came in a low consistent rattle, like a generator.

I slipped from the Studebaker and went to piss in the brush. Leaning on a tree, I constructed a plan: I was going to say I was sorry, a lot, to everyone. If I needed to, I would beg. I was going to make everything okay. I had to make everything okay.

Stumbling footsteps carried Steven beside me. "Howdy," he said, and began to urinate.

"I should go," I said.

"Well, don't be a stranger." Steven saluted me with his free hand, and sighed in relief. "And tell your grandfather no hard feelings. Being a paperboy sucked anyway. Tell your grandfather I hope he catches that Nixon guy."

"What?" I asked.

"The guy in the Nixon mask." Steven tucked himself back into his pants. "Tolson and I saw him one night. The guy who sprays shit all over your grandfather's sign."

It took me twenty minutes to jog to the Beachcomber Motel where I stopped to use the pay phone. While I waited I paced the gravel lot. I hoped my father would hurry.

Before this, the last time I talked to Ty Claiborne was on the day of Nana's funeral, at the reception.

I was tired of condolences, tired of thinking. So, I had decided to clean the pool in the backyard, using the net to skim the dead bugs off the surface. That was where I was when my father came out to see me.

"Hey, George," he said. "I wanted to tell you how sorry I am. And that's just for your Nana, for starters."

Ty wore a dark blue suit and sipped a Diet Pepsi while I walked around and around, skimming off the insects, not talking to him. He was a thin, gray man with straw-colored hair. He looked the way I imagined an undertaker should look, drained of blood, sort of dusty. (In fact, the undertaker at Nana's funeral had been a rotund and almost cheerful man, bustling around the funeral home with boutonnieres.)

His appearance had changed a great deal since our previous face-to-face meeting, four years ago, at the incident in the parking lot in Blue Hill. That was when he threatened to kill my mother, and Paul broke his nose with a snow shovel. His hair had been very long then, and he'd lain in the snow, bleeding everywhere, and even after my mother rushed me inside and locked me in the bathroom, I was able to hear him howling.

Looking closer now, I noticed the distinct bump on his nose.

My mother had told me about Ty's two years of sobriety, his new job, the college degrees he earned in prison, and the social work he did at the YMCA. Emma told me how he wanted to talk to me. She said she thought I should. (It was around this time that I had, in fact, stopped speaking to my mother.)

"I know 'sorry' sounds like an excuse, but it's not. It's the fact of the matter. There are no excuses in the program, George. I was a lousy husband and a worse father. I'm an alcoholic and a drug addict and a recovering piece of shit. That's the fact of it. I threw twenty years of my life down a hole and I pelted everybody who looked over the edge with my garbage." He took a deep breath. "And I am sorry. I am so sorry."

Mrs. Desjardins had come out smiling with a garbage bag and collected Ty's Styrofoam cup, then patiently held open the bag as I shook out the net full of dead bugs.

"Nana taught me how to clean the pool," I said to my father when she left.

"Well, then I think that's a fine thing to do today," he said.

We stood around for a couple more minutes, and I didn't say anything else. The pool was clean. Then he tried to give me his phone number. "If you want," he said.

"I'm not taking it unless you promise not to call me," I said.

Ty promised, and kept his promise.

16.

When the taxi pulled up to the curb in front of the Beachcomber, I wasn't thinking about the promise. I was thinking about the island of Rhodes and the article by the divorced professor. I remembered the writer's bizarre notion that the Knights of St. John had transformed into voyeuristic stray cats, basking in the sun and admiring the ripe brown breasts of European tourists. I remembered the cashier at the Citgo, the Goth kid with the fork on his Adam's apple who took so much interest in the Desjardins. "Dammit. Janet."

The wheels of the station wagon crunched over the gravel and I ran from the phone booth.

I threw the door open and dropped into the cracked leather of the backseat. The car smelled like pine and cigarettes.

"Hey," said Ty, "I'm glad you called. You know your mother's looking for you?"

"I need to go to my grandparents' house," I said.

"Are you going to call your mother when you get there?"

"Yes." Then I added, "Please don't talk to me."

"Sure," he said. "Are we in a hurry?"

"Yes," I said.

Ty swung the car around the lot, and onto Route 5. He flicked on the tape deck. Bob Dylan piped up in a honky-tonk clatter. Bob said he couldn't believe it; just last night they had been together, and now she acted like they never had met. The car rolled over a fallen branch in the road, gave a bounce. Without looking around, Ty reached back and pointed at the seatbelt by my shoulder. I pulled it down and locked it.

"'Dammit. Janet.' Mean anything to you?"

"*Rocky Horror Picture Show*. I projected it."

"Mean anything else to you?" I asked.

"Not unless you really like cross-dressing, or Tim Curry."

"Thanks," I said, still not exactly sure what I was onto, but beginning to feel the edges of it.

"Sure." My father turned onto the interstate. Ty reached back again and made a window rolling gesture. I told him to go ahead. He put down his window. We streaked past a rig pulled over to the shoulder and blinking its hazards; water glistened off the cut granite that walled the road. The morning air was sharp and sweet.

"Do you have a cell phone?" I asked.

"Uh-huh," he said, and passed it back.

I called my grandfather. The phone rang five times and Nana picked up. "Don't mourn, organize," she said, and gave a wheezy chuckle. "And leave a darn message, too." The machine beeped. I clicked off.

The taxi whooshed up the off-ramp, made a left onto Dundee Avenue. I stared at the back of my father's head, his short-cropped orange hair, sprinkled with gray. There were just a couple of more miles before we got to where we were going. I was nervous and afraid and ready. I wasn't really thinking of him as my father. That was a good thing, maybe.

My father was a bad guy; he was an addict and a felon, a wild man screaming and gushing blood in the snow. Ty Claiborne, however, was a middle-aged taxi driver who had given me a lift when I was in a pinch. A guy reached out, you gave him hand—and vice versa.

We slammed to a stop at the curb and I saw Papa lying there on the lawn. I had my seatbelt off and the door of the taxi open before it stopped.

I stumbled forward, pinwheeling my arms for balance, and pitched onto the damp turf. I got up and ran, dropped to my knees beside him.

He was on his back, the tails of his bathrobe spread out in the grass. The breath came from his mouth in a whistle. His eyes were glazed, holding the billboard at a diminishing angle, like the plane of building's façade. There was the grave etching of former vice-president Albert Gore Jr., followed by the bold, true statement:

THE REAL PRESIDENT OF THE UNITED STATES.

But one could not fail to notice what had been scrawled across the legend in green spray paint: **VOTE NADER SHITHEELS!**

"It's going to be okay, Papa," I said. "It's going to be okay." Nothing in his face gave a sign that he heard me. He had eyes only for Al Gore.

I had my father's cell phone. I started to punch the numbers.

"We already called an ambulance," said Mrs. Desjardins.

Gil and his wife were standing there, too, of course.

*   *   *

At that point, I wasn't aware of the details; that Gil had been writing travel articles for obscure newspapers for years (under the pseudonymous name G. T. Flowers); that, typically, he wrote these articles about places he had never visited; that these articles often included references to naked Europeans, stray cats, his ex-wives, and a very few other things that were of lasting interest to him; that he had been so surprised at being accepted for publication in the Sunday *New York Times* that he had been unable to wait the time it would take to drive to the supermarket and instead, rushed next door and plundered the Travel section of my grandfather's delivered copy.

Nor did I yet understand that one of the main reasons Gil had continued to pluck sections from my grandfather's newspaper was simply because he was too cheap to subscribe and too lazy to drive to the Citgo for his own copy; that another reason he didn't like to go to the Citgo was because the manager (he of the fork-tattooed Adam's apple) had once encountered Gil in an entirely different venue: one night at the USM campus movie theater at a midnight showing of *The Rocky Horror Picture Show*, when Gil was dressed in leather chaps with the cheeks cut out, and riding a tricycle up and down the aisles.

Above all else, I couldn't see that the vandalizing of Papa's billboard had nothing at all to do with the Sunday *New York Times* or Steven Sugar. I was not wise to the history of Gil's relationship with Ralph Nader, to the depth of his wild devotion for the man. It was only a few months later—after the filing of Gil's fifth divorce—that we received a letter from Mrs. Desjardins that filled in the final blank:

To put it succinctly, she said that Gil believed with absolute certainty that he had once stroked Ralph Nader's naked thighs at a masquerade orgy. This mystical union had, according to Gil, occurred following a lecture on the applications of Kant to the Watergate scandal at an all-night bash at the Beverly Hills Hyatt in 1973. The man he swore to be Nader had worn a purple Zorro mask, but Gil was nonetheless utterly convinced of the fearless consumer advocate's identity. Furthermore, Mrs. Desjardins wrote (in a manner of phrasing which in no way belied a hint of jealousy), that it was Gil's testimony that the masked man had returned his thigh-stroking in kind, and with all the compassion and attention that one might have expected from a person who had selflessly dedicated his life to the public good.

At least, that was what she said.

But above and beyond such talk, I could never have guessed that Gil—funny old, dirty old Gil—possessed the capacity for the sort of pique which he must have nurtured over the course of the years, as my grandfather carried on and on, about his unions and solidarity and the common good. I could never have guessed at how it must have grated on him.

Which is to say, I didn't know Gil at all.

I gaped at the man. The name Tom Hellweg came to my mind, and just as quickly blew away again, like a bad smell.

Small and frail, Gil stood wearing his wife's kimono, his hands sullenly jammed in the pockets. The Richard Nixon mask sat on top of his bald skull. There was red paint splattered on his neck and on the mask, from where my grandfather hit him with the IL-47, a killshot from the sniper's nest in the guest room.

Mrs. Desjardins wore a pair of leather overalls, elbow-length gloves, and a driving cap emblazoned with a pink swastika. "The ambulance should be right along." She was, as always, smiling brightly. "I think it's just a stroke."

"He wouldn't shut up about the politics," said Gil. "He couldn't take a little teasing."

I said the obvious thing, the only thing that mattered. "You were his friend."

"He never chipped in for any of my grass, either," said Gil.

"You were his friend," I said again.

He worked his hands deeper in the kimono. The Nixon mask sat on his head like a deflated pie.

"And, furthermore, Ralph Nader never owed Al Gore a goddamn thing."

The car door slammed. Ty's shoes beat across the pavement.

The old man in the kimono glanced over with a grimace.

Ty stopped beside me. "Costume party?" he asked.

"That's it. I'm going home," said Gil, and he turned, walked rapidly down the driveway, and disappeared around the hedge in a whisper of silk. Mrs. Desjardins followed him, giggling as she tottered away on her motorcycle boots.

We were alone then, my father and my grandfather and I, on the lawn, the three of us crouched in the shadow of the billboard of the man that should have been president.

"Papa," I said, "Papa, can you hear me?"

His eyes slid slowly over to look at me, like rusted screws being wrenched loose. The skin of his face was slack and ashen. He opened his mouth, but he could only produce a croaking noise.

"Don't talk," I said. I pulled the flaps of his bathrobe closed.

Ty jogged out to the street to wave down the ambulance so they didn't miss the split in the avenue.

Papa stared at me. His eyes were blue and scared. A tear welled and rolled down his cheek, grooving along a wrinkle before falling to the ground.

I grabbed his hand. "You're going to be fine, Papa," I said. I squeezed to show him exactly how things were going to be. "I'm with you. I'm here."

He opened his mouth to speak—and coughed again. There was a hitching noise, a wet clicking, and I could see he was trying to swallow. He started to blink rapidly, deep color filling his cheeks.

This was it; this was the part where my grandfather died.

This was the part before the part where we went to another funeral. I saw the old men in the black vinyl Local 219 jackets lingering at the back of the funeral parlor. I heard them whisper about the time Henry McGlaughlin stuck out his thumb and asked a big-shot defense contractor if he needed any help climbing up on it. I watched us lower another coffin into the ground and heard everyone sing the "Internationale" while the priest stood there looking nervous.

I saw it all, and I felt it.

I still had Ty's cell phone. I dialed home.

*   *   *

"Hello?" I felt a surge of relief at the sound of Dr. Vic's voice.

"I think he's choking," I blurted. "I think Papa's choking."

There was a moment of silence. On the ground, my grandfather's entire body had started to tremble, to vibrate like a tripped wire. His eyes were rolling. I heard the ambulance siren in the distance.

"What makes you think that, George?"

"His face is turning purple. He looks like he's trying to swallow."

"Okay, I believe you—"

"—thank you, I'm sorry," I said.

He cut me off. "Not now—I'm betting that what your grandfather is choking on is a peanut. I want you to open his mouth, and put your finger on his tongue. I want you to get your finger down as far as you can and pull that thing loose."

Papa's mouth was already agape. I plunged my index finger in, stabbing the back of his throat. I hit something hard and dug at it with my nail. In the next instant, he gasped, and chomped down on my finger.

The ambulance whooped to a stop and the EMTs came running across the lawn.

I brought my finger up to my face, and looked at it, and saw it was crooked. I put it down and breathed and lay there. The sun was up over the house, lighting the shingles gold. I lay there some more.

Ty squatted down beside me. "Your mother's on the phone," he said. "She wants to talk to you."

I sat up and nodded at him. He was almost an old man. When I looked at his face, I could see how I would look when I was old. That was okay. We both had time. People live a ton.

"Mom?"

Her voice came in a rush. "Are you okay? Just tell me that you're okay, George. I need to know that you're okay."

I was fine. "I'm fine," I told her, and she gasped, and then we both started talking.

ORGANIZE!

The day the skyscrapers fall we are at the hospital. Papa has been moved into long-term care, where therapists are helping him learn to speak and walk again. My mother, Dr. Vic, and I sit around his bed and watch the television in the corner of the ceiling. We eat our way through Papa's untouched lunch in shocked silence. The old man's face is frozen in a lopsided half smile; he always look drunk now. He doesn't try to speak. None of us does, really. On the television, a reporter attempts to describe the sound that a human being makes when it free falls one hundred stories and strikes the roof of an automobile. This description is inadequate.

At some point, the president comes on. He tells us to be calm. He tells us everything is under control.

My grandfather begins to cry. He speaks with a helium voice through a mouthful of cotton. "The president looks strong, doesn't he? I think he's going to be okay. I really do." The half smile is grotesque, and I hate myself for not wanting to look at him.

Emma turns off the television and goes to him.

"Can I have my Jell-O?" he asks.

"I ate it," I say.

He sobs. He half smiles. "It's okay, George. They give us all we want."

At their wedding, my mother and Dr. Vic's first dance is to a song by the Flying Burrito Brothers. If nothing else, I have come to appreciate my stepfather's solidity, his consistency. He loves comestible bands, and my mother loves him. I accept it.

For their honeymoon in December, the newlyweds tour the islands of the Mediterranean. I have Christmas with Ty and we go to see Bob Dylan at the State Theater in Portland. Bob is as spindly as a grasshopper. "Do you think Bob kind of looks like the Queen of England?" asks Ty. We seem to get along, my father and I.

On the drive home I ask him about his polydactyl toe. He laughs. He says his fell off the first time he was in rehab. "I found it in my sock. It just fell off."

I don't believe him. But he pulls over and shows me—and it's true. There's a fine scar at the edge of his foot, nothing more.

"Did it hurt?" I ask.

"No," he says, "but I miss it."

"Why?"

"Because it was a part of me," he says.

I am the last six-toed man in my family.

We visit my grandfather at the assisted living center where he has been moved. There is an orange zeppelin of a cat that wanders among the infirm and the elderly, and Papa has become the creature's greatest friend. The cat's name is Softball. While we try to engage Papa in a conversation about the weather or the seniors' bowling league, he ignores us and talks to the cat. "Softball would eat any terrorist that tried to kill the geriatrics, wouldn't he? Wouldn't he just kill those terrorists?"

In the halls at school, I nod to Steven Sugar and his former lieutenant, Tolson. They flip me vague salutes. Tolson's face has healed, but one side is dark, as if he is always thinking bad thoughts.

My mother tells me that the Mediterranean was beautiful, and that "yes, the reports of numerous naked breasts being on display in Rhodes were true." *She laughs like crazy about that, but I'm embarrassed. So I only let her kiss the top of my head. The last thing she says to me is,* "I'm going to be late for work."

My mother and Charlie are locking up the clinic late that afternoon when the rusted blue minivan comes screeching into the parking lot. The GFA woman, the one who likes to scream about whoremasters, and wears a baseball cap emblazoned with a sparkly crucifix, leaps out of the van with a bucket. My mother steps forward, and Charlie fumbles for his gun. The GFA tosses the bucket, drenching my mother in a spray of dirt and earthworms, and then catching her across the mouth with the plastic rim. Emma tumbles to the pavement, and there is the sound of something cracking just right, like an egg on the rim of a bowl. The egg is my mother's skull and the rim is the curb, and in a moment she is gone.

She feels nothing, they say, but no one could know that.

And then, my vision becomes real, and the three men meet at the Beachcomber in their black suits, and my father and Dr. Vic and I pick them up. Dale has come in from Boston where he moved with his new wife and family, and Paul has come from Blue Hill, and Jupps has traveled from the hydroponic farm in the Netherlands.

Jupps presents me with a beautiful tomato that he snuck through customs. I return his suitcase. "We took it everywhere," I tell him, and he starts wailing and drops his beautiful tomato in the mud.

"Man," says Paul in the car, "oh, man."

"I have been bummed before, but this is brand fucking new. This is a kick in the nuts to end all kicks in the nuts." Dale unrolls the window and sticks his head out like a dog. Jupps gives Dale the tomato and tells him to throw it.

"I'm sorry very much about that," says Jupps.

Paul tells him not to sweat it, man. "These things happen, you know?"

Instead of the "Internationale," we sing "Amazing Grace," for obvious reasons.

After the funeral, Myrna Carp insists on speaking with me privately. She pushes me down on a couch in a dark room. She has mascara all over her face. She sniffles and cuddles my head against her breasts. It is her duty, insists Myrna, unbuckling my pants, something she owes to my mother.

"No," I say. "Do you have a condom," I say, and Myrna reminds me that she's on the pill, but I insist, and on the night I bury my mother, I ball up my dirty shorts and throw them under the bed. I do not believe in an afterlife, but I know Emma would be pleased that I used a condom.

I do what anyone would do: cry like I'll never be able to stop. No one comes to check on me.

Three years later, my grandfather has lost interest in the news. It is unclear how much he remembers, but he likes to pet Softball and to be wheeled around the grounds of the nursing home. He is sleeping now beside me, the two of us seated beneath the boughs of an elm tree. I am home on vacation from my freshman year of college.

I don't know how I feel about it. I wish someone could explain it, make it all neat and simple, like a ballot. I could just check off a choice, and never worry about free will again.

I wonder where Steven is at this moment. He joined up right after graduation, just like he said he would.

It must be night over there, a night like blue silk over the desert city, and the dust and the sand and the quiet between outbursts.

"Okay," says Captain Sugar. "Okay, men." His troops are gathered around him in a circle. From the wrecked town square there are crooked little lanes running in all directions, pointing a dozen different routes out of the combat zone.

The captain's face is scorched and haggard, but he meets every gaze in turn. "If we work together," he promises, "we can still get out of this mess."

Frozen Animals

The three men moved in a close line, tied to one another by a hemp rope: Kosskoff, the biggest man, took the point; second in the procession was Funt, the other trapper; and third was Pinet, a dentist. A heavy snow was falling, thickening the pass, and slowing their trek. They carried lanterns, and from a distance, if any creature had observed them, it might have conceived of the three men as a single beast made of flickering light, shambling and swaying, perhaps wounded. But no creature observed them.

They were on their way to Kosskoff's wife. The trappers kept a cabin and a carving shed on the south side of the mountain, three or four miles up. Kosskoff's wife had something wrong with her teeth. She was pregnant; it wasn't safe for her to travel.

The way between the two cliffs was a bottleneck of snow curving gradually up and out of sight. Whorls of deep freeze marked the rock faces on either side. Rising hundreds of feet, the cliffs folded in jutting piles of slate, stopping only where they seemed to meet the sky—a sliding gray-black mat of clouds—as if the weather were made of something solid. The snow fell over and across everything.

Several times the third man, the dentist, seemed to lag. He would pause, appearing to collect himself, and rub his arms through his jacket. The dentist would press the flaps of his hood tight against the sides of his head, as if he were trying to hold something in. Then he would plod forward.

Behind the travelers, their tracks walked away on the wind.

*   *   *

Powerful, intermittent gusts obscured Funt, the second trapper, from Pinet's window of vision. The dentist was still feeling the effects of his morning dose; he heard the snow too loudly: to his ears it was like the sound of metal scraping on metal, a sound that had nothing to do with falling snow or gusting wind. Pinet was used to such incongruities, but this situation was unusual, and the noise added to his discomfort.

His greatest concern was that something would cause the line to break, and he would be separated from the other two. In his life Pinet admitted that he was far from guiltless—he had, for instance, been unfaithful to his wife—but he felt a death by freezing was a punishment that should be reserved for sins greater than his own. He understood that he was a weak man, susceptible to temptation, cringing in confrontation—and wasn't the knowing of it punishment enough? This was the way the dentist was thinking as he walked, putting one heavy boot in front of the other, the nose on his face like a stalactite, and his head filled with the idiot sound of a fork being dragged across a tin plate.

And beyond this lay the morbid prospect of spending the night—or God forbid, even longer—with the two trappers and the woman. There was no chance that he would be able to return down the mountain until the weather cleared.

Pinet knew Funt vaguely from Limestone's only tavern, and found him typically repulsive. The tavern, a nameless black belly of a place, windowless and airless, held only a few tables and on a couple of the occasions when the dentist had made his bimonthly pass through town, he had been forced to sit with the diminutive trapper. Funt was crude and bad smelling, and talked of nothing except whores and killing animals; he seemed emblematic of everything Pinet loathed about the dismal life of the encampments that his itinerant practice condemned him to. Once, over pints of half-rancid potato vodka, Funt had regaled Pinet with a horrific story about a legless prostitute in Ontario who specialized in obscene magic tricks. For a period of weeks the dentist suffered from recurring nightmares about the poor woman.

Kosskoff he didn't know. The other trapper was certainly very large, and Pinet guessed, very stupid. But he did seem to be in charge.

When they woke the dentist from his stupor—Pinet had passed out again, and the tavern keeper had deposited him in the hayloft again—it was Kosskoff who explained the situation: the woman had a sick mouth, she was pregnant, and Pinet would have to go up the mountain to see to her. Then he stuffed the greasy wad of dollar bills into the dentist's shirt pocket, and demanded they be on their way. His size and manner seemed to brook no refusal, and ten dollars meant a great deal to a man like Pinet, a man of needs.

In the lead of Funt and Pinet, Kosskoff climbed tirelessly, and the black train of his fur coat seemed to slither along behind him.

Moving directly against the wind, the snow stinging his eyes, Pinet tried to imagine the life of the woman who was stuck—*trapped,* by his way of thinking—in the same cabin with a pair of men like these. A toothache probably seemed like relief to her. The dentist shivered; he was tired and he needed a dose. The shiver collected in his groin, and Pinet realized that he needed to piss, badly.

He yanked on the cord. The other two stopped, and waded back to the dentist.

Kosskoff drew the other two men into a huddle, and they put their arms over each other's shoulders, lowered their heads together. In the circle of bodies they could speak with relative ease while the wind rose and snapped at their backs. All three men wore the flaps of their hoods knotted tightly beneath their noses, so their talk was muffled.

"You stopped," said Kosskoff.

"I have to piss," said Pinet. "Stand there, please. I can't go in the wind—I'll freeze up. Just give me a minute." He bit his ice-stiff mitten to pull it off and spat it onto the ground.

"Just do it in your drawers, *mon ami.*" Funt sounded merry.

Pinet ignored him, and fumbled under his jacket for the buttons of his fly. The tips of his fingers were numb.

The snow dropped in sheets, powder rolled off their shoulders. In Pinet's head, the fork was scraping faster, the tines jerking back and forth, scribbling and screeching.

Digging the buttons free, he found his penis and winced at the sharp cold.

He looked up, suddenly aware of the closeness of the other two men looming around him; they still had their arms over his shoulders. He could see their eyes through the gaps of their hoods. "Back up a little," said Pinet. "I've got to piss."

Kosskoff blinked a few times, but said nothing. There were flakes of ice on his eyelashes.

"Back up," said Pinet. "It'll only be a moment. If you don't back up I'm going to piss on your shoes."

Funt chuckled and elbowed his partner.

"What?" The dentist clutched his penis beneath the skirt of the jacket. His bladder throbbed. The fork scraped around and around.

Pinet looked again at Kosskoff. The big trapper shrugged and took a couple of steps back. Funt took a couple of steps back.

"Thank you," said Pinet. The dentist had heard stories about trappers, about men who lived together in the mountains. He didn't like them standing there, but it was too cold to piss against the wind.

The dentist raised the skirt of his jacket slightly. He felt his testicles tighten up and ground his teeth against the accompanying swell of nausea. He focused himself on the act, the release of the water. Nothing happened. For a second he thought a piece of ice had lodged itself into his urethra, but when he looked down at his penis—a tinge of blue colored the head—he saw there was nothing.

"Turn around!" Pinet swung his lantern ineffectually at them. "Fucking turn around—I can't go with you watching me."

The two trappers exchanged glances. Pinet saw Funt's jaw move, but the sound of his laughter was torn away by a gust. The two men turned slowly around until their backs were facing the dentist.

Pinet was trembling and there was a wobbly feeling in his knees. He threw his head back to steady himself. The cloud cover was the turgid gray of laundry water. It seemed ready to fall. He had a sensation of vertigo, of himself being slammed down and flattened by the solid sky. Pinet wondered what would come first, the piss, or the vomit.

The water came loose in a series of painful spurts. The urine pattered in the snow at his feet, and a few droplets blew onto his boots.

Pinet stuffed himself back into his pants, and took several deep breaths. Maybe he wouldn't be sick.

He hauled on the rope and the other two men turned around. They huddled up again.

"You think that's bad," said Funt, "the clap, *mon ami*—it's like broken teeth chewing—"

Pinet bent forward, gagging, but managed to hold back from vomiting. The bile was coppery on his tongue. He dropped to his knees in the snow. He wanted to lie down and hug himself. Kosskoff grabbed the dentist's elbow and pulled him up straight.

"Not much farther," said Kosskoff. "My wife will make food. You can get a drink then."

The snow rained against their bodies. The weather seemed to be getting heavier. Pinet's groin burned from the exposure to the cold. He wasn't used to this kind of exertion.

"Not much farther?" he asked.

Kosskoff shook his big head: No.

"And there's something to drink there? Something strong? I'll need to warm up."

"You bet," said Funt, winking, "we got vodka and whores and cards and an accordion player who sings out his ass. Steaks, too. Big fucking steaks. Yessir, we got a saloon up there, and it's a pretty nice one."

"Do you hear a metal sound?" asked Pinet. "A scraping noise?"

Kosskoff stared at him. Funt snorted.

He wanted to explain. "It's like metal, metal cutting on metal." Pinet put a hand against the side of his head.

"You got knives in your head, doc?" Funt laughed.

Pinet nodded.

"Go," said Kosskoff, and put a hand on his chest, and shoved him.

Pinet stumbled and fell onto his backside. The other two men turned and started to move away.

As he watched the rope play out, cutting the new snow, a memory occurred to the dentist. It was often like that these days. An odd association would rush up at him from nowhere, and accost him, like a panhandler, or a mad person. Pinet would find his heart crashing, his breath catching, his head crowded. The shelves of the rock gathered around them, bearded with ice, and the snow turned and spun and ghosted.

As a boy, he'd been a great keeper of pets, and beneath a floorboard in the barn he once discovered a pair of baby mice. Look, Laurent. They're twins, his mother said.

Pinet named them Molly and Polly after two girls in a storybook, who ran away from home, and freed a witch, and won a magical object, a golden eye that winked whenever it heard an untruth. It was Pinet's great hope that the mice were witches—this might explain the absence of their mother—and that he might be the one to reverse the spell that bound them. *Two witches*, he thought.

He kept the mice in a wooden box he hammered together himself from scrap. Sometimes, after dark, Pinet snuck them little fragments of venison that he secreted from the supper table.

Pinet let Molly and Polly scramble up and down his arms, bright eyed and squeaking. He stroked their fine brown fur with great care, using just his index finger, because they were so small and fragile. He studied their tiny paws, and the eager way they sometimes rubbed them together, and believed that he detected something human in the movement. The future dentist prayed for his pet witches to be transformed and to make him a gift for loving them so well: a pair of golden eyes, one to wink at liars, and the other to wither them.

But an illness claimed one of them—he couldn't recall which—and when his mother discovered the corpse, she also found the living mouse nibbling on its dead sister's leg. Of course, his mother explained, because it had undoubtedly taken the sickness from the dead flesh, they must dispatch the living mouse, as well. For mercy, she said.

Pinet observed dutifully as his mother put the survivor in the steel icebox. She permitted him to give the mouse a few strokes to say good-bye.

It wouldn't suffer, his mother had promised, but thinking of it now, he wondered.

*   *   *

The dentist pulled on the cord again. Kosskoff came back. Funt threw up his arms.

"Yes?" asked Kosskoff.

"We're not going to freeze, are we?" asked Pinet.

Kosskoff eyes narrowed.

"I don't want to freeze," said Pinet, "I just want a drink." He knew it was unreasonable, maybe even mad, but the memory of the second mouse, curled up in a comma, fur stiff with ice, black eyes clouded white, seemed like a premonition.

"You'll live," said Kosskoff, "you'll have a drink. But only if you move your ass." He reached forward and gave the dentist a firm push, square in the chest. Pinet staggered.

The big trapper turned and went forward. Funt let him get ahead, then followed.

Dragging his boots—one step and then another—Pinet started, too.

The snow thickened, and even Funt disappeared. The dentist concentrated on the cord. One step and another. It was like sleep-walking, but he did not dream.

Over and across everything, the snow fell.

When he awoke, they were banging on the door for the girl to let them in, out of the storm.

Funt asked him if the mark on his neck was a love bite. They were in the cabin.

"No. My wife went away. Home. To her people." To suggest Mrs. Pinet's departure the dentist made a flapping gesture with his hand.

When they came in, the girl had helped the men out of their frozen layers, and draped them in dry furs. Now they sat in their long underwear on a bearskin in front of the stove.

The trapper's wife had busied herself cooking fish and the room was close with the smell. She was only a girl, and delicate anyway, so that her great pregnant stomach seemed not so much a part of her, as her a part of it. Her features were smooth and flattened, her complexion light. She glanced once at the dentist, but the look was almost perfectly blank, and conveyed nothing . . . except, perhaps, that Pinet was not an especially notable presence, an evaluation with which he could not disagree.

Pinet sipped vodka from a tin cup. His head still throbbed, but this was not unusual. The sounds of scraping metal had receded, and he was feeling optimistic. After the business at hand was resolved, he had promised to administer himself a double dose as a reward for not freezing to death.

The cabin was a single room. The stove commanded the center of the space, while several shelves, haphazardly stacked with jars and dented pans, lined the walls. Furs were piled on the beds. Two oil lamps hung from the main rafter.

Pinet could imagine Kosskoff humping the girl, and Funt in the next bed, watching, working at his mustache with darting flicks of his black tongue.

Outside, the wind pounded at the walls and trembled the boarded windows.

"Reckon you must've learned your lesson, then," said Funt. He was still on the subject of the dentist's wife. "Stick to whores, keep it business. I always approach a whore just the same. 'Whore,' I say, 'I got a small piece of business I'd like to transact with you.' Keep it simple."

"I don't patronize brothels," said Pinet.

"Yeah, but you can still fuck em." When he smiled, the trapper's sparse mustache stretched like a caterpillar.

The dentist drank steadily, unconcerned about his ability to examine the woman's teeth.

Kosskoff's wife served them the fish on tin plates and stood watching them eat. She hadn't spoken, yet, and Pinet supposed she wouldn't.

The food was blackened and tasteless, and even if the dentist had had an appetite, he doubted he could have eaten much. The sound of Funt and Kosskoff, barbarically crunching the tiny bones, eating the creature whole, nauseated Pinet. He didn't want to be sick. It embarrassed him to think of the way he'd behaved on the mountain. The dentist poured himself another cup.

When she was certain that he was finished poking at the food, the girl took his plate and went to sit on one of the beds. She ate with her fingers.

When the plates were cleared Kosskoff decided it was time for the dentist to work. "Fix her mouth now," he said.

Pinet instructed the girl to sit in a high-backed chair. The dentist placed his satchel on the bed and removed the headrest and his instrument case. He went behind the girl and locked the vise grips of the headrest onto the chair.

The leather cradle of the headrest was cracked and torn in places, and it conveyed a distinct odor. Pinet calculated that in the course of his travels through the villages and encampments and lumber towns more than a thousand unwashed heads had settled into it.

"Lean back," Pinet told the girl.

From his instrument case the dentist picked the single tool that lay on the worn velvet lining, along with a series of interchangeable headpieces. The tool was two-pronged, with one prong slightly longer than the other, and the other prong hooked and sharp; it looked something like a nutcracker.

"What's that?" asked Funt.

"Forceps," said Pinet.

Funt scratched his grizzled cheek.

"They're like pliers," said Pinet.

Funt grinned. Pliers were something he understood.

The dentist turned to his patient. The trappers gathered close behind him.

Face-to-face with her now, Pinet saw that the girl was not quite plain. She was dark, probably a full-blooded Pasamaquoddy, and had striking blue eyes. Her nose, slightly crooked to the left, had been broken once and never set. It was pretty in a way, the dentist thought, and he would have liked to touch it, to run his finger over the healed place where there was a tiny bump.

"What seems to be the trouble?"

The girl blinked at him.

"She can't sleep. Her mouth hurts her all the time," said Kosskoff. "It hurts to eat."

Pinet nodded, sipped from the cup. He noticed a puffy swelling on the left side of her jaw, just below the mandible. "Open wide," he said.

Her breath was bad; this didn't surprise or bother the dentist, who was, at this stage, well accustomed to the unhappy mouths of rural folk. The girl's teeth were stained in the typical red and yellow tints of the chronic tobacco chewer. Pinet doubted if she'd ever brushed her teeth in her life. The discoloration of the gums indicated the beginning stages of gum disease. Jammed between the upper right cuspid and the upper right lateral Pinet noticed a tendril of meat.

He estimated ten years before Kosskoff's wife needed a full set of replacements, and maybe not that long. It was a shame, thought the dentist. He could visualize the nice straight set of teeth that she might have enjoyed with proper dental treatment and care. Pinet could see the yellowed, meat-jammed upper right cuspid as it ought to have been: a tiny pinnacle of glistening enamel, blemished with just a speck of chocolate—before a sweet girlish tongue swabbed it clean. Pinet lifted the cup to his lips; it was empty.

But her current predicament derived from a pair of caries, one of the lower left first molar and another of the lower left lateral. The lateral wasn't as bad. He touched them with the dental pick at the end of the other prong: the telltale rotten softness of each tooth gave a little with the press of the needle. The girl winced, but stayed still.

"Where do you hold your pouch?" asked the dentist.

The girl touched her mouth in the area of the infections.

"Well. You've got two caries." Pinet lightly prodded each tooth. "Here and here."

After making this diagnosis, the itinerant dentist straightened up and allowed a few seconds of silence to fill the single room of the cabin. In the pale light of the two oil lamps, the thirty-seven-year-old man could have passed for sixty. He was clothed in a grimly stained pair of long underwear that a widow had bartered him in exchange for lancing a sore on her tongue. And if his ruined complexion and the dead man's gamy long johns were not enough to convince an observer of the absolute dissolution of his character, then Pinet would have cheerfully directed any interested party to the more conclusive evidence which could be provided by his ruined marriage, his drug addiction, or even the tiny ghosts of his long dead pets. These things were undeniable; he accepted them, and kept them close to his heart.

But, still, he was a professional—a graduate of Baltimore College, and the veteran of seventeen years of practice in the field. Pinet was a real dentist, not some mountebank. So he let the few seconds of silence explain this authority to the mountain people, let it tell them that he knew what he was doing.

Pinet put the situation forward succinctly. "A caries is a sickness of the tooth. It's a kind of rot, if you will. I would hazard that these two caries are related to your diet—you eat too much meat—and likely from your tobacco use as well.

"The one in the back has to go. It's dead as well as infected. I can probably dig the other one out, fill it with a steel bit, but in your case I wouldn't recommend it. The procedure is unpleasant and I don't believe that your lifestyle lends itself to the necessary preservation techniques."

The girl blinked and gave a sniff.

"Pull them both," said Kosskoff.

"Very well," said the dentist. "Now, how far along are you?"

"Eight months," said Kosskoff.

Funt hooted. "That makes one month and thirteen years until I take the little critter down to Maisie's and treat him to the whole house. Those girls'll work him until his pecker falls off."

"Be quiet," said Pinet.

"Is she too far?" Kosskoff sounded worried. "Is it safe?"

"*Pardon, mon ami,*" said Funt.

"It'll probably be fine," said Pinet. "But I don't dare give her anything really strong for the pain. And, of course, there's always a chance that something could happen with any procedure. But I don't—"

"Take them," said Kosskoff's wife. The girl gave an eager nod. "Just take them out."

* * *

Doing what he could to numb the tissue, Pinet dabbed vodka around the girl's gums. He also soaked his forceps in vodka. He set out some strips of clean cloth and requisitioned a Hickum Brand cigar box for the pulled teeth. An illustration on the side of the box showed a fat crow tatted up like an English dandy and puffing a huge stogie. "The rest is for birds," said the caption. "Hickum's my brand, friend. Just stick one right in your craw and see if you don't agree!" The crow was snapping his braces and twirling a cane.

Pinet told the two trappers not to stand so near behind him.

The girl's head was tilted back against the headrest for the surgery. She arranged her hands neatly and calmly across her pregnant belly. To Pinet's eyes, the dark face, with its blue eyes and sweetly misshapen nose, registered nothing. She waited with her mouth slightly agape, like a child expecting a candy drop. Pinet thought she would do very well.

The dentist was drunk, but not overly so. The metallic scraping sounds were regathering in his skull, but he could wait until the surgery was completed. Pinet remained confident of his abilities under far more impaired conditions.

He went around the back of the chair and looked down at her. "Open wide."

When she did, he quickly found the first tooth, and fitted the forceps around it. To tighten his hold, Pinet turned the screw at the crux of the instrument's handle; he kept turning the screw until it whined in its grooves, and then something cracked; this was the sound of the rotten tooth fissuring from the vise pressure.

Some of the infection drooled over the girl's lip in a gray-red pus. She flinched, but that was all.

"Stay still," said Pinet.

He hooked his arm around her neck, braced himself, and yanked: the tooth pulled loose cleanly. There was a pop, and the girl gasped, and that was all.

"Good," said the dentist.

The bad tooth rattled into the cigar box.

Pinet reached into her mouth and with his bare fingers squeezed the infected gum area. More of the gray-red pus oozed out. The girl clenched and unclenched her hands. He continued to press until the blood was clear. He disinfected the area with vodka and gave her a strip of cloth to ball against the area of the wound.

"It was ready. You practically didn't need me at all."

She smiled to display the bloody new gap to her husband and Funt.

Kosskoff exhaled. Pinet noticed that a film of sweat lay on the big man's forehead and cheeks, and glistened in his beard. "She's doing well," the dentist said to reassure him. In reponse, Kosskoff gazed at him blankly.

Funt tapped the dentist on the shoulder and handed him a fresh cup of vodka. "You're doing good, doc."

Pinet thanked him and took the cup. "One more." He resoaked the forceps. He took the piece of cotton from the girl and peered at the empty socket.

"Okay," Pinet said. "Very good." He removed the forceps from the cup and took a healthy draught to ready himself.

Kosskoff had come up close again, scratching his beard and looking with something like amazement at his wife. Pinet ordered him again to back up.

The girl opened her mouth, and the dentist proceeded as before, this time fitting the arms of his forceps around the girl's lower left lateral tooth. He turned the screw. It was more difficult this time; there was living material still left in the bone; he turned the screw again. The girl shivered. In his skull the dentist heard a thousand needles abruptly fall onto a plane of steel, and then go skittering wildly, crying and screeching across the metal surface. His hand shook and his fingers locked on the screw, turning it a quarter inch farther. There was a wet pop as the tooth splintered. Pinet staggered back. The forceps slipped from his hand and spun through the air, cracked against the far wall and clattered onto the floor. A fine spurt of blood shot from the girl's mouth, spilling down her chin; blood spattered the front of the dentist's long johns. The girl shrieked.

Funt caught Pinet before he could fall. Kosskoff gave a yell of rage and shoved the other trapper out of the way to get at the dentist. The big trapper's fist, like a giant mallet, was drawn behind his head, ready to slam down.

"I'm sorry," said Pinet, "I'm sorry, Jesus—the tooth—that happens once in a while—Jesus, I'm sor—"

The girl's laughter froze her husband's fist. He let it drop to his side.

"Look," she said, her voice garbled by the blood in her mouth. The three chips of the lateral tooth lay on her palm. She laughed with her lips very wide, revealing the new bloody space. A couple of tears dribbled from her eyes.

Her laugh was rich and startling; it had a fine, tremulous quality; Pinet recalled his wedding reception, how his father-in-law called for attention by tapping a silver fork against a crystal champagne flute.

The girl patted her pregnant belly. "Pretty soon, he have more teeth than me."

To celebrate the successful surgery, the trappers uncapped a jar of brown liquor, while Pinet worked quickly to prepare his inhaler. "Excuse me," said the dentist, although no one asked. "It's for my asthma." From a plain medicine bottle he poured three thimbles of clear liquid down the spout of the inhaler.

Kosskoff's wife mixed the liquor with maple syrup and snow, and finally garnished it with brown sugar. "Yes!" cried Kosskoff. "Make it thick!" They started in with long wooden spoons and shared a single bowl.

Pinet cradled the inhaler in his left arm, and worked the small pump with his right. He sucked on the spout, taking deep but carefully measured breaths. From the first inhalation, the sensation was one of pure release, of every weight being lifted away.

When the dentist set the inhaler down, the laughter was already boiling at the top of his throat. He found that the others were grinning at him; he grinned back.

One of the lamps sputtered out, dimming the room. The wind whistled through an invisible crack.

"So," Pinet started, and broke into cackles. Then they all began laughing. Funt rolled around like a happy dog, banging into things.

Pinet told the girl about how he tried to urinate outside in the storm. She snorted and showed her bloody gums.

Kosskoff excitedly banged a pot with a spoon. "It's true," he said, "it's true."

"I thought it was gonna freeze clean off," said Funt, reaching over and slapping Pinet's knee.

"Then you could have sent it to my wife!"

Kosskoff whooped and drummed the pot.

The girl laughed, too; laughed and laughed. She also cried, because it made her mouth hurt even more to laugh.

For comfort she brought out her bag of chewing tobacco and took a pinch. It occurred to Pinet to warn her that it was bad for her teeth, that it would surely aggravate the raw gums, but instead heard himself asking for some.

He had never chewed before, and the sickly sweet taste revolted him. He spat it out. "Shit," said the dentist, "that's shit."

The others laughed. Kosskoff beat the pot.

From his satchel the dentist retrieved his toothbrush and jar of paste. He briskly scraped his teeth until foam came from the corners of his mouth. Some of it dripped over his chin.

It was not until he finished, rinsing his mouth clean with water and spitting it into a cup, that he realized that the two trappers and the girl had been watching him, fixated.

"Does it hurt?" asked the girl. Her cheek bulged with tobacco.

"No. It cleans. It feels good."

The girl shook her head, and seemed to doubt him.

"I knew a whore, scraped her teeth all the time," lied Funt. "She had a whole collection of fancy tooth scrapers. It was something to see."

For whatever reason, the spectacle of the tooth brushing quieted the group. The girl chewed her tobacco, seeming to think. Funt and Kosskoff drank, and appeared to think of nothing. Kosskoff's beard was as big and wiry as an eagle's nest.

The dentist felt oddly embarrassed, as if he had done something wrong. He was reminded of the unfortunate episode with his wife, the one that resulted in his ignominious dismissal as a spouse: Mrs. Pinet caught him with another woman, another widow, as it happened, who suffered not only from a pained jaw but a generous nature. There was nothing Pinet could do for this widow—she needed a surgeon, not a dentist—but she insisted on completing her end of the bargain anyway, although the agreed-upon sexual act could only have exacerbated her condition. It was then that Mrs Pinet walked it.

"I ought to have insisted on going to her rooms," said the dentist. He made the announcement abruptly, and without any preamble. He chuckled. No one had any idea of what he was talking about, nor did they appear to care.

"Who is going to deliver the damn child, anyway?" Pinet was suddenly offended at their lack of reaction. He hiccuped. "The child?" he asked again. "Who will deliver the child?"

Opening his mouth wide—the dentist saw rows of crooked yellow-green teeth—Funt let loose a long, pungent belch. The small trapper screeched with laughter.

Kosskoff hit the pot several times.

Fresh cups were poured all around.

The dentist made no further effort to speak. The drug was settling into his system; his mouth seemed to disappear; his eyeballs felt as though they were hardening to stone in their sockets; a corona spread out from the wick of the remaining oil lamp and Pinet stared into a winter sun ten years gone.

In college the dentist traveled west with his wife-to-be and her brother. They went by train, and it was difficult for the dentist and his lover to find privacy, but they were imaginative and persistent. Once, they made love in the luggage compartment, rolling around on top of bulky pieces of portage, handles and strap buckles jabbing them in their backs and buttocks. In the frenzy the dentist kicked over a parrot cage, and the bird escaped. It smashed around the cabin for a few moments and then began to screech for gravy. "Where's m'gravy? Where's m'gravy, you old so-and-so?" The bird continued to howl for its garnish, but Pinet's future wife held him fast, and told him not to dare stop.

Somewhere beyond the Rockies, at a desert pit stop, the lovers shared a bag of nitrous oxide. "For science," Pinet said, although it was not, in fact, his first experiment. They staggered away from the train and took shade beneath the depot platform. They lay in the sand and gazed up through the slats at the boots and shoes of their fellow travelers.

The dentist had a vision, but he sustained no memory of it. Later, his wife related it to him: "You said you saw a giant mouth and that it was going to eat everything. 'It's eating the world!' you screamed, and then you started crying, and just a minute or two later, you said, 'Oh, oh, I'm sorry! It's on our side. The mouth is on our side.'"

"You were crazy," said his wife, making eyes. Then, as she was telling him this a little time later, they had only recently been married.

"Crazy. It's true. I was crazy." He grabbed her wrists.

"Was?" she asked, and opened her throat to him.

"I asked you about your wife," said Funt. "Is she ever coming back, *mon ami?*"

Pinet stared at him. "Fuck you." He smirked. He fell asleep.

But the trapper was not insulted. He pondered a ragged hole in his long underwear, plucking the threads with a blackened finger.

The dentist opened his eyes to find himself propped between the other two men. Pinet heard his limp feet scrape across the floor, and looked down at them. Yes, those were his feet. They laid him down on one of the beds.

He blinked up at the large faces of the two trappers: Kosskoff bristling with beard, Funt licking at his mustache. Then the girl appeared. She bent over the dentist, until her lips brushed over his nose, chin, mouth. Pinet smelled the tobacco on her breath. Fingers gently peeled back his lips. A tongue slowly licked across his teeth.

Pinet groaned.

Her bloody mouth stopped at the sore mark on his neck. She kissed it.

The earth shook below him. Pinet realized that the two beds were being pushed together. The dentist's limbs flopped about him.

"Please," he said, croaking the word so thickly that only he could have translated the sound.

Somehow his long johns were stripped away. The dentist supposed he had been skinned alive. One had to skin a fish before it could be cooked. Mice did not require skinning. Mice could keep their skins. Mice could be frozen. Mice were best eaten cold. "Please."

Kosskoff slid in beside him, and began to kiss his ear. The wires of the big trapper's beard tickled Pinet's ear.

The pregnant woman's belly pressed against the dentist's thigh. Her breath was near, but he could not find her mouth.

A hand reached between his legs, accompanied by a voice of perfect reason. "Here it is, *mon ami.*" It was, Pinet realized, a doctor's voice. He also knew from the doctor's tone that the diagnosis was grave.

The doctor put a hand over Pinet's mouth.

"Will it hurt?" he asked into the palm, tasting the doctor's sweat. But no answer was necessary. When it came to pulling teeth, no one was more aware than Pinet of the procedure's inherent discomfort.

In the morning he awoke alone in a single bed. Someone had shifted the dentist onto his side, perhaps to keep him from choking if he vomited. Shafts of daylight stabbed through the gaps in the boards that covered the windows.

The dentist was naked and achy beneath the furs.

He stumbled to the bathroom closet. There was a bucket of cold water and he washed himself as best he could. He came out, feeling no better, but thinking more clearly. There was no one else in the cabin. His clothes were folded on a chair.

After dressing, Pinet searched for a bottle of something to pick himself up. He came across the Hickum Brand cigar box; the crow's cigar was enormous, disproportional. "The rest is for birds. Hickum's my brand, friend. Just stick one right in your craw and see if you don't agree!"

The dentist put the box on the floor and stomped on it. He kicked the pieces under the bed.

There was no liquor and Pinet was forced to settle for some weak, icy tea left unfinished on a sideboard. For all he knew it might have been days old. He considered his options and made the courageous determination to wait until he made it back to the boardinghouse in Limestone to take a fresh lung.

The dentist gathered together his instruments and stuffed them into the satchel.

Half out the door, Pinet leaned against the frame and squinted at the vista of snow and light and line and sky. In the clarity of day he saw the small distant shape of the pass they had walked through the previous evening; the cliffs were merely outcroppings. Farther off, much farther, he saw the lake where the local children went to swim in the brief northern summers. The spire of the town's Methodist church was visible through a copse of winter-stripped birch.

A little way off the ice-sheathed, clapboard carving shed puffed gray smoke from a stone chimney.

Pinet approached it, walking in their tracks.

He found them just inside, scraping down a mink skin. Funt and Kosskoff held the skin taut across a table, while the pregnant girl dragged a blade, nicking off the bits of gristle and muscle. A fire burned in the chimney grate. The guts and body of the mink were in a pail on the ground. Steam rose from the bucket.

Watching them, Pinet decided that he had imagined the previous evening entirely. He was an addict, he told himself, and the mind of an addict was easily confused. The pregnant girl chewed on her lip as she worked the blade, inching it over the flesh parchment. Her cheeks and forehead were fever red.

"I have to go," said Pinet.

Kosskoff glanced up, looked away. "We paid you."

"*Tabernac,*" swore Funt as he strained to hold down his end of the skin.

The smell of the animal guts drifted to the dentist.

Mrs. Pinet, a careful shopper, had often bought tripe rather than the butcher's more expensive meats. Pinet never complained; in fact, he liked it, liked the taste, the richness and the salt. Over dinner his wife giggled, and made a comment that when the tripe was raw, it smelled to her like it did when they made love. Pinet had been confused. "Do I smell?" he had asked. "No, Laurent, no," said his wife. "I wasn't talking about you. I was talking about—about the love we make together—I was just saying—it's not a bad thing, that smell . . ." She pinched his cheek and kissed him. His wife had fed him chunks of the meat with her fingers.

This occasion took place years before, in a previous life, and he was sorry to remember it.

"Why are you standing there?" asked Kosskoff.

"It smells like fucking out here," said Pinet, and gave a short screechy laugh, pointing to the bloody bucket. The dentist slapped his hand down, but couldn't contain another giggle.

The girl spat something dark in the snow.

Wonders

Game 1

The best contact wasn't like contact at all; it was like swinging straight through, the baseball only an echo of the bat's motion. The game was so hard, but that moment was so easy—the ball flew, Eckstein ran, and there was no chance they were going to catch him. Much of the time, Eckstein felt out of sorts, rushed and uncertain; often, when it was time to go to sleep, he could still feel the dull ache of the morning's alarm bell, a faint thrumming at the back of his neck. Playing was the only part of his life that had ever felt completely natural. Except tonight. Tonight, even the notion of knocking a true one and watching it fly didn't soothe him. He had made a real mess of matters and didn't want to so much as tighten his laces, let alone take a swing.

Eckstein, the second baseman for the Coney Island Wonders, was sitting out that night's game against the Hoboken Gentlemen. He told Gordy Wheelock, the manager, that he was sick, a sour gut.

Wheelock didn't like it. "You better invest in a couple of seltzers, kid. I ain't here to rub your tummy." But the manager wasn't about to take any chances with a talent like Eckstein, the best hitter they had—the old bastard gave him the night off.

So now Eckstein slumped on the bench, watching the game from under the bill of his cap. He tried not to think about what a sorry human being he was, but it was hard to ignore the tiny steel teeth grinding his insides. And on top of it all, the heckler was at it again,

giving an earful to Burnham, the Negro who played left field for
Coney Island.

Cleatus "Woodpecker" Burnham stood at his position with a placid
expression. Between pitches he folded his arms, and rolled a toothpick from one corner of his mouth to the other. He might have been
waiting in a line, or riding the subway. His bearing seemed to be the
very essence of patience, or maybe it was just resignation.

But only a deaf man could fail to hear the heckler's bray, which
seemed to rattle endlessly around the ballpark, like a bumblebee
pinging off the walls of a sealed jar.

"You're horrible, Burnham! Not only do you look like you got
struck by lightning, you play like it, too." The heckler was a spindly
creature with a patchy black fungus of beard. "A big damn wind
oughtta blow you back to Africa. Not a typhoon, *a ty-coon*." There
were a few guffaws, and the heckler bowed to the people around him.
Eckstein wished the jerk would shut up; the screaming hurt his ears.

When the Wonders trotted off the field for the bottom of the
inning, the groundskeeper came on to rake around the base paths
and the pitcher's mound. It was time for the seventh-inning stretch,
and the nightly Vaudeville Intermission; two attractions from the
freak show, the Backwards Man and Jenny Two Heads, clambered
onto the field. They raced miniature tricycles around the warning
track while the organist played "Muskrat Ramble."

Woodpecker sat down next to Eckstein. The bench creaked. He
was the oldest guy on the team, and pretty well past it. There weren't
any other Negroes in the Hudson League; it was against the rules, but
Coney Island had an entertainment exemption for special attractions.
(The previous season they had used the exemption on a strongman
dwarf called Udolfo the Unstoppable Force, who resembled nothing
so much as a single, enormous bicep, strutting about on stump legs
and threatening to bite people's balls off. "I going to gnaw off your
berries from you!" he would scream at almost anyone who happened
to block his path. He drew a large number of base on balls, but
Udolfo couldn't really field or run, and besides being a drunk, his
Germanic accent—not to mention the ball-biting threats—failed to

endear him with either the team or the front office. Coney had finally traded the dwarf, for future considerations, to a Utica sideshow that needed a chicken man.) Which was how this season, the Wonders came to bring in Woodpecker Burnham, a Negro who could play baseball.

And, apparently, at one time Woodpecker had been a hell of a hitter. Sometimes he could still turn on a ball, and knock it a good distance, but his average wasn't much. In the outfield, he was flat-footed and seemed to move through thick mud.

They called him Woodpecker because he was always chewing on a homemade toothpick. He had a pocketknife that he kept on his person at all times, and used to chip shards from whatever was around. There were hundreds of gouges in the dugout bench, like a beaver had gone at it.

A few of the guys liked to have some sport with him. For instance, Pelky, the third baseman, asked Woodpecker to autograph a water-melon. The Negro had been decent about it, too, signed Woodpecker Burnham, real big and clear. Now Pelky displayed it on the top shelf of his locker, a Wonders hat stuck on the dome and a toothpick poking out of a drawn-on mouth.

He was a different sort, Burnham was, but Eckstein liked him. For one thing, you could always have a talk with him about the pictures. Almost any time Eckstein went to the Odeon, if he looked up to the balcony Woodpecker would be sitting in the front row, hunched over the railing, toothpick dangling from his lower lip.

The second baseman watched as his teammate turned an old broken Louisville Slugger over a few times on his knee before selecting a spot high up on the barrel, and with a flash of the knife blade cut away a neat toothpick. Woodpecker spit his old toothpick on the ground and inserted the new.

In the outfield, beneath the flare of the light stanchions, the Backwards Man tumbled from his tricycle. He stood up, confused, and ran in the opposite direction, away from the finish line. The freak handlers hurried to correct him, but it was difficult to get the attention of the Backwards Man; his cross-eyed peanut of a head was set on his neck looking over his spine.

"You get a good one?" Eckstein asked him.

Woodpecker rolled the pick around in his mouth. "It ain't too fine."

"That son-of-a-bitch out in the bleachers never shuts up, does he?"

"I don't pay him no mind," said Woodpecker. He scratched his belly, rubbing his long dark fingers, their whitish tips, over the soft bulge of flesh.

"You see anything good lately? At the Odeon?"

"I seen the new one. It's pretty good. Vampires."

"Much killing?"

"Some."

"Girls?"

"Just one. She don't show much," said Woodpecker, "Little leg. No thigh."

Woodpecker cut a pick from the Louisville Slugger and gave it to Eckstein. To the second baseman the pick tasted like dust, but wanting to be polite, he chewed at it diligently.

When the seventh-inning stretch was over the freak handlers guided the Backwards Man and Jenny Two Heads off the field. One of Jenny Two Heads' heads was asleep. This head, the bald one, was rarely awake, and never spoke, but the other head lewdly wagged its tongue at the Backwards Man.

In the bottom half of the inning, Woodpecker slapped a hit in the right field gap, but was thrown out lumbering into second base.

The heckler started howling before Woodpecker had even dusted himself off. "You fat bastard! Get the lead outta your ass!"

Woodpecker appeared not to notice him and jogged back to the dugout still nibbling on the pin of Louisville oak.

In the ninth Wheelock told Eckstein to "tie up his guts, put em in a bow," because he was pinch-hitting. Eckstein could see that the pitcher was tired, the zip gone off his fast one, and nothing but spin left on his curve. He figured on banging one, no problem. But as he swung, his feet slipped in the batter's box and the ball dribbled to the mound. The pitcher pounced. A snap throw to the second baseman, and over to first. Double play.

"C'mon, Eckstein! C'mon!" Once, Eckstein had seen a racehorse break a leg at the Steeplechase, and watched as the jockey himself in his tattered racing stripes stood over it, and used a pistol to put the creature out of its suffering. The clarity of the gunshot came to him now. The heckler had a voice like a foghorn. "What is this, Eckstein, are you a nigger now, too?"

The crowd—families on holiday, boys in yarmulkes and short pants, men in shirtsleeves and boaters, girls in summer dresses, a couple of nuns, the seven or eight Negroes standing outside with their fingers in the right field fencing—exhaled, and began to file out, heading home, or back to the boardwalk. The scoreboard operator put up the final score: Hoboken Gentlemen 4, Coney Island Wonders 3.

Eckstein returned to the dugout and dropped down onto the bench. The other players, Woodpecker included, departed. The scoreboard operator replaced the digit placards for each inning with the advertisement boards for Red Giraffe Extra-Long Hot Dogs. There was a series of cranking noises as one after another the switches were thrown on the three light pylons that towered over the field. As the filaments cooled, the night filled in around the banks of lightbulbs, and turned the grass black.

After, Eckstein walked to the Odeon. Lillian scowled and let him in for free.

The movie was called *Black Mansion*. The prospect of it made Eckstein feel somewhat cheered. You couldn't do much better than a vampire picture.

Two hobos, Gooch and McMasters, are riding in a boxcar, making it for California, when they decide to jump off outside a little town somewhere in Texas, and find something to eat. This part is funny, because Gooch is just a happy-go-lucky tramp, and a real wetbrain. "If they ain't got some real chow here, Mac, heck, I might try an eat you," says Gooch, and at the same time, he hallucinates a giant pork chop all dressed in McMasters's duds and wearing McMasters's hat.

Except, what's not so funny is the horde of vampires who haunt the little town and live in a mansion on the hill, surviving on the blood of human sacrifices. It's to placate this enclave of bloodsuckers that the townspeople lure Gooch and McMasters up to the mansion that night, promising them a big baked bean supper and a couple of warm beds. The only thing that the vampires aren't counting on, though, is McMasters, the tough-as-nails ex-boxer who wears a crucifix from his uncle, a priest, and never takes it off, even though he stopped believing in God when his kid sister died of polio. That's how McMasters manages to ward off the vampires and somehow escapes. Meanwhile, Gooch is cornered, and the vampires are coming for him; we see things from their point of view, and all of sudden it's a pork chop wearing Gooch's duds and Gooch's hat.

Lillian sat down beside Eckstein.

"The town's being run by vampires," whispered Eckstein. "One of the hobos got away."

"Trash," was all Lillian said in response.

McMasters tries to raise a posse to storm the mansion, but the people are all vampire bootlickers. The only one who will help him is the mayor's daughter, Kelly-Anne. McMasters sneaks back into the mansion while Kelly-Anne sets up dynamite, and makes her promise on his kid sister's soul that she'll set off the whole load in thirty minutes if he doesn't come out. Inside, McMasters kills the king vampire, stabbing him in the heart with a chair leg. But he takes so long that Kelly-Anne has to set off the dynamite. She's broken-hearted, because she realizes that she loved the lug, never mind all his tough talk. That's just before he uses his crucifix to dig out of the rubble and the sun comes up on a new day.

Throughout the movie Lillian made small, sighing noises of dissatisfaction, but Eckstein hardly noticed. It was the sort of picture a person could maybe see two or three times. His favorite scene was when McMasters pushed over the huge vampire throne and trapped the screeching, squealing bloodsucker underneath. The hobo had torn off a throne leg—the foot shaped like a bear's claw—and plunged it into the vampire's black heart.

While he waited for Lillian to close up, Eckstein paced the curb, kicking at pebbles. He was feeling guilty again. After what he'd done, Eckstein figured he deserved the same fate as Gooch. He knew it was supposed to be funny—a joke on a joke—but the part where the vampires looked at Gooch and he was a pork chop, that part made him sweaty, and brought back his nausea. He remembered something his father had said to him once: "I do believe that life is going to make a meal out of you, boy."

He thought of how the vampires surrounded the hobo, moving in slowly, slowly, hunching over the man, and lifting their capes, shrouding the cringing figure, seeming to melt down the wall, until they became one dark undulating mass, a living shadow.

"What's so funny about that?" Eckstein asked himself. He decided maybe he didn't like the movie so much, after all.

Down the arcade a barker was running a quarter pitching game against a brick wall. A beat cop stood by, collecting bets in his Keystone cap. At the mouth of the alley across the street, a bum sat cross-legged and stirred a puddle with a stick. A Model-T clattered over cobblestones. The big wheel at the top of Luna Park blinked green and white, green and white, green and white.

Lillian came outside and started to draw down the steel shutter. He went to help her, but she told him to get out of the way. The metal sheet clanked down, and she locked it. "I'm hungry," she said.

They walked without further discussion to the diner around the corner. Her heels clicked on the sidewalk. Lillian was a big girl, heavy around the hips. She wore her hair in a fashionable wave that flipped with every step, and she always smelled fresh, of talcum and lilacs. Tonight, however, they walked too far apart for Eckstein to catch even a whiff of sweetness, and her perm appeared sodden.

Taking a booth in the back, Lillian let the waitress pour their coffee and then move away before she started in: "I know what you want to ask and the answer is no. It didn't come. That's nine weeks, buddy boy."

She stared at him hard and he looked out the window.

That first night, back in April, she'd seen him at a game. Her face had been flushed when she leaned over the grandstand railing and handed him a ticket for that night's show. The film turned out to be a love picture, about a beautiful girl with amnesia and a millionaire playboy. Eckstein never did see how it turned out, though. "I'm bored," Lillian said into Eckstein's ear as the playboy brought the beautiful amnesiac to consult with a fortune-teller. "Something awful happened to you," said the fortune-teller. "I see a wicked stranger. I see him searching for you, even now." The girl gave a cry. "Now, now," said the playboy. "That's quite enough of that."

But by then, Lillian was tugging Eckstein from his seat and they were going through the side door, and up the stairs, to the dark closet where the movies came from.

Steam crawled out of a cracked manhole cover in the middle of the street. Eckstein fogged a corner of the window and wrote an E.

The waitress came over. Lillian ordered a steak, a potato, and strawberry pie. Eckstein asked for coffee. The waitress moved away.

"It was an accident," said Eckstein. "And you knew what you were doing—"

"It's all your fault. I was just sweet on you, and I get this." She blinked several times, and rubbed at the corners of her eyes.

It had been his first time, that night in the projection room. "Don't do it inside me," she told him. There was hardly space for them both in the tiny room. "Don't do what?" asked Eckstein. A moment later he groaned, and spent himself.

The ecstatic moment was cut off by Lillian's frantic shoving. Eckstein tumbled backward into a shelf of movie reels. She said he was an idiot. Eckstein said he hadn't been thinking, that was all. And it was the only time they had ever done it; she barely let him kiss her since. One desperate evening, willing to do anything for another taste, he offered to marry her, pregnant or not. "That's a laugh," Lillian had said. "My family'd love you, a ballplayer with a Jew name."

"I ain't a Jew," said Eckstein, "I'm German."

"Sure." Lillian gave him a sneer. "Sure."

Then he blurted that he loved her, purely loved her. Lillian's eyes had widened, gathering him up, and Eckstein felt her looking deep inside him. His throat caught. Her eyes narrowed. "You're a monster," Lillian finally said very quietly.

"I'm gonna get fat and lose my job," Lillian said, and began to cry.

The waitress brought the food. Lillian's face was streaked with tears. She looked at her plate with disdain, shoved it away. "Did I ask for gravy? And what about napkins? Don't I look like someone who needs a napkin?"

He escorted Lillian home, to the apartment she shared with three other girls in a women's boardinghouse on Mermaid Avenue.

"The part in that movie, where the guy, the hobo—where the vampires looked at him, and then he looked like a pork chop, I didn't think that was funny," said Eckstein, hoping to start a conversation.

"Stupid," she said, but nothing else. They went the remaining four blocks in silence.

"After you're done work tomorrow, I'll get it taken care of," said Eckstein. Lillian blurted a sob, and struck him weakly with her purse.

"Bring a change of clothes," said Eckstein, because he had heard it was something that a girl should do in a situation like this one.

That night, Eckstein felt so terrible he told his roommate, Bobby Pelky, the Wonders third baseman. Once it was out, though, Eckstein immediately regretted having spoken. Saying the words aloud made it worse. He was guilty; the truth was as bright as a lamp.

Pelky didn't see the problem. He was from the South, Alabama or someplace, and sometimes he dictated letters for his mother to Eckstein. "She got a brother or some people? A cousin? Someone could kill you?"

"No," he said, "I don't think she has any people."

"So, then," said Pelky. "You're peachy." In his letters to his mother Pelky always promised that he was keeping his shoulder in on the spitters and curves, and to let him know right away if that farmer Garrison from up the road was causing her anymore trouble, asking her out to the county fair again. *That old clodsplitter better mind his manners*, Pelky had dictated once. *I will shoot his dog and that is just for starters.*

Now Eckstein tried to change the subject. "I saw the new picture at the Odeon, the vampire one."

Pelky sat in the window and lit a match. He was wiry, sneaky fast, a slick fielder who was so unhurried in his movements that it sometimes looked as if he might drift off to sleep somewhere between catching the ball and throwing it over to first. His swing was long, though, and sometimes he had trouble with the inside pitch.

"But you've got some pity for her." It wasn't a question.

"I got twenty bucks."

"That's not enough." The flame went down to Pelky's fingers and he pinched it off. "You need forty, maybe fifty."

Eckstein shrugged.

"You know where to go?" Pelky went to his nightstand, found his wallet, and took out three or four dollars.

"Yeah," said Eckstein. "Sure, I heard."

"Okay, Eck. We'll canvass the boys for the rest. It's shouldn't be a problem." The third baseman dropped the bills on Eckstein's table and went back to the window. He lit up another match.

"You know we took up a collection last year, for the dwarf, the Kraut dwarf. Not for a broad, though, for a doc. The Kraut dwarf caught a dose. From some whore. Or so he said. I'd like to see that whore."

Eckstein tried to force a chuckle, but he could only manage a cough, and his eyes stung. His quickly blew his nose.

Beyond the open window, over the third baseman's shoulder, the lights of the midway spun and flickered and raced. There were singing drunks somewhere below, and calliope music, and laughter. "Can you imagine if that big roller coaster came down?" asked Pelky. "Just fell right in on itself, like a bunch of sticks? The people who were on the roller coaster sure would scream, wouldn't they?"

Eckstein sagged in his bed. He reached out from beneath the covers, touched the bills with a finger, and then withdrew his hand. "Yeah. I bet they would give a holler."

The man in the window blew out his match. "Come on, Eck," he said, "cheer up. Let's write a note to my mammy."

Game 2

In the third inning, as Woodpecker was camping under a high fly ball, the heckler threw a bottle. "Stone-hands-nigger!" The bottle struck Woodpecker in the side of the head, and he crumpled to the ground. Before anyone thought to stop him, the heckler was already up the grandstand, and scuttling down the exit ramp.

A couple of the guys on the team propped Woodpecker up and helped him from the field. Eckstein was shocked to see the blood on the left fielder's temple, staining the rim of his cap, and dripping down to the collar of his pinstriped uniform. Woodpecker's eyes were glazed and dumb with pain; when they met Eckstein's gaze there was nothing between the two of them, they were strangers.

In a few minutes, after the new left fielder warmed up, the game resumed.

Eckstein had hoped playing would take his mind off Lillian and what they were going to do—to *undo*. But the thoughts were impossible to stop: he imagined Lillian, obscenely sprawled on a table, crying and screaming, blood splashing from all directions; and when he finally forced the image out, his mind jumped to Gooch's death in *Black Mansion*. Except that instead of Gooch, it was Eckstein who was sliding down the wall; and the vampires lifted their capes above him, blocking out the light.

On one of the last nights, after the tuberculosis had wormed into her brain, Eckstein's mother told him, "I should have got you taken care of. Now look at me." By that time, his father had been gone for three years, and hadn't sent money in two, and it was just the mother and the son in the fifth-floor room. He didn't listen to her, and stared at the wall, and mostly she didn't say much. It was in this bare room that his thoughts finally came to settle, and to fix on the brown stain on the wall above his mother's bed.

By the seventh-inning stretch, along with going hitless in three at-bats, the second baseman had committed two errors.

"You're garbage today," said Wheelock. "Nobody throw out Eckstein. He's garbage but nobody throw him out. You hear me? No matter how damn much Eckstein looks like a damn piece of trash sitting in a dugout full of baseball players, nobody throw him out. If I find that little son-of-a-bitch in my clubhouse trash can I just might not be accountable."

Eckstein spat on the ground, but didn't say anything.

During the seventh-inning stretch, for the Vaudeville Intermission, Jenny Two Heads and the Backwards Man raced across the outfield on pogo sticks. The organist played a crazed version of "Sugarfoot Stomp," accompanied by the Purple Girl on recorder, and Three Ton Timmy on trumpet. A nun in the crowd threw a hot dog at the Purple Girl; the Purple Girl danced out of the way, flashing her gams at the crowd. Three Ton Timmy wailed on his trumpet, the size of a harmonica in his giant mitts, and his jowls bounced around like the saddlebags on a horse at full gallop.

The Backwards Man fell over again in a heap, pretzeled around his pogo stick, the small eyes in his dainty head rolling wildly while the crowd howled. Jenny Two Heads took a bow; the head that was awake licked the ear of the bald head that was asleep, but the bald head did not respond. The crowd cheered and rippled. A milk truck transported Three Ton Timmy out the service gate in right field. The Purple Girl blushed green at the catcalls that fell down and around her.

In his last at-bat, Eckstein got hit in the hip by a pitch. "Fuck you, you goddamn busher," he said to the Hoboken pitcher as he hobbled to first.

Final score: Hoboken Gentlemen 9, Coney Island Wonders 1.

In the clubhouse Pelky asked each player for a donation, dollar minimum. To the shortchangers, he said, "Don't you Jew around with me now, boy," and he warned them with a little smile, and they would fork over the rest. Even the manager, Wheelock—after a headshake in Eckstein's direction—gave two dollars.

For his own part, Eckstein sat and bit his nails. Then he fled to the showers and stayed beneath the hot spray until his skin felt as though it were shrinking around his bones.

When he returned, Pelky was standing over Woodpecker.

His head wrapped with a bag of ice, Woodpecker lay stretched out on a bench. The flesh around his right eye was swollen and meaty looking. A shard of red wood, cut from the locker room bench, pointed from his mouth.

"This all you got, spade?" Pelky held up a dime. He was grinning his little grin. Everyone was watching.

The black-skinned man turned his head away and stared at the wall.

"Well, then. What are we going to do, Woody?"

"I get you the rest tomorrow."

Pelky dropped his fist into his teammate's soft belly. Woodpecker gasped and curled up. The standing man slapped the toothpick from his mouth. A couple of guys shifted uncomfortably, but nobody spoke.

"Okay," said Pelky, "bring it tomorrow. But you just better make it five, old boy. How's that sound?"

Woodpecker didn't say anything.

"I guess it better sound pretty good, or you know I'll have your balls, don't you, nigger?" Pelky nodded to himself. "And that's just for starters."

Towel around his waist, Eckstein had frozen up. It was a small dirty room, humid from the showers. The men sat on stools in front of their lockers. They were mostly naked, their bodies pale suits, faces and arms brown from the sun. Woodpecker, also naked, was a black smudge in the middle of them, chest rising and falling, and the ice pack in a turban around his head. Pelky yawned and the silence broke. He turned away from the prone figure on the bench and went to take donations from the last couple of guys on the team.

The miasma of the locker room—sweat, mildew, liniment, and tobacco—filled Eckstein's nose, and he felt like vomiting.

When the second baseman was dressing, Pelky came over and pressed a wad of bills into his hand. "That's thirty, not counting the spade's five." Pelky threw his arm around Eckstein's shoulder and pulled him into a huddle. "It's a little short, but I don't guess they're the kind to turn down a decent amount of dough."

It took a few seconds for Eckstein to find his voice. "Thanks. I owe you."

"Well," said Pelky. "You know how soft I am."

He went to the movies, hoping to find a mistake. Once, in a cowboy picture, he saw the fender of a Ford sticking out from around the back of a building. The movies were full of mistakes, and usually

such carelessness merely irritated the second baseman—except tonight Eckstein wanted proof that it was all make-believe, that *Black
Mansion* wasn't true . . .

. . . The hobo's eyes swelled as the monsters closed around him.
Tiptoeing forward, nearer, nearer still, the vampires' capes followed
across the floor, oozing and curling like living animals. White-faced,
black tongues licking their black lips, they did not bare their teeth,
but the shape of them—tiny swords beneath the flesh—was visible at
the skin of their tight, ghastly cheeks. The viewpoint shifted and
suddenly the screen showed things the way the vampires saw them:
Gooch became a man-sized pork chop, stuck inside a tramp's
patched suit, and wearing a tramp's battered old bowler.

Several people laughed; one man down the row from Eckstein
cackled and pounded the seatback in front of him.

Gooch moaned. "Lord, lord," he said, "Lord, lo—" Capes and
shadows enveloped his body.

Eckstein bolted up, jostling past the cackling man at the end of the
row. It was the heckler. He threw a couple of pieces at popcorn at the
ballplayer. "Watch the knees, shitbird."

In the lavatory, Eckstein finally did vomit. It was mostly coffee, but
he recognized a fragment of that morning's bacon, floating at the top
of the murky expulsion—and then he dry-heaved some more.

When he felt better, he stood and washed his hands, splashed
water on his face. When he pissed, the crackling of the ice in the
urinal made Eckstein shiver.

He went outside to walk around until the theater closed and Lillian
got off.

The weekend crowd was thick and boisterous. Children chased
each other. Tinkling piano keys echoed from the dance hall. Two
vagrants wrestled feebly with each other, arm-locked and lurching
while passersby stepped around them. A man pulled a giggling girl
into an alley. Eckstein unbuttoned his shirt a couple of buttons, and
pushed his hat back on his head in a way that felt good. He let the
flow of the crowd carry him to the end of the boardwalk. There were
colored lights and touts hollering out the latest attractions. Eckstein
bought a bottle of pop. The vendor recognized him. "Is it a slump?"

the man asked. "No," said Eckstein, "just giving Hoboken a break. We'll put the wood to em tomorrow, I believe." He tipped his hat to the vendor, and the vendor tipped his red-striped paper cap in return. Eckstein found a baseball tossing game. He fired one ball after another through the dangling hoops, while the operator smoked a cheroot. "Get outta here, ringer," said the operator. "No prize for you."

A while later he wandered back to the avenue and found Woodpecker seated on a curb, carving toothpicks from a chunk of driftwood across his lap. Before Eckstein could slip away, the outfielder looked up and grinned and waved his teammate over. Eckstein felt a burn of embarrassment in his cheeks.

At his feet, Woodpecker had built a little pile of new toothpicks. He flicked at the gray chunk of wood with his pocketknife, popped loose another fragment, and gave a grunt of satisfaction. "Good wood," he said.

"I bet," said Eckstein.

"I got that five dollars," said Woodpecker.

"No, it's okay. I don't need it," said Eckstein. "I'm sorry about Pelky, he was just trying to help me out and—well, he got too hot."

"It don't matter," said Woodpecker. He took out a bill and pressed it into Eckstein's shirt pocket.

The sounds of the boardwalk were distant and faint. Reflecting off the night clouds, the big wheel splashed green and white, green and white, green and white.

Lillian would be closing up soon.

"Thanks," said Eckstein. "But I guess I oughta scoot."

"You see that movie?" asked Woodpecker.

"Yeah," said Eckstein, "Scared the heck out of me."

"Looked real didn't they, them vampires?"

"Hell," said Eckstein.

"That's right," said Woodpecker, "that's right." With an air of contemplation, the black-skinned man slowly rolled his toothpick back and forth in his mouth—but said nothing more.

* * *

Lillian avoided Eckstein's eyes as they left the theater. He slouched along beside her. Frequently pretending to scratch an itch at his nose, he dabbed at his eyes, which were teary. Away from the boardwalk, the houses on Surf Avenue narrowed, the slats peeled and grew scabby, the lawns wilted; mounds of garbage lay in the gutters and the air was rotten with the smell of fish. The howling of two fighting dogs startled him. "Dammit," he cursed, and Lillian did not scold him.

When they reached the alleyway Eckstein recognized it by the infamous street sign: a broken scrap of crating nailed to a twisted lamppost, and painted in chipped black letters: WRETCH LANE.

Lillian hiccuped, and began to sob. "Someday I'm going to have beautiful babies," she said. Her voice rose and broke with the hiccups. "You'll just be a used-up ballplayer in some jerkwater town."

There was an empty bottle lying in the street. Eckstein went and picked it up, then flung it as far as he could, over the rooftops on the opposite side of the road.

She stopped crying, and he held her purse while she applied fresh makeup, using her compact and the light of the moon.

He offered her his hand and she took it. Their palms suctioned with damp.

At the end of the alleyway they emerged into a small courtyard littered with trash. A twisted unicycle was propped up against one wall. There was an animal cage pushed up against another wall, big enough to hold a lion. Something very large lay in it, unmoving or dead. The courtyard gave way to a darkened, sagging house; the shutters were battened; a porch leaned before it, giving access to two doors, one black, one red.

"It's the red door we want," said Eckstein.

He knocked hesitantly while Lillian waited at the bottom of the stairs, holding her elbows. Eckstein's eyes had dried out very suddenly. He found himself blinking rapidly, shifting from one foot to another.

After a minute, the second baseman heard steps, a slinking, one-two-*shhh*, one-two-*shhh*. His hands clenched.

The door opened. "You come for a screw?" asked the Purple Girl sleepily. "It's after hours. It's extra now." Her skin looked bruised in the moonlight. For some reason she held a broom, which had been dragging behind her, which accounted for the *shhh*-noise.

Eckstein couldn't speak. He blinked and looked at the broom.

The Purple Girl followed his gaze. "Sometimes, I just feel like sweeping," she said. "I can start sweeping at almost any time."

She took the broom and brushed it over Eckstein's shoes. The Purple Girl wore a white nightgown and her skin peered blackly through the material. Eckstein felt a fearful stirring of arousal.

"We need the surgeon," he said, abruptly finding his voice.

The Purple Girl looked out over his shoulder, spotted Lillian, and wrinkled her nose. "Follow me," she said. She turned and swept away down the hall.

They followed the Purple Girl down a splintered hallway. At the foot of the hall a naked bulb hung above an open basement door. The Purple Girl nodded down a set of wooden stairs, then swept away. Lillian clenched Eckstein's hand. They went down the stairs.

"You'll have to wait till he's done munchin," said Jenny Two Heads' wakeful head. The two-headed freak was standing beside the table in the middle of a dim, dirt-floored room. Sitting in a chair that was turned away from the table, his body facing the wall, the Backwards Man opened and closed his mouth obediently as Jenny fed him, spooning soup to his lips.

From somewhere above their heads came the sound of the Purple Girl sweeping, *shhh-shhh-shhh*, like an admonition.

But the Backwards Man had no use for admonitions. "Munch, munch," he said, in his tiny voice that was like air whistling through a cracked window. His hands rubbed his thighs happily, while his head ate soup behind his back.

"Excuse my brother. He can't feed hisself properly," said Jenny. Her sleeping head, the bald one, lolled at her shoulder, sickeningly.

"Munch, munch, munch," sang the Backwards Man.

Eckstein and Lillian stood without speaking, their hands squeezed numb together.

When the feeding was done, Jenny Two Heads took the Backwards Man upstairs.

She returned with a large dusty jar and a lamp. She set them on the floor beside the table, and nodded to Lillian. "You get your ass up there." To Eckstein, she added, "And you gimme the money."

Lillian went to the table and climbed awkwardly onto it. She began to cry again.

Eckstein gave the freak the money.

"Wad it worth it?" Jenny cackled and stuffed the bills between her breasts.

He squatted, hoping that it would be easier to breathe at floor level. It wasn't, though, and he stood back up, the room turning dizzy.

Eckstein noticed something move inside the jar. He wiped a hand across the film of dust. A knot of thick white worms, like ropes of taffy, squirmed at the bottom of the glass.

"What are those for?" he asked.

"They eat it," said Jenny Two Heads. "That's they job."

He took a place by the table and held Lillian's hand. The freak flipped up Lillian's dress, and with a savage swipe, tore away the girl's underwear. "You won't want em after this, honey," she said.

Jenny set the lamp on the table between Lillian's legs. From a drawer she took out a pince-nez and two instruments—a battered spoon and a rubber nozzle.

She fixed her spectacle and set the probe down close by. Jenny leaned over with the spoon and studied the girl's genitals. "Wider," the freak growled and slapped the girl's heavy pale thigh.

Lillian moaned and stretched herself open.

Eckstein thought of a baseball, clean and white, soaring into a high, bright night, soaring farther than any other baseball before it. He thought of it still rising, of the droplets of dewy air sliding over it, and of its long, grand descent, *plunk* into Sheepshead Bay, down, down, sinking down, and settling gracefully into the silt, between stands of waving seaweed. For a moment, Eckstein was far beyond the basement, beyond the city, beyond himself. He was all movement and ease. Eckstein was perfect then, the way he had always been perfect when the plane of the ball met the plane of the bat and made a third plane, the one that cut through the sky and lifted the second basemen to sanctuary. He was in control then, and safe, and no trouble to anyone at all. He was a hit.

With a snort, Jenny Two Heads straightened. The bald head suddenly lifted, its eyes opened, and it burped. Just as abruptly, the head shut its eyes and fell back, and cracked on her shoulder.

Shhh-shhh-shhh, came the sound of the Purple Girl's broom.

"Your lucky day, sugar."

"What do you mean?" Lillian curled on the table, clutching her knees.

"Your works ain't no good. Your works don't work. Rotten fruit. They ain't no babies ever comin from there. Fuck all you want and there won't never be any."

Lillian let go of the second basemen's hand.

"Munch, munch, munch," echoed the distant song of the Backwards Man from somewhere above.

"All right," said Jenny. "Fine." She plucked the money from between her breast. "You can have half back, but that's all. We don't do charity around here."

When they got outside Lillian ran away from him, stumbling through the courtyard and down Wretch Lane.

The massive thing in the cage called pitifully to Eckstein as he passed. "Please don't let them make me eat any more. They won't let me stop. They keep feeding me. Please. I'm not hungry. I haven't been hungry in years. Please. Make them stop. Make them stop."

Game 3

The first pitch came to him in black and white, and the slump was over; Eckstein saw the white ball as a black spot and the colored world around it as a blank mat. He swung and the ball rocketed off the barrel of the lumber club, straight up the middle of the diamond. It ricocheted off the ankle of the Hoboken pitcher and squirted into foul territory. By the time the third baseman tracked it down, Eckstein had trotted into second.

In his next at-bat the kid drove the ball on a flat arc, hissing through the air, and not stopping until it boomed off the scoreboard. He dug into second with another double. Eckstein stood on the base and ground his teeth.

"You knocked that one," said Gordy Wheelock when Eckstein returned to the dugout. "That was a frozen rope."

"Stick it up your ass," said Eckstein.

His third time up, Eckstein was able to see the fear in the Hoboken pitcher's face. The pitcher's cheeks glistened with sweat; he bit his lip and took off his cap, brushed his hand through his hair. Eckstein watched the man fiddle and waited patiently. When the pitcher finally did throw, the kid hit the baseball up and away, over the scoreboard.

The Wonders were winning 7 to 1 by the seventh-inning stretch and the kid had batted in all the runs but one.

On the bench, Woodpecker offered Eckstein a pick. "Good wood," he said. "Real piney."

The second baseman grunted no.

Woodpecker looked Eckstein over and shook his head. "You aren't exactly here, are you?"

"No." Eckstein shook his head. He thought of the worms in the jar, hungrily squirming over each other. Maybe his mother had been lucky after all—maybe there were worse things even than Eckstein. "No, I don't guess I am."

There was no race in the outfield today. Instead, the cart with Three Ton Timmy unloaded the giant freak in right field. He sat there like a small mountain. The Purple Girl, the Backwards Man, and Jenny Two Heads ran circles around him. Three Ton Timmy roared and made histrionic grabs at them, as if he wanted to devour them. The organist played "The Moten Swing."

With one out in the ninth, a Hoboken batter hit a high fly into shallow left field. Woodpecker got a bead on it, tracking the ball into foul territory, heading for the grandstand. He stumbled against the wall, straining to catch the ball as it fell about two rows back. At that moment a hand reached from the crowd and plucked Woodpecker's cap from his head.

"Got your hat, nigger!" The heckler jumped up and down in the aisle of the grandstand, waving the cap.

Woodpecker stood by the wall, but made no move.

Eckstein bolted. "Come on, you bastards," he yelled at the rest of the Wonders infield. Pelky and several of the others looked around at each other, shrugged, and started to jog after him.

The heckler swatted the cap across Woodpecker's face. "Down boy! Sit boy!"

Eckstein reached the wall and vaulted over it.

The heckler turned, dropped the hat, and bolted up the grandstand stairs.

Four more Wonders pushed past Woodpecker, pouring over the wall. The black man watched them go. A spectator handed him back his hat.

"Thank you, sir," said Woodpecker.

Eckstein caught the heckler just in front of the exit. He jumped onto the man's back and rode him to the cement floor. The heckler wailed. "Nigger lover! Nigger lover!"

But Eckstein's fist stopped the man's mouth. The first blow split his lip, and the second made something in the heckler's face snap. The heckler crumpled to the ground. Eckstein grabbed the man by his hair and slammed his head against the ground. Blood spurted onto the cement. Twice more he banged the man's face off the floor.

Eckstein looked at his bloody right fist. There was a yellow chip of tooth embedded in his knuckle. The heckler was moaning and making sucking noises, trying to find air. "Well," said Eckstein, half to himself and half to the heckler, "well, you asked for it."

He stepped back, wounded hand cradled against his belly and staining his jersey with blood. "Well, you asked for it," Eckstein repeated again, just so it was perfectly clear, and so that everyone— not least of all himself—understood his innocence. It was a good line, he thought. It was something he planned, then and there, to get used to saying from now on.

Meanwhile, the other Wonders had gathered in a loose circle around the heckler. They began to close in, nearer, nearer still. Pelky delivered the first kick. The heckler made a shocked gurgling noise. They all started kicking him.

Snake

After Frank's father dropped him off at the curb, he started doing doughnuts in the parking lot. Frank could see his father, Ken, in the Honda, stabbing a cassette into the tape player, and immediately starting to sing along and drum the dashboard, bopping his head and rolling his shoulders. His father punctuated this exercise by wrenching the Civic—a tapioca-colored box that with its Clinton/Gore '96 bumper sticker and mismatching salvage-yard-gray passenger side door, practically screamed "public school teacher"—into a shuddering figure eight, weaving between a rusted Impala and a long black van, and nearly clipping the van, before bouncing out the exit. Ken honked a good-bye song, *beep, ba-beep-beep-beep, beep!*

It was Sunday, a few minutes before noon, when the Jetport Mall opened. Frank sat on the curb and gathered a small pile of stones. When he deemed his ammo dump large enough he began to throw them at the rusted Impala. Frank aimed for the fissured windshield, and the sound of tinkling glass. The car was a wreck, sitting on flats.

The light was high and the morning frost had burned off the roofs of the housing development across the street from the mall. The row of identical pale green boxes stretched along the crest of a hill, and then over the top, which gave the odd visual suggestion that they were being led somewhere—or maybe sneaking off on their own.

Frank was sixteen years old, a junior in high school, but his long, stringy black hair made him look older. He wore a water-stained trench coat and old canvas sneakers with ripped soles. His parents were divorced and it was one of his father's weekends.

However, on this particular weekend, the usual festivities of father-son bonding—sports bar burgers, rented movies, bowling—had been cut short by the Penobscot Union Touch Football Championship, the Teachers' Association against the Public Works Crew. His father had asked Frank if he minded, and Frank had said no, and his father had said come on, and Frank said, "Seriously, Dad, I don't give a shit," and his father had accepted that.

"Okay," Ken had said and, with a groan, removed a packet of roast beef from the fridge.

"You can just drop me off at the mall." Frank took the pot off the burner and poured his father a cup of coffee in a mug that was printed with an elementary school picture of Frank. In the picture, Frank was wearing a plaid tie and a grin with no front teeth.

Ken popped a slice of meat into his mouth, and pressed the rest of the cool packet against his swollen nose. His father's eyes were bloodshot, and the bags beneath them looked—as Frank had once read in the hard-boiled prose of a Bernie Varrick crime novel—"like a pair of matching black hammocks." Frank didn't know if the swollen nose was from his father's new girlfriend, or a simple fall. He understood innately, though, that the distinction was unimportant.

"How much to keep your mother from taking a piss down my back?" Ken asked.

"Forty," Frank said. He handed his father the coffee cup.

"Twenty," said Ken, "and you warm me up."

Frank pulled the flask of Dewar's out of the bread box. His father looked up at the ceiling, sighed, rolled his neck, and then took the flask. He administered a healthy splash to the coffee. "Thanks, Frankie. But, remember, someday when you tell your psychiatrist about this episode, I didn't ask for it. You offered."

He tossed the packet of roast beef in the garbage and went to dig the football out of the closet.

They played catch in the sun-glared driveway for about twenty minutes, mostly in silence. His father directed Frank to hit him on the run, and Ken awkwardly jogged one way, and then the other, pumping his arms and breathing hard, but managing to flag most of the balls down.

"These public works guys," Ken said, pausing between words for breath. "Half of them are picking up disability. But get them on a football field. They've all been to visit the fountain at Lourdes since their last checkup. They're healed."

Frank squinted in the light and smiled. His father could still make him smile, could make anyone smile, even Frank's mother.

In the car, before he climbed out, his father told Frank he was sorry.

"For what?" Frank asked.

"For a lot." Ken patted the steering wheel. "For a hell of a lot, but listen—" and then he explained his plan for the winter. He was going to take a leave from the high school, let someone else hose down the monkey house for a few months, and in the meantime, really settle into his old study carrel at the university library, really buckle down, and finally put a big pink bow on his dissertation.

The rocks chimed off the Impala's corpse. Weekends with his father invariably put Frank into a mood; the mood was hard to pin down, though; it was that Sunday feeling, a sort of general ickiness, the way you felt after watching television for a few hours and then looked outside to see that the day had turned into night before you even got started. Those kind of days felt good while they were happening, while you were doing nothing, but when they ended, you felt like a slob. Of course, here Frank was, broad daylight, all the bright hours in front of him, but the feeling was with him just the same.

He imagined his father in front of a lecture hall, giving them the Ken Ackerly Left Eyebrow of Skepticism^{TM}, a bushy black eyebrow that he could raise so high and sharp that it was worthy of Groucho Marx. The college kids would love that; Frank could hear them laughing.

At noon the security guard rattled open the glass doors. Frank dumped the remaining stones from his pockets and slouched inside.

The Jetport Mall wasn't much of a mall, just one level in the basic stenciled C-shape. There were a couple All-For-A-Dollar Stores, a dingy hobby shop, a Mr. Paperback which mostly sold greeting cards and miniature stuffed animals, a pet store, the local DMV, a florist, a hairdresser, a Dexter Shoe, a Nathan's hot dog stand, and an arcade of old and semifunctional video games.

Ken called it the Reagan Mall, and if he was hammered enough, he could be counted on to give a lecture on the subject, about how ever since Ronnie the country was like a dumb kid who had eaten a bunch of lead paint chips. (This diatribe, of course, inevitably featured an appearance by the Ken Ackerly Left Eyebrow of Skepticism™.) "Those All-For-A-Dollar Stores," Ken said. "What they really ought to call them is Cheap-Shit-For-The-Gipper Stores."

This had been before the divorce, and Frank's mother, Catherine, had responded, "Fascinating, Ken, just fascinating. Why don't you have another beer, and then fill us all in on what the real problem with the Middle East is?"

Frank turned right at the end of the entrance wing and made a beeline for Mr. Paperback—about the only store in the mall that interested him. He planned to burn the afternoon reading, maybe even catch some z's in the armchair in back of the store. This single piece of furniture—certainly of thrift store origin, smelling permanently of damp, and so deep that when Frank rose from it, he almost had to kick his way out—was an almost poignant response to the enormous new chain bookstore at the mall in Bangor, which not only had several brand-new armchairs, but a café. Frank was in the mood for a crime novel, something swift and tough. The kind of story that put a strong feeling in his chest, gathering speed as it wound through the dead-ends and false leads, the inevitable violence, but always the certainty that one way or another, the mean truth was going to come out. Twenty bucks could sometimes buy as many as three or four crime novels; Frank figured that should be more than enough mean truth to keep him satisfied for a few days.

There was an unspoken arrangement in his acceptance of the money from his father. If his mother asked, Frank would say that he and the old man went to the movies, or the library, or did something constructive. Not that he would have tattled even if his father gave him nothing. That was a fast track to more family counseling, something no one deserved any more of at this point, least of all his mother.

The last time they went to a group therapy session at the YWCA, the therapist had gone on and on about how when there was strife within the family unit, it was as if the phone got disconnected, and that by the time the phone was ready to be turned back on everyone had already made different arrangements. "Before all the shit went down you were all on this big party line, and now, now everyone is jabbering away on their own cell phones," the therapist had said. "I mean, sometimes the party line was a bummer, right? There was one time you couldn't call your buddy in Fresno when you really wanted to, and you couldn't, right? But that's part of living together. That's how it goes with the party line. So, we've either got to get that big party line hooked up again, or else learn to deal with all the bullshit that goes along with having a cell phone."

("What the fuck is a party line?" Frank had asked.)

A few days after the session Frank had come into his mother's room and found her sitting on the bed and crying, rocking back and forth and hugging an Opus doll. "I'm forty-two, Frank. I can't start over. I can't even get a cat. I'm allergic to cat hair." She had let loose a sob then, and belched, spitting up a little yellow something onto the head of the Opus doll. "And look at this," she said, holding out the doll, "now I've puked on my penguin."

Frank thought what everybody really needed to do at this stage was get on with it—and in a way, that was why Frank was at the mall. His father was getting on with it by knocking back some beers and playing some football with his buddies. Frank was getting on with it by browsing for books at Mr. Paperback. And since she didn't know any better his mother was probably getting on with it back home, meditating or dealing tarot cards to herself and Opus. If there was anything he'd learned from reading crime novels it was that there wasn't any sense in making a stink. The stool pigeons never made it to the sequel. They ended up wearing the razor necktie, or buried in a shallow grave, taking the dirt nap. The best chance you had was to take it on the chin, do your time, keep quiet.

*   *   *

Frank was down the hall from the bookstore when a booming voice jumped him. A big man over at the exhibition area waved him over.

The exhibition area was a raised platform at the center of the mall's main passage, where special events were held—a kiosk selling airbrushed T-shirts in more than a hundred designs, a taxidermist's display, the Easter Bunny or Santa Claus, a trainer from Gold's Gym giving five-dollar neck massages in an orthopedic chair—but never anything interesting. Today, the big man was standing in front of a skeletal arrangement of plain wooden beams.

The wooden framing made a rectangle, six feet or so high, and around twelve feet long. A couple of crates were arrayed on the tiled surface of the exhibition area, and some hay had been strewn across the floor beneath. It was an odd setup; the man was maybe a contractor or something, Frank thought, although it was difficult to say what the wooden framing was meant to display.

"Yeah?" asked Frank.

The big man was about fifty, goateed, a biker-looking type with a straining belly and the dark shadow of a tattoo beneath the hair of his forearm. He wore brown leather chaps and a T-shirt that said, I HUNT WHITE-TAILED DEER. The T-shirt showed a man with a wolfish grin taking aim with a very long elephant gun at a girl in a bikini who had been treed high up in a pine.

A Polaroid camera was draped around the man's neck and a pair of highwayman sunglasses was hooked onto his collar. Frank thought he looked like some sort of post-apocalyptic tourist.

"Hey, bro, you got a lighter?" The man shook out a pack of cigarettes.

"Sure." Frank took off his backpack and fished out his lighter. "You can't smoke in most malls."

"Fascists. There's more of em everyday. It's like that old sci-fi flick with the psycho plants—dweebs in ties keep on popping out." He lit his cigarette, not bothering to offer Frank one.

A woman was slowly pushing a stroller. They both turned at the sound of creaking wheels.

"Hey, man, I don't want to offend your civic pride, but this is a pretty shit-ass mall, ain't it? Most places there's at least a few people waiting to get in. So far it's just you and her." He thumbed toward the woman with the stroller.

"She's crazy," said Frank. "All she's got in that stroller is a two-liter Coke bottle wearing a wool hat. I've seen her here before. She sort of does laps with the stroller."

The man shook his head. "She ever spend any money?"

"I don't think so," Frank said. "Sometimes the Coke bottle wears different hats. Maybe she buys those."

"Fuck," said the man. "I don't sell hats."

Frank could smell the guy's b.o., a funky odor that he associated with dogs. He looked irritated, and made a juicy sound as he sucked on his cigarette.

"So what are you doing here?" Frank asked.

The man raised an eyebrow. He coolly blew smoke out of the side of his mouth. "I'm a snake man. This is a snake show."

"Oh, yeah?" Frank wasn't sure what he meant until he spotted a piece of posterboard taped to the wall:

Jimmy "Leatherneck" Federicci
and The King Boa Of The Amazon:
Julius Squeezer
Photos with Julius Squeezer $5
Feed Julius Squeezer $20
Warning: Julius Squeezer WILL eat ASSHOLES!!!

A fearsome snake threaded through the letters, rearing up with hypnotic green eyes.

"You wanna see?" asked Leatherneck Federicci. He didn't wait for an answer. "Stay there."

The big man went to the largest crate. There were several holes punched in the side and a heavy metal latch with a padlock. He took a key from his pocket, unlocked it. Removing the lid, he squatted down and put his arms into the wooden box.

Frank felt little anticipation. He had seen snakes before at the zoo in Portland and the experience had not been a memorable one. The idea that a mall snake would be any more interesting than a zoo snake was unlikely.

Leatherneck lifted the creature from the box and draped it nonchalantly over his neck. From the distance of a few yards it looked like nothing more than a thick green cable.

He came back to Frank wearing the thing, hung around his neck and twisted down the length of his left arm in a practiced way. Along the side of the snake a band of darker green diamond-shaped markings appeared glazed beneath the mall's fluorescent lighting. The snake looked very heavy, swelled somehow, although Leatherneck carried it with ease. Its eyes were yellow chips of glass; it might have been dead.

"This," said Leatherneck, "is Julius Squeezer."

"Cool," said Frank. He was mildly impressed.

"Fuckin' A cool," Leatherneck said. "That right there is a big badass snake. An emerald boa constrictor." He held up his hand and squeezed a burly fist. "Choke you right off."

In fact, the snake didn't appear all that active.

"What's it do?" Frank asked.

Leatherneck gave Frank a disdainful look. "What's he do?" He stroked the creature's head with a single finger. "He's a giant boa constrictor. He does whatever he wants."

"I mean, he seems like he's sleeping."

"Yeah, well. The Squeezer keeps his own hours. He's not a dancing bear."

Frank wondered where the animal had come from, and how it had ended up playing scarf for a beefy biker. It wasn't much to wonder about, but for a Sunday, it wasn't bad.

"Where'd you get him?" asked Frank.

"That's an interesting story." Leatherneck petted the dark flesh where it wound around his bicep.

"Yeah? Tell me."

"You like a good story, huh?"

"Sure," Frank said.

"You got five bucks in that backpack? Five buckaroos for a Polaroid, kid. This ain't a charity. I'll tell you all about the Squeezer while I snap your portrait."

Frank figured why not. He had a few dollars to spare, and there'd be enough left over for the bookstore. There was certainly no hurry. The crazy woman with the stroller had gone past and they were alone again, the surrounding storefronts open for business, but quiet.

"I guess I can spare five bucks."

"Right on," said Leatherneck and led Frank over to the poster, positioning him so that it would be in the background. "For copyright purposes."

Leatherneck gripped the motionless creature at a point underneath the jaw, and pulled it loose in one smooth motion, as if he were taking off a belt. "Just look tough, and we'll get a nice one. The Squeezer knows you're with the good guys."

Something skipped in Frank's throat; it occurred to him that he was about to wear a giant snake, however docile, or even deceased, it appeared. "So, where did you get him?"

"Originally, the Squeezer hails from Costa Rica," said Leatherneck as he gently set the animal against the back of Frank's neck. It lay against his collar, weighing less than he expected. He had imagined the snake would feel wet and clammy. But it didn't really feel like much, a small pressure against his nape.

"Like, you found him in the jungle?"

"Nope. A girlfriend of mine was trying to kill me," said Leatherneck matter of factly, and drew the ends of the snake over Frank's shoulders.

"What?" Frank registered only vaguely the slight tensing of Julius Squeezer's body, making certain of his hold.

"Your girlfriend was trying to kill you? Are we talking a murderous rage kind of thing, or are we talking about a professional hit?"

"You're one of those morbid little bastards, huh? I should have been able to tell by the trench coat." Leatherneck dropped his cigarette on the tile and ground it out. "Well, I'll give you the short version: a buddy of mine from the service had a little place on a strip of beach down there and invited me to come check it out. Me and this girlfriend of mine took him up on the offer. Sun, snorkeling, beer on the beach, maybe some dope, what could be better, right?"

"Right," said Frank.

"But this girlfriend of mine thought I was cheating on her, snagging a piece on the side from this island gal. It was a totally bullshit rap, by the way. I never touched this island chick. I pleaded my innocence, made my case like Perry Mason. At which point, my lady friend, she says, 'Fine, I believe you, sugar baby.' And I thought that was the end of it, everything's cool. Big mistake. Never trust a broad when she starts talking to you like an infant.

"Turns out my lady goes and makes a deal with this fucking witch-dude. No kidding, a fucking witch. One of these characters who goes around wearing a big fucking bush on his head.

"This guy, he gives her a snake to do the job, make it look like the thing crawled in through a window or something, which is perfectly believable down there. I'm dead fifteen minutes after the poison hits my bloodstream. Fifty bucks for a shroud, drop me in the ground, and my lady and the witch go have piña coladas. She heads home with some extra luggage, but otherwise no big hassle."

"Holy shit," said Frank. He glanced down at the creature where it was knotted around his arm, supple and silent.

"Pretty fucking sinister, huh?" He raised the camera, lowered it, checked the flash, and raised it again. "Thing was, the guy was an idiot. He gave my old lady a boa constrictor, which he thought was a viper. A significant difference, my friend.

"So, she slips the old Squeezer in bed with me after I'm asleep one night, expecting him to bite my ass or something. I wake up, feeling a little tickle around my feet, and think I've kicked off the sheets. That's when I see Julius here, curling all over my legs. For a second, I think I'm fucked, but then I realize he's only a boa, and I sit right up and start cuddling with the big son-of-a-bitch. The witch snookered her."

The flash snapped. "And there it is," said Leatherneck. "You have proved yourself to be a worthy mantle for the greatness of the Squeezer."

Frank blinked at the spots of color against his eyes, and felt Leatherneck remove the weight from his shoulders. The snake trainer carried Julius Squeezer over to the wooden frame and hung it up. The snake dangled limply, as harmless as a damp towel on a rack. In the next moment, it curled up, wound itself out along the wood. The snake froze in this position, a hard green spiral.

Swishing the square of celluloid back and forth in the air Leatherneck said, "It's gonna be a nice one. I got the Squeezer's handsome side."

Frank found the five dollars in his wallet and they made the exchange. In the photograph, the snake appeared even deader than in real life.

"That's an incredible story," said Frank. "The double-crosser got double-crossed. I love stories like that."

"I'm glad you enjoyed it, brother," said Leatherneck. "But let me tell you, it wasn't that funny living it. Every time you wake up with a snake in your bed it takes five years off your life, minimum." He went over to one of the other crates and started rustling around in it. "Anyway, have a good one. Tell all your friends about the Squeezer."

Frank pulled a couple of books from the shelf and retired to the pill-spotted armchair in the rear of the store. These first two paperbacks were well titled—*The Gold Stamp Murders* and *Checkfate*—but almost immediately disappointing.

These were the kind of his books that Ken, an English teacher, called "cops and robbers crap."

"Jesus, at least you're reading something, though," he had said once. "I've got kids in my senior class who wouldn't be able to decipher a draft notice. When I was eighteen there were guys I used to play Little League with coming home in pine boxes, and meanwhile their nuts were being chewed on by jungle rats in Southeast Asia. It was college or death, kiddo—hey, what have they got you reading in class?"

Frank had shrugged. *"Great Expectations."*

"Dickens!" his father cried. "That's tremendous, Frankie. Can you believe how funny it is? I mean, the language."

"It's boring," said Frank.

"C'mon," said his father. "Pip? Joe? Miss Havisham? *Magwitch,* for god's sake? Darlin', you gotta get with the program. Don't you love it when they eat 'wittles'?"

"But what are 'wittles'?" Frank had asked, and his father had heaved a sigh of disbelief. "Ah, forget it," Ken said. "You want to go and shoot a few strings?"

The trouble with *The Gold Stamp Murders* and *Checkfate* was that neither was particularly believable. The first book was about a gangland war. In the second chapter, a hired gun backed over a private investigator with a garbage truck. Then, after the garbage truck pulled away, the P.I. was able to crawl off with only a fractured leg. Please, thought Frank. It was common sense that after one pressing by a garbage truck, that was it, your ticket was punched.

Checkfate was about a chessmaster caught in a game of international intrigue: Frank knew several guys on the chess team at school and the notion of any of them seducing a female MI6 agent strained his suspension of disbelief. If it didn't seem true, what was the point? That was the way Frank looked at it.

Luckily, he had an ace in his pocket, a sure thing—the latest paperback by Bernie Varrick. There was a small picture of Varrick on the back cover, showing an old man with a head of windblown snow-white hair and a scowl. The author's note said that Bernie Varrick was a retired Florida sheriff. He was one of Frank's favorite writers. In Varrick's books when people died, they stayed dead; there were no brilliant madmen, just desperate people and tough cops. The new Varrick was called *Some Things Float.*

Frank began to read: a plane goes down in the Everglades, carrying a congressional candidate and his brother. There's no chance that anyone survived, and no way to recover the bodies; anything out there in that swamp was gator bait. And that would probably be the end of it, except for a sheriff from a nearby township, an alcoholic hard case named Charlie Gunther, who stumbles across a packed suitcase belonging to the congressman's dead brother in the closet of an overdosed prostitute.

It was vintage Varrick stuff: *Gunther played the flashlight over the walls of the basement. There was a smell in the room. It was a humid smell, tangy and overdue. He thought about meat turning from red to white in the sun, drawing gnats. Rusted hooks lined the walls.*

Gunther listened, the smell rising up to his eyes. After a moment it came to him: it was the reek of old bait, fish guts. Something scraped in the darkness. "Who the fuck?" he asked, trying to keep the stutter out of his voice . . .

But Frank's mind wandered. Maybe at that moment his father was chasing down a pass, perfectly timing the parabola's end, loping in for a touchdown. He could hear his father tell it: "I gave the d-back a bump, broke left, caught it in stride, and hustled my ass into the end zone. Thought I was going to bust a gasket, Frankie, keel right over." This was followed by what seemed to Frank a somewhat likelier image: his father leaning against a sapling a few yards north of the field, releasing a long, sighing beer piss in the bushes.

Gunther reached for the grip of his thirty-eight, strapped tight underneath his armpit. His fingers recognized the cap of the flask, the one he had stowed away last night, in case of an emergency. He swung the flashlight across the room. The white circle spotted something on the ground, something moving. Gunther took a step forward—the light caught two tiny spikes of yellow—and the old cop clutched his chest, staggered back, wheezing, and popped like a balloon. Julius Squeezer, the King Boa of the Amazon, slithered into the circle of the flashlight.

Frank set the book down. Maybe he wasn't in a reading mood today. The bookstore was empty except for the counterman and a woman in the greeting card section. A piano plunked from the tinny store speaker system. He pulled the Polaroid of the snake from the inner pocket of his trench coat. He ran a hand through his hair, dragging at the knots. After studying the picture for a minute or two, he used a sharp corner to pick at his teeth. Then he looked at it again, looked hard.

Leatherneck's story had come to him, and something about it suddenly bothered Frank. He was reminded of his father, of the way the old man described the plays he made in his football games, or the arguments he won when he was out drinking. The conspiratorial delivery, the casual intimacy as he talked and worked the camera at the same time. It even had the hallmarks of his father's stories: sinister women, startling confrontations with rampant ignorance, the frustrations of being a simple man. What was troubling him now,

Frank realized, was that as a general rule, his father, like most crime novels and paperback thrillers, was not to be believed.

Leatherneck was sitting on a crate, forlornly eating a hot dog.

"Hey," said Frank.

The snake handler sighed. "The chick with the stroller came back through. You were right—totally fucking batty. I tried to convince her that it might be cool to get a picture of the Squeezer in the baby carriage, maybe even see if we could get him to wear the Coke bottle's hat, but it was like talking to a television."

"Yeah," said Frank.

There was a pause; Leatherneck chewed his hot dog, raised an eyebrow. "Don't tell me there's something wrong with your picture."

"No, no, it's fine," said Frank. "I was just wondering, well, I got to thinking about your story. About you and the Squeezer and your girlfriend."

"It's all true," said Leatherneck. "What else you want to know?" He stood up, glanced around to make sure no one was watching, and disposed of the remaining segment of hot dog and bun by dropping it into a nearby plant pot. He came back and stood in front of Frank with his arms crossed.

"I couldn't figure how you got him through customs. The Squeezer, I mean."

"What?"

"He's an exotic animal, right? That's not legal, is it?"

"Sure it is," said Leatherneck. "Just had to lay some cash down. It's a different world over there. They don't accept American Express, if you know what I'm saying."

"What about your girlfriend?"

"She took a hike, got her ass on the first plane back to the States and away from me. I was ready to kick ass. Probably went home to mommy. Anything else you wanna know, Sherlock?"

"What happened to the witch?"

Leatherneck drew a thumb across his throat.

"You killed him?"

"I'm not saying that I killed him." Leatherneck paused. Even his goatee looked fake, Frank thought, with that fine white line. "But I will say that Julius prefers the finer meats, as opposed to rats and birds."

Frank felt himself break into a wide grin.

Their eyes met; the snake handler's were green and soft, lake pebbles flashing under clear water.

Frank broke the gaze, glancing at the ink ghost of the old tattoo on Leatherneck's forearm. A small, careful gnome, blowing a long smoking pipe. The cloud of expelled smoke spelled a word: WOOD-STOCK.

"No, you didn't," said Frank, "you didn't kill anyone. No way, I don't believe you." He was surprised at his own voice, and uttered a nervous giggle, meaning to sound friendly. Although he wasn't exactly sure that he felt friendly to the man who had tried to pass off the ridiculous story, like Frank was a moron. "And that snake *isn't* from Costa Rica," he added. "No way, José."

Leatherneck rolled his eyes. He let his head fall back, so that he stared up at the ceiling. The stubble on his neck was stiff, and rat black. Bringing his hand close to Frank's face, he gave him the finger. There was a moon of black dirt beneath the long fingernail. "Fuck you. Fuck you, fuck you, fuck you." He said it like he was singing to himself.

Frank took a step back.

The snake handler grunted disgustedly, and sat down on his crate.

Frank plunged his hands in his pockets, searching for the five dollars he still had left. "I'll get another Polaroid," he said.

"Nope, get lost, fuck off," he said. "I don't need any smartass kid shit." He made a sweeping gesture. "Fuck off. Begone."

Frank walked off, checking back over his shoulder as he walked away: the snake trainer didn't watch him go, just sat chewing a fingernail and looking pissed. The snake was still curled thickly around the same wooden beam, unmoving, eyeless.

It was after four, and the light was failing. His father had promised to pick him up around closing time at five o'clock. Only a dozen or so cars were parked in the lot. Another busy shopping day at the

Reagan Mall. The wind spun wrappers and leaves across the parking lot. Frank hugged himself as he crossed the pavement.

The driver's side door of the Impala was locked with rust, but with a wrenching creak, Frank dislodged the back door and slid inside. The ancient, torn leather of the interior crackled under his weight. There was a pervasive scent of urine.

From the bottom of his backpack he withdrew the zippered plastic bag with the two joints. Stretching out, he lay on the backseat and fired one up. Frank took a long pull and blew smoke at the dirty felt ceiling of the car.

He had busted an old hippie for lying. It had been a nasty thing to do, Frank thought. Leatherneck wasn't really like his father, he was just a guy trying to make a living. A part of Frank wished that a cop would come along and haul him off for possession. On the ceiling of the Impala he could make out grubby fingerprints.

Someone had driven the car, driven it a long way, from dentist appointments to malls to schools to who knew where else. Driven until the Impala rusted and wouldn't drive anymore. Finally, it had stopped and that was all. Just stopped.

His father wasn't going back to finish his Ph.D., and this car was never driving anywhere again. And that was okay, maybe. You just had to be honest about it.

A tapping on the glass woke him. It was dark, and it took Frank a moment to remember that he was in the abandoned car in the parking lot of the mall. He had fallen asleep and now it was time to go home.

He sat up groggily and flexed his hand, which was sore. The joint had burned down to a cinder after he drifted off. His backpack thumped onto the floor of the car.

The door of the Impala opened from the outside and a man's head stuck itself through. It wasn't his father, but Leatherneck, the snake handler.

"Oh," Frank said. "Hey."

"What are you doing, brother?" A cigarette glowed in Leatherneck's mouth. His breath was white in the night air. He wore a tight black winter stocking hat. "It's cold as fuck."

"I fell asleep," said Frank. "My dad was going to pick me up. He had a football game. I must have missed my ride."

"You want a lift?"

Frank rubbed his eyes and shivered. He blinked at the older man. Leatherneck grimaced. "I'm not going to rape you, kid," he said. "But I'm not going to stand out here, either. Your call."

The snake handler closed the door and walked off, boots jingling.

After waiting long enough to show he wasn't desperate, Frank gathered his stuff and climbed from the abandoned car, not bothering to close the door. The long black van—that must have been his with the light on—was only a couple of empty parking spaces away.

Leatherneck pushed open the door for him. "Hop up," he said. Inside, the radio was blasting classic rock, galloping guitar solos and a charging bass line.

Frank climbed the step. Immediately, he felt his cheeks tightening in the sudden warmth. The vibration of the big-watted stereo rumbled through the seat. He raised his voice to be heard. "You like a lot of heat, huh?"

"That's how it's got to be for the Squeezer." Leatherneck smiled at Frank and put a hand on the teenager's shoulder. "Say, I thought I smelled the distinct tang of some domestic bud in the back of that hulk. Don't suppose you'd care to roll another one before we drive you home?"

Frank laughed. "Sure, okay."

Leatherneck pointed an elbow at the back of the van. "Let's retire to the Enchanted Garden." A homemade wall of plywood separated the cab from the body of the van. The snake handler slipped between the seats and opened the narrow door set in the middle of the wall. "Close it behind you," he said.

Frank followed, crouching through, and shut the door as he was told.

The walls of the van were obscured by a small jungle, slick twisted branches and heavy green and glazed leaves, a few small flowers, all glowing under a low purple light. Frank stood for a moment, startled by the change in environment. The music hummed through the plywood and filled the tight space. He recognized a long, dark tube lying on one branch, shrouded in foliage: it was Julius Squeezer, or some part of him.

"Let's fire that bad boy up," said Leatherneck, sitting down on the leaf-strewn floor. He put on his highwayman sunglasses and rubbed his hands together.

Leatherneck patted the floor. "Sit, sit."

Frank shrugged off his backpack and rummaged through it for the joint.

"So, the old man forgot you, huh?"

"Yeah. He's a drunk." Frank lit the joint. It was like a sauna inside the van. He felt sweat gathering under his shirt collar. He took a drag and passed it.

"Shit. Forget I mentioned him." Leatherneck didn't sound overly concerned, though.

Leatherneck took a deep pull and hung on to the smoke for a long minute before releasing it. The snake handler cackled. "This is some fucking schwag all right."

Frank grinned.

"I'll tell you what, my man, you're young to be such a ballbuster." Leatherneck sucked on the roach.

"I didn't mean to. I just couldn't help it," said Frank. "I can't stand lying, you know."

The big man passed the roach. "Well, fuck you very much. I thought it was a perfectly good story."

Frank tried to take in some more smoke, but started to cough.

"It is true that the guy I bought the snake from was Costa Rican. Or half Costa Rican or something. He was foreign, anyhow. And my girlfriend wished it would bite me. That part was true, too. I will admit, though, that I was the jackass who thought it was a viper."

"Whatever," said Frank. "It doesn't matter. I can be an asshole." He coughed, once, twice, and caught his breath.

Leatherneck took a fresh hit. A new song came on. "The Allmans," he groaned. "Ah, fuck, I hate dead bands. This just gets me down."

The coughs were flapping in his chest, but Frank held it in. He breathed deeply; the air was wet and smoky. The good feeling was already hitting his brain, lifting everything up, brightening the corners.

There was a quiver of movement, a shift in the long shape on the branch.

"This place is amazing," said Frank.

"Nothing but the best for the Squeezer," said Leatherneck.

Frank watched Julius Squeezer slither along a branch, rattling the leaves. The reptile's skin flashed and warped with reflected light, and Frank thought of an old Cadillac, restored, all the chrome buffed.

"You're a good kid, Frank. Only sale I made all day. You didn't even want a Polaroid. I could see that. You were just being cool, that's all. Your dad is missing out." Leatherneck blew rings of marijuana smoke.

"He's okay," said Frank, hearing his voice from a distance. The snake whispered smoothly back along the branch. "He takes me bowling. He's got some good stories."

"Hey, that's something," said Leatherneck.

The snake's eyes were finally visible, yellow flashing purple flashing yellow, as it wound down the bole of a tree, moving with the effortless consistency of water finding its way. It was real, it was alive. Frank reached out to touch it.

My Second Wife

When my wife left me for another man I called my brother Wayne.

"I can't work, I can't sleep," I said. "If I was an essay I would have no thesis, no conclusion. I'd fail a student for producing something like me." I used to be a history teacher. I was crying.

I had an image of a parade, one of those ragged, snaking affairs that trickles through brick-hearted middle American towns on the Fourth of July: starting with the fire trucks and the police cars and the harvest float with the pretty girls wearing costume shop overalls and chewing on big pieces of straw; and then come the war veterans in their pressed blues and top-down convertibles, and the pomp of the high school marching bands in their white boots and spangles, trombones stabbing and batons twirling; but after that the procession begins to grow uneasy, because the labor guys are next, strutting and drinking from paper bags, trying to knock off each other's mesh baseball caps, throwing pennies at the ass of the fat boy with the bass drum at the back of the band; and following them are the doom-faced Little Leaguers with their stirrups yanked up to their knees, and the tiny, dazed ballerinas; and their parents keep pace, shoving down the crowded sidewalk like federal agents in an action movie, snapping pictures and occasionally leaping into the street to grab someone's shoulder and give it a firm shake of warning; and finally it dwindles to a freak show of uninvited tagalongs, halfway house loonies signed out for the afternoon and waving around their ice cream cones, street kids throwing snapdragons and shouldering into parked cars to set off the alarms, and, worst of all, the disciples of the local religious sect, dressed in black ties and handing out intricate diagrams of the secret universe that lies beneath our own, like the table beneath the cloth; and at the parade's end, there stumbles a filthy busker, crowing "Love Me Do," over and over again, up and down every street; all of these poor people, growing blisters and getting sunburned, acting as if they were actually going *to* someplace, and not just to the last stop sign in town. I saw my life dragging on the same way, through years and holidays. I saw myself marching in a parade that no longer existed.

"I am going to die alone," I said to my brother.

"No," said Wayne.

An ancient sexual episode suddenly came to mind, from college, when we first moved in together. My future wife had come home, and she was intoxicated, absolutely ripped, out of her mind. Without saying anything, she pushed me onto the couch, dropped between my knees. Then, as she fellated me, she began to laugh, and then to hum and garble, "Love Me Do."

At the memory, I felt my gorge rise.

"I'm not going to die alone?" I asked. "What, are you coming over to watch?"

"You are not going to die, period," said Wayne. "But I am coming over. To help you pack. We have to go Starke, Florida, to get a car."

It was Wayne's plan to drive to Starke in his mustard-colored Chevy Malibu, sell it, and drive back to Maine in the mint condition 1974 black Jaguar convertible that was waiting for him. I wanted to know how Wayne could afford a mint condition 1974 black Jaguar convertible. There had to be a catch, I said. I was a cuckold; I knew about catches.

"Your problem is superstition," said Wayne. "Don't get me wrong. You have a lot of other problems, like your haircut, and your wife fucking around, but superstition is the elephant in the room." My brother was on the other end of a phone, in his rented room at the YMCA, but I could see him, relaxing with one hand on his crotch and the other on the rod of the venetian blinds, flicking it back and forth, turning the street on and off like a light switch.

Wayne could do that. He was overweight; he was bankrupt, had always been bankrupt, in every sense; he was tattooed and divorced, poorly read and hepatitis-B positive; he was the last man in the Western world to wear a handlebar mustache with non-ironic intentions; he was my older brother, and the only human being I had ever known who was capable of existing in a state of absolute certainty, who never suffered a single misgiving, who never faltered.

"I love you," I told him. I had stopped crying, but now I started again.

Wayne explained that the town of Starke was the seat of the Florida electric chair, and the car belonged to Virgil Pendergast—the so-called Sportscar Splatterer—a psychopath of no small renown. Four summers earlier the Sportscar Splatterer had run down three squeegee men in Tampa before a neighbor spied Virgil Pendergast out in his driveway, digging clotted meat from the grille of his Jaguar. "I woulda thought he just hit a deer or some other varmint," said the neighbor in a newspaper account, "but I was pretty sure I saw a finger sticking out of the grille." (In fact, it was a thumb.)

Despite having been used as a ram, my brother informed me, the car was hardly nicked. "Pendergast was a superior body mechanic. Hitting a human being at sixty or seventy miles an hour can really do a number on an automobile, but he did an incredible job maintaining the chassis. It's a peach, Stan. I'll show you photos."

The genesis of the deal came about in an on-line chatroom for the relatives of serial killers, where Wayne befriended Pendergast's wife, Yolanda.

"What kind of a place is that to go looking for conversation?"

"I thought I would find some interesting viewpoints."

"Jesus, Wayne, do you even know if that could be considered a violation of your parole?"

"I know that if someone tries to tell me who I can or cannot talk to, it'll be a violation of my fucking civil rights."

I continued to cry.

"It's fine," said Wayne. "My parole officer buys pot from me. We went to see String Cheese Incident together. I'm not going back to jail."

"I don't care if you go back to jail."

"Hey. Fuck you."

"I can't stop. I wake up this way."

"You want a reason to cry? Cry about the car. I did. This car is a hard-on with wheels. When I saw the photos I cried like I caught my dick in a zipper."

Several collectors of serial killer memorabilia had made Yolanda Pendergast substantial offers for her husband's Jaguar, but she didn't want to profit from the murders. Now, with the execution scheduled for April 1, she was holed up in Starke until the big date. Yolanda's offer to Wayne was to sell the car for half its estimated value on the vintage car market, so long as he never attempted to cash in on its history.

I wanted to tell my wife about Wayne's latest crazy scheme. My wife loved Wayne. "Why can't you have a little levity, like your brother?" she used to ask me. But my wife was gone. There was only an empty kitchen to relate the story to.

"Okay," I said to Wayne, "I'll go with you to Starke."

We took I-95 down the East Coast. It was early spring. We drove with the windows open to try and blow out the dead raccoon smell.

Before going to prison, Wayne parked his car at the end of a fire road and concealed it in a stand of underbrush. But something about the four pounds of Northern Lights in the trunk proved irresistible to the local raccoon population, and they chewed their way into the Malibu's trunk. Three months later, upon his parole, Wayne returned to find the weed devoured—and a half-dozen overdose victims in various states of decomposition in the Malibu's trunk. (After initially recounting this tragedy, Wayne had asked me, sounding very casual, "Do you think it's wrong—I mean, morally wrong—to try smoking, like, only a small portion of a dead body?")

This was not the first time that my brother had been involved in the gruesome death of an animal: as a kid, Wayne had been something of a prodigy, and he used to fashion circuits from tinfoil and pen parts, and shock the dog. Once, he built an electric mousetrap and it electrocuted a mouse exactly the way it was supposed to. The smoke cleared, and Wayne and I stood there, appalled, watching the tiny creature sizzle.

As we drove south to collect the condemned man's car, I thought about the raccoons and the smoldering mouse. Zooming through Worcester in a downpour, I gazed out at the muddy hills and the needles of the churches. On higher ground, a factory chimney jutted up, gushing pillows of white smoke. I thought about cremation. I thought about leaving a request in my will for Wayne to roll my ashes into a joint, and smoke me. Would I become a part of Wayne? Would I drift into the atmosphere and become pollution? Would I become a piece of someone's cancer? I had a lot of thoughts like these. At rest stop urinals I felt an urge to push men for no reason, and whenever I saw a skinny woman I imagined what it would be like to kiss her.

And I thought about my wife, and her lover, a man named Albert Michalkiewicz. He was a baker. My wife and I used to eat his bread with almost every meal: wheels of hard-shelled French country rounds and soft, lumpy asteroids of black rye that lingered on the palette with soporific sweetness. I loved his bread; he loved my wife. "These things happen," she said.

On my worst night—drunk, but not really drunk—I had called her phone at work after hours and played a complete recording of "Love Me Do" into her voice mail and made crazed slurping noises.

Wayne punched my shoulder to snap me out of it. "What do you think this is about, Stan? Do you think this is about love? Do you think she left you because she loves this guy?"

That was, in fact, what my wife told me. "I love another man," she said, and then, "These things happen."

"These things happen," I repeated to my AP American history class when I announced my leave of absence. "But I know that my wife will get better. These mental illnesses are not the locked door they once seemed to be." A couple of my students were teary-eyed from the story of my wife's condition, the hallucinations, how I fended her off, how I visited her every day and brought her coloring books. "But I want you to know that I'm truly sorry to be leaving you all before the end of the semester. You're a first-rate bunch of kids. A goddamned first-rate bunch."

"That's what she said, that she loved him." Baltimore was bristling up around the Chevy's windows, miles of windowpanes and billboards of giant, smiling heads.

"Negative," said Wayne. "That ain't it."

"What, then?" I asked.

"For the thrill of it, Stan. For the screwing-on-top-of-the-chopping-board-and-then-running-around-naked, squealing-and-smearing-jelly-and-powdered-sugar-all-over-each-other, pigging-out-and-getting-fucked thrill of it. Plain decadence, sib, that's all it is."

He swung over to the breakdown lane and decelerated so I could vomit and not get too much on the side of the Chevy.

"Do you think she's going to want to spend the rest of her life with a man who gets up at four in the morning every day? A man who could drop dead tomorrow, and if you dug him up in twenty years, he would still smell like yeast?"

We drove in silence for several hours and now I was left to contemplate grave robbing, someone pulling my corpse from a casket. "Aw, Christ! This one reeks of solidity," said one of the thieves in my mind, a handkerchief clutched to his mouth. That was what people said about me: "Stan, he's solid. He's someone you can count on." I thought that my wife had grown lonely; or maybe she just grew bored, which was surely worse. I worked, and I tried, and I always shared the television controller. "Put him back," said the other body snatcher in my mind, "He's worthless," and I watched the thieves scurry down the garden row, to the richer tomb of a squeegee man.

At a campsite that night, my brother and I smoked marijuana with a retired couple from Reno who were on their way home after visiting relatives on Prince Edward Island. "My sister's in a home there," explained the old man. "Woke up one day and her memory stopped at age ten. Thinks I'm our father and FDR's president."

"I'm sorry," I said.

"Why?" asked the retired man. "She's happy. She's daddy's little girl again. Think about it. She's got her whole life in front of her."

Wayne told them the old nugget about his two-year acid trip, Austin and Belize and the remote utopian settlement of the deaf where a couple of corrupt policía had stranded him after a trumped-up disorderly charge. "You don't just go bulling into some strangers' utopia, you know? It pisses people off. Even a bunch of very mellow deaf people with a huge organic farming operation. So, I was on a short leash from the get-go.

"And, meanwhile, all over the place, I'm being constantly distracted by these tiny animals that no one else can see."

"Been there," said the retiree, and then used his hand to demonstrate the way a tiny, invisible animal would come after you. "Grrr, grrr," he said, snapping his hand at Wayne's knees.

Wayne nodded. "Yup. I hate that shit."

I woke near dawn, stumbled from the Winnebago, and pissed on woodchips. When I finished, almost without thinking about it, I started to masturbate, still half asleep and propped with an elbow against a birch tree.

A few years before, I had had an affair with the mother of a student. I didn't tell anyone. She was not a pretty woman, not even remotely good looking. The second time we had sex was on my desk after the school was closed. Her heaving body pinned me across an open-mouthed stapler. The pain was incredible. After that I ended it.

While I masturbated, I envisioned the same scenario, but this time it was my wife who slammed my back onto the stapler.

The sun, cold and smoldering, slowly ascended the trees. The light fell on me, on the trees, and on Wayne's camouflage tent. I nerved up and went limp.

I wanted to see Appomattox Court House, where Lee surrendered to Grant. At some point, years before, I'd had the idea I might like to write a book about the Civil War, but I never could settle on a subject. My wife thought it was something I could do, if I put my shoulder to it. Now, of course, I knew better.

We spent the night at a Motel 6 with a plaster statue of Lee in the parking lot, gallant on a rearing Traveler.

The next morning I sat on the old courthouse steps while Wayne slept in at the motel. People went by and bought tickets for tours at a window at the top of the steps. On the sidewalk a television reporter was being filmed doing a segment. A juvenile delinquent was jumping back and forth behind her, trying to get into the frame. The cameraman told him to beat it.

"Put me on, bro. Put my shit on television," the kid said.

Finally, a courthouse guard came down. The kid ran to the bottom of the steps. "What you gonna do now?" asked the punk.

The guard shrugged. "Nothing," he said. "Long as you stay where you are."

I closed my eyes and heard the sound of Traveler's hooves on the frozen mud of that early morning, the mist ghosting from the torn street, the lace curtains limp in the windows of the townspeople's empty homes.

The Confederate officers milled about the steps in their heavy wool coats and black boots, talking in whispers, as if there was something sacred about this patch of mud and clapboard, that was no different from the thousand other places they had stopped to rest and bleed. But at the echo of the hoof beats, the whispering stopped, everything stopped. From out of the mist, the old man and his horse appeared. How old Lee looked, as if his proud, straight spine might snap at any moment, and his body crumble to twigs inside his uniform; and Traveler looked like a phantom of horse.

Lee reined in, but did not dismount. He said: "Men, we have fought through war together. I have done my best for you; my heart is too full to say more."

The officers on the steps realized that their general was weeping. It was over. Without even knowing it, they had all surrendered.

A sudden gust shredded the mist, and Traveler reared up. The general tightened the reins, but the stallion replied with another sharp kick, and the general pulled again, harder this time. The animal whinnied, snorted. Then, the old man bent down, and whispered something into the beast's velvet ear—perhaps some secret that, after all, even General Lee's great, defeated heart could not contain.

"Hey, mister, buy me a pack of Marlboros from that dude over there." The kid who had been bothering the cameraman was standing in front of me. He pointed at a vending kiosk at the foot of the courthouse steps.

The kid gave me five dollars and I bought him his cigarettes.

"Thanks," he said when I handed them over.

"Stanley, what are you doing? He's a minor. What has happened to you?" I could hear my wife saying these things. It seemed reasonable to me then, that she should love another man, a simple baker.

Clip-clop, clip-clop.

I knew what it felt like to surrender. I sympathized with both man and horse.

My wife's upbringing had been strict, and religious. For most of her formative years the only toy her parents permitted was a Bible; and the only way she could play with the Bible was to make book covers for it. (My wife could knock out a perfect book cover in about thirty seconds; take a paper bag, snip-snip, six precise folds, and there you had it.) To this day, the walls of her parents' home were decorated with these childhood book covers, lovingly framed and hung alongside family photos. The book covers showed elaborately painted action scenes: Jesus smashing the moneychangers' table with a kung fu kick, and David taking a chainsaw to Goliath's spewing jugular, and "THE BIBLE" in bullet print above the pictures, like it was a Steve McQueen movie. Each night, her parents contentedly ate dinner at their kitchen table, beneath a framed cover of Cain dismembering Abel with a machete.

Throughout our wedding, these good people never took a seat on a pew, but remained side by side on their knees, praying for their daughter to marry a God-fearing man, someone with an honest haircut.

My wife told me that she believed that her childhood stunted her imagination, and maybe that was the reason she never felt quite whole. The only stories she knew were the stories in the Bible; her own story didn't begin until she went to college and met me.

"But what about the time you escaped from those wild bears?" I asked her. We were lying in the dark. It was years before, when we were poor, when my haircut could still be considered mildly corrupt, and when she still slept in the nude.

"What do you mean?"

"I mean, how did you get away? There were wild bears. They could have killed you. They wanted to kill you."

She blinked. Then my wife said, the words coming out quick, breathless: "It was the honeymooners. The honeymooners saved me. Without even knowing it."

"Yes?"

They advanced upon her, the stinking, shambling monsters, the wild black bears with claws like scimitars, eyes rolling and blood crazed, their steps shaking the ground. "I knew that my only chance was to show that I was one of them," my wife said, and she leapt through the arched legs of the biggest bear, and fell upon the disemboweled and still-steaming bodies of the two young honey-mooners. My wife yanked out an organ and tore away a massive bite of tissue. The wild bears became confused; after watching her devour an intestine, they realized she was one of them, and the beasts all went to sleep. "Later," said my wife, "I killed them, skinned them, and sold their pelts to gain passage back to Sri Lanka."

The game became a regular part of our evenings. "Give me a question," she'd abruptly demand, as we lay in the bedroom dark. Then, after a moment, I'd ask, "How about the banditos? The Spanish gold, the old mission, the blind girl? How did it play out?" I turned on my side to watch her recount the escape and the crooked deal and the sweet revenge; and her eyes brightened, and it excited me, the abandonment in that expression, but now I realized that I had made a mistake. I never included myself in a scenario, or asked my wife how I would save her. I sent her into peril alone.

I tried the game on Wayne. "How did you escape from the wild bears?" I asked him.

"This is the screw game you played with the bitch, isn't it?" He was eating a roadside barbecue sandwich with one hand, strings of juicy meat spilling down the front of his shirt, and driving with the other, tearing through Virginia at just under a hundred.

"Yes," I said. I could already see it wasn't going to work.

"Okay. I shot the shit out of the bears."

"Nice," I said, "that's really inventive."

"Sorry, but that's how it happened. Shot the fuckers. You asked, I told you."

"I cheated on her, Wayne," I said. This was something I had never told anyone.

He groaned. "Are you going to eat that?" he asked.

"No," I said.

Our third and last night on the road, we stopped at a drive-in in South Carolina to grab some shut-eye, but neither of us could sleep. Wayne and I walked around the lot, trying to peep. We thought one guy was getting a hand job, but it was hard to see; we couldn't tell for sure. Both ends of the double feature were about people dying of cancer, but in the second show, the cancer gave the protagonist superpowers.

"You really torture yourself, thinking about it, don't you?" Wayne asked. He didn't have to tell me what "it" was.

I imagined my wife and Albert Michalkiewicz having sex atop the steel counters of his bakery kitchen. I saw the flour caked to my wife's ass as she sprawled beneath him; the powder turning his chest hair white, making him old and repulsive and powerful, like Anthony Quinn, like Zorba the fucking Greek. When they were done, I supposed they would feast—naked and ghostly and utterly famished—gobbling pastries and pies with lusty abandon. I pictured Albert Michalkiewicz squishing a cannoli on my wife's chest and smearing the cream filling all over.

"Well?" Wayne had discovered an almost full bag of popcorn lying in some weeds. On the movie screen, the superhero was terribly withered from the disease, but still strong enough to shoot lasers from his eyes, and knock down buildings to block the tidal wave. Crickets chattered, a girl giggled, protesting no, but giggling yes.

"Can I still buy my bread there? From *him*?"

My brother shook his head. He held out the bag. I took a handful of stale corn and chomped.

*   *   *

We arrived in Starke on a Friday evening. We passed a bar marquee proclaiming, THIS SATURDAY: CRISPY CRITTER DRINK SPECIALS! It seemed that Virgil Pendergast was still waiting for his stay of execution.

The penitentiary squatted in a barbed wire nest on a hill above the interstate. A half-dozen spotlight beams pointed ineffectually into the gathering twilight. A few strip malls slept in intervals along the main street, advertising valuable merchandise at low prices.

Pendergast's wife was staying at a Days Inn a mile or so from the penitentiary. We took a room of our own for two nights, because the deal did have one catch: if Pendergast did receive a stay of execution, Wayne couldn't buy his car. The widow-to-be didn't actually own the car until he was dead.

Wayne called her and she turned out to have the room next door.

Yolanda Pendergast was a lanky woman, pushing fifty, but not that hard to look at. First, she shook my hand, and then she gave my brother a hug that lingered a little too long and clung a little too tight around the waist to be just sisterly. I immediately realized how it was going to be, and a part of me wanted to slug my brother; only a couple of miles away a man sat on death row, and here was Wayne, preparing to pork his wife, and take his Jaguar for a song. In the next instant, I found myself wondering how I could think that way: Wayne was my brother, and Virgil Pendergast was a psychopath who had run down squeegee men, and who had smugly informed his court-appointed psychiatrist that he had never run over an actual man, just frogs. ("And then, in reference to the squeegee men, Mr. Pendergast stated, 'They's just frogs in disguise, that's what you all are overlooking right here,'" testified the psychiatrist during the penalty stage of the trial.)

So the man's wife was moving on. These things happen.

Yolanda had a six-pack of beer and we sat on plastic chairs around the motel swimming pool.

"Last time they turned on the juice it knocked out the power all over town, blew the top clean off the penitentiary generator. Apparently there are some circuits mixed up with the chair's battery, but the county engineer is plum perplexed," said Yolanda, not appearing especially concerned herself, as she sipped from a longneck and reached over to trace Wayne's TCB belt buckle.

"I don't have to tell you that Virgil is some concerned."

Wayne clucked his tongue. "It's an ugly business."

The evening was mild. Venus was bright. Another guest was watching a war movie; a soldier was screaming for his mother. The sergeant told the grunt to shut his hole, pronto.

"I miss Paula. I miss my wife." I blurted the words, almost spitting them out.

Either they didn't hear me, or they pretended they didn't, because no one said anything. Wayne stroked Yolanda's blond hair. She squinted at the last light and smiled, and scratched a cold sore in the corner of her mouth with a long purple nail. The war ended.

We finished the beer and Wayne suggested we go out for a few more drinks. Yolanda knew a great place.

In the motel parking lot I noticed the canvas-covered body of Virgil Pendergast's murder weapon. Only the bottom curve of the Jaguar's silver hubcaps was visible beneath the tarp. I thought of secret eyes, peering between the gaps of a venetian blind.

We took the Malibu to the bar.

The painted awning of the bar pictured an alligator in a Florida State letter jacket munching on a Union soldier. The Yankee soldier's tongue lolled grotesquely from his mouth.

We took a table on the veranda, which commanded a view of a balding hillside of scrub grass and the northbound side of the highway. A couple of tall gawky chickens milled aimlessly on the dark slope, picking at the dry grass, occasionally producing a raspy squawk.

There was a round of shots, a round of beers, another round of shots, more beers, and Wayne told the story about when we were kids and the mouse got electrocuted. Only this time, I made the mousetrap and the mouse blew up. "In the next second, the little bugger was gone, and there was nothing but a real fine vapor of blood hanging in the air."

"Oh, I just hate mice," said Yolanda.

"My point," said Wayne, "is twofold: first, Stanley was a sicko growing up; and two, electricity has a mind of its own."

"I used to shock the shit out of the dog, too," I said.

She gave me a glassy, pinched smile. "You know, Stan, I think you and Virgil would have a lot in common. He's real good with science, also."

Wayne announced that he had a dick full of piss and tottered to his feet.

When he was gone, Yolanda put her hand on mine. "I can't tell you how supportive your brother has been to me during this difficult time. Wayne met me every day for lunch at the chatroom—I just hate to eat alone. I swear, without him I think might've just gone crazy, and lost control of my body completely: just stopped talking and crapped in my pants like a baby.

"And as a woman, I want you to know—because Wayne said your wife was thin—I want you know that a lot of real thin women will fuck just about any old Joe. It's not your fault. They just can't help it."

"I ought to write that down," I said. Yolanda said I sure should.

Wayne came back and I went to the bar and played a video game where you had a screen with two almost identical pictures of sexy men, but things—little bow ties, tattoos—were missing from the second picture, and you had to press the screen to put a circle on the missing spots.

A dark-haired girl in red jeans and cowboy boots sidled up to me. "That old boy on the right there doesn't have the black band on his jock."

"Thanks," I said.

"Sure," she said, and informed me that her name was Jesse and that fate had chosen me from all the gentlemen in the bar.

"Yeah? What's he want from me? Fate, I mean."

"To buy me a Tom Collins. That's a peculiar drink, but Fate is peculiar."

I had no reason to doubt her. After all, some kind of fate had brought me to Starke, Florida, where the government killed men with massive shocks of electricity for running down other men with their sports cars. That Fate should now be guiding me to purchase a Tom Collins for a stranger in tight red jeans seemed far less unbelievable.

"I'm Stanley," I said, and bought her drink. We played through a dozen studs, pointing at the missing socks and eyebrows, before a Hawaiian beefcake in a towel stumped us with a vanished ponytail.

Jesse came over to the table with me, and Wayne regaled the group with a history of his two years at Cornell, and how he'd been expelled for trying to crossbreed marijuana with seaweed. I found myself studying Jesse's pretty face, her nub of a nose. My gaze drifted down to the tight draw of shirt across her small bra-free breasts and back up to the jagged incisor at the corner of her mouth.

"There's thousands of beach caves up and down the northeast coast where you could grow a versatile plant like cannabis. Of course, you'd still have to worry about federal agents and informers, but it could be a big cash crop for disenfranchised farmers." Wayne took a meaningful pause to sip his beer. "I was getting close—certain people got nervous."

"The government is one big conspiracy." Yolanda was stuffing her third pint glass of the night into her purse.

"I didn't know you went to college, Wayne," I said, and slipped my hand onto Jesse's thigh.

She picked up my hand and examined my palm lines. Jesse massaged my fingers, cracked my knuckles. She drew my index finger to her mouth and gnawed on a hangnail, bit it loose. "Got it," she said.

I was nauseated, confused, but undeniably erect. I told Jesse. "I feel kind of—you know." I made a vague circle in the air, which signified nothing.

But she understood. "It turned you on, didn't it? But it was gross, right? I don't know where you've been, or where your finger's been, but I went and gnawed on it just the same. Pretty sick, right?"

"But I liked it," I said, "even though it was awful."

"Sometimes love's like that," she said.

I sipped my drink. I stared out at the hillside, and the giant chickens strutting around in the scrub grass. I wanted to explain to this woman about my limitations—about my infidelity, about my cowardice, about my unwritten book, about the desire I still harbored for his food, for the good bread that my wife's lover shaped with his hands. I wanted to say all these things and more, but the words were snakes.

I licked my lips. I grinned. "Those are big chickens."

"Not chicken. Emu," said Jesse. "They're emu."

Wayne's head hit the table.

"You pussy," said Yolanda, sounding cheerful.

"Emu?" I asked.

Jesse sighed. I could see that she was becoming disillusioned with me. In my mind, I told her that she was going to have to get used to it.

"People make hamburgers from them down in New Zealand," Jesse said. "Some dude around here tried to ranch a few thousand, but it didn't work out. Emus eat for shit, I guess. Dude lost his farm and the emus went wild. You see them around. People hit em with their cars sometimes. Whatever."

"You big old pussy," said Yolanda.

"F," said Wayne. He gurgled, and then repeated the letter. "F."

"Are you angry?" I asked Jesse.

"I thought we had something, that's all." Jesse pinched her little nose, and sighed again. She casually dug at the crotch of her red jeans. "You just better figure yourself out is all I'm saying, mister."

So I went to collect my thoughts.

I stepped out the back door, to the foot of the hill. I started to climb. I wasn't sure where I was going, but I knew that the interstate was somewhere beyond, and if nothing came to me, eventually I would find traffic. The moon wobbled at the top of the rise.

Before long my shirt was plastered to my torso. I paused to catch my breath and looked back, to the bar and my friends on the veranda. Jesse lifted a hand. Yolanda lifted my brother's head by the back of his hair.

"Good-bye," I said, and waved. "Good-bye! I'm going to run into traffic! Good-bye!" I screamed it, knowing they would never hear it over the music.

I turned, and took another step, the first last step—and then I stopped:

An emu's silhouette was drawn against the moon. The emu was man-sized and thickly feathered. The long, bony profile reminded me of my wife.

The bird, no more than thirty feet away, raised its head from the ground and seemed to sniff. The head swiveled, the beak coming around like a rifle barrel, and the creature's eyes locked on me. They were bright, those eyes, pooled with moonlight. I had seen those eyes before: every night I asked a question, and Paula told me how she cheated death.

The emu let out a howl, a half squawk, half honk.

It charged.

In a second of clarity I came to a series of realizations: I realized that my only weapon was my hands, that my only chance was to somehow get close enough to gouge out one of the beast's eyeballs; I realized that even this move would only disable it; I realized I would have to choke it to finish it; I realized I would have to squeeze the breath out of it with my fingers; I realized I was fucked.

I stood and waited for the end.

Kicking up spurts of dirt, the emu's claws chewed across the ground, rapidly covering the space between us. Two small wings fluttered angrily at the bird's sides. The bright tiny eyes bored into me, and demanded I remain still, and listen to the story that was about to unfold.

Paula, I thought again, and the bird was Paula, her black hair streaming out, her red bathrobe whipped up into a cape, pale skin exposed, fingers clenched to tear. This was my story. But how could I escape? How could I save myself from the kind of love that could rip you to pieces, the kind of love that in the end still loved you enough to tell you the last hard truth, to tell you that things had changed?

Die, I thought, and shot her with my eye lasers.

Feathers tickled my leg as the bird burst past me in a rush of air. Four or five more steps and it collapsed in the dirt with a puff of dust.

I went to the bird and knelt down. I searched for a pulse. The animal's neck was like a giant, feathered pipe cleaner. It was warm, but I couldn't feel anything.

Dust had settled on its black eyes and there were a few burst blood vessels around the edges. I traced the deep hollows at its clavicles. It must have been starving. I doubted that when it charged, the poor animal even saw me at all. A few brown feathers lay scattered about the corpse.

I put my hands under the long bird, expecting to lurch under its weight, but it was light in my arms, no heavier than a child. I carried it away.

My companions were waiting for me when I got to the door, the dead emu cradled in my arms. They had observed the whole thing from the veranda and they were nothing short of amazed. The bird had been about to kill me, but I stared it down, stunned it dead with an icy gaze.

"You got the voodoo," said Yolanda, shaking a finger at me like I was a naughty boy.

"Bruce Lee," said Wayne. He leaned against Yolanda. He shook his head and licked his lips. "Bruce Lee."

"It was his heart, I think."

"It's okay to cry," said Jesse, already grabbing my hand and guiding me to her truck across the parking lot.

"Bruce Lee," said Wayne one more time and slipped down to the ground, where the bird lay. Yolanda waved. "What you want us to do with it?" Yolanda called after me.

"I didn't mean to kill it," I called back. "I don't mean to hurt anyone."

"Shush," said Jesse, and shoveled me into her car.

We drove away and I looked out the back window to see Wayne, sprawled in the dirt and the neon light, clutching the dead bird like a fallen comrade.

Jesse said we needed to get married before we consummated our love. Her Uncle Bob was a minister and he could do it. "I cannot lie with you unless we're married. Those are the non-negotiable rules. That's the tenth commandment, and you get the other nine for free."

"I'm already married," I said.

"That's not important," she said. I had no idea where we were driving. There were fewer streetlights. Insects seemed to hurl themselves at the windshield.

"Okay," I said. I placed my head on her lap while she drove. I looked up into her nostrils. They were hairier than I expected. "Maybe it's the angle, but it looks like you could do with a little edger work up in there."

"Sugar," she said.

The car stopped. My body sat up, and my head followed after a second or two. We were in a trailer park. My attention was drawn to a palm tree planted on a green island in the center of the park's looping drive. It was festooned with white Christmas lights. I blinked at the lights, and found myself struck with a brief but pleasant sensation of amnesia, which carved away the six months since Christmas, and left me only a few moments away from Paula. She was home, waiting for me; we had presents to open, a birth to celebrate.

In my next blink, I was here again, in a trailer park, in Florida. Christmas: gone. Wife: gone. I banged my head against the dashboard, once, twice, three times.

Jesse popped open the door and pulled me from the truck. My legs walked to a trailer—a clean, white-sided, black-roofed trailer no different from any of the other trailers that were spread out around me. The alien star of a penitentiary spotlight flickered above the field of rectangular domiciles.

"I didn't kill the emu," I said. This point suddenly seemed vital. Hairy nostrils or not, I was down to my last option. I didn't want her to think that she was marrying a serial killer like Virgil Pendergast. I wanted to make it work this time. "It was a bad ticker, that's all."

Jesse banged on the door of a trailer. There was the sound of something falling over inside, and a curse. A tall, grizzled man in a bathrobe appeared. His red jockey shorts flashed from between folds in the robe. His face seemed to convey both boredom and exhaustion, as if he had been awakened from a deep dream of secretarial work.

"Uncle Bob, I need to be united with this gentleman in holy matrimony," Jesse said.

"Oh, okay." Uncle Bob put a finger in his ear, picked, studied it, wiped it, and gestured for us to come inside.

I clung to Jesse's arm. "Is he a real minister?" Even in my current state of intoxication, the red underpants raised certain doubts.

"As real as life," said Jesse. "But no more questions." With her index finger, she lightly touched my zipper. "This is a somber and beautiful moment that we will remember for the rest of our lives."

There was a large cross on the wall at one end of the trailer. Uncle Bob pushed a couch out of the way and told us to wait. When he came back he had a shoe box of plastic rings. "Pick one," he said. I took a shiny blue one. Jesse selected a yellow for me.

Uncle Bob told us to take each other's hands. He read the service from a wrinkled piece of typing paper. When it was done I gave Jesse her ring and she gave me mine. We kissed. Uncle Bob snapped a picture of us with a Polaroid camera.

Jesse guided me into the bedroom. It didn't occur to me to ask where Uncle Bob was going to sleep. Nothing occurred to me, really. I looked on the floor, expecting to see little rumpled dunes of red underwear in every corner. But it was too dark to see into the corners of the room.

The next thing she was pulling off my clothes and I was naked, lying on the bed, and she was on top of me, and I was inside of her. There was a silver chain around her neck, dangling with maybe two dozen plastic rings. It bounced against her chest; her tiny nose wrinkled; her boy's hair bobbed.

"How did you escape from the wild bears?" I asked, knowing she wouldn't understand.

Except, she did understand. "Sugar," said my new wife, and reared up, "I am the wild bears."

I woke up in the parking lot of the bar. My clothes weren't on the right way. It was day. I blinked. The maniacal Florida State alligator and the Union soldier loomed above me, dusty in the morning light.

I walked back to the motel. Several times I paused to dry-heave into the brush along the side of the road. Bugs bit me and I was too weak to scratch at them.

Wayne's bed was undisturbed. There was a note on the night table:

out with yolanda to see her old man get the juice. Some local wit told me that yolanda was not kidding when she said the hot seat was a little cranky. said the head popped clean off the last dude they fried. probably bullshit but i'd like to see it.

that said, stan i hope you know that if you got sent to the electric chair and your head popped off, i'd raise bloody hell. (truth: i might keep your old noggin in a jar and show it off, tho. just to mess with folks. i give you permission to do the same, bro.)

will report on head-poppings or whatever else occurs.
wayne.

I went in the bathroom to wash my face. The dead emu was in the bathtub. A few flies darted around his head and beak. I puked again.

I lay down. The earth moved; I listened to it moan. I moaned back. We were both pretty tired.

I woke at twilight. My head and my stomach hurt. I ordered Chinese food and asked them to bring some aspirin, too. I took the emu to a Dumpster around back and laid him to rest.

The food came, but no aspirin. I ordered a pornographic movie on the cable box and ate dinner.

There was a part toward the end of the movie when two women were taking a bath together, soaping each other's breasts and slopping water out on the candles on the floor. I knew they were just acting, but it looked like a lot of fun.

"I'm still dirty down here," one girl pouted.

"Looks like Dr. Sponge will have to operate," the other replied.

I called my house. The machine picked up. My wife told me to leave a message.

*   *   *

At 12:03 A.M. the state of Florida electrocuted Virgil Armistead Pendergast, the Sportscar Splatterer, for three counts of first-degree murder. I know this because the power in my room went out in a sudden flash, along with the rest of the electricity in Starke. I read the time by the Day-Glo digits of my watch.

When he called, Wayne told me that as the electricity coursed through him, Virgil's feet burst into flame. No one could figure out why. "But," said Wayne, "it doesn't take a rocket scientist to figure that the man didn't clean much in there, in the toe crevices."

"Are you saying that toe jam is flammable?"

I took his silence as an affirmative.

"I'm on a boat," said Wayne.

"I see," I said.

"I'm not coming back," he said.

"What am I supposed to tell Mom and Dad?" I asked.

"I mean, I'm not coming back right away. Yolanda and I are going to Haiti. So, I need you to drive Virgil's Jaguar home."

"Haiti?" I asked.

"She knows a voodoo guy that says he can bring Virgil back from the dead."

This information caused a number of questions to cycle through my mind, but I picked, "Do you want that?"

"No, not really." Wayne sighed. "But I don't want to be one of those pushy fucking guys, you know? One of those pricks who never shares the remote control?"

"Well, if she's going to raise him from the dead, where does that leave your relationship, Wayne?"

"We're still trying to figure that out. We're taking it slow, you know?"

Wayne told me to cheer up, and then he said good-bye.

I packed my things and started home.

On the way, I stopped in Appomattox again and hung around for a few days. A few days turned into a week, and at some point I decided that I was waiting for something to happen—a sign, some kind of permission.

I visited the statue of Traveler and rubbed his nose for luck. I loitered around the steps of the courthouse and made myself available to other tourists who needed someone to take their picture. But, mostly, I waited, and drank diet sodas, and spoke to no one who knew me.

Finally, one afternoon, as I sat on the hood of the Jaguar, staring up at the statue of Lee and the rearing horse, a man with a bucket of soapy water and a squeegee approached me. He had his cap pulled low so I couldn't see his eyes, just the gristled wedge of his jaw. I could smell the booze on him. "Awright," he said, and held out his hand, "you want me to take it from here?"

I handed over the keys, and hopped a Greyhound back to New England. When he finally did come home, two years later, and missing his left eye, Wayne acted like he had forgot all about the car, never even asked.

Albert Michalkiewicz turned out to be an alcoholic and my wife left him not more than three months later. Not long afterward I read in the paper that he'd declared bankruptcy. Of course, I never went to his bakery again, but when I walk by the boarded-up storefront, I sometimes pause to sniff; three years later, the sweet smell of his bread still lingers on the sidewalk.

My wife does not talk about this time. Nor do I bring it up. I did not reproach her when she came home. What right did I have?

We are happy, I think, the way people like us are happy: sometimes we share a bottle of wine at the local excuse for a French restaurant. We watch television together. We have a dog we take for walks. Now that Wayne is home, sometimes the three of us will sit around and laugh, and play Trivial Pursuit. He's never told me what happened in Haiti, or where Yolanda went, or if they used voodoo to raise Virgil Pendergast from the dead, but the elbow stump of his left arm and the picture of a beige-skinned baby in a polka dot jumper that he carries in his wallet tell me enough. These days Wayne works as a parking attendant at the airport, and lives alone. Once, I drove out to surprise him with a sandwich, and saw him sitting in the booth; he had removed his glass eye, and he was fingering the photograph of the baby in the polka dot jumper, and staring off into space. I did not disturb him.

Paula and I built a birdhouse, and on weekend mornings we like to watch the finches flap down, then strut around, and bicker with one another, and preen, and fly away again. Yes, I am convinced that we are happy enough.

Only the other day my wife and I were curled up on the sofa, nearly in love, nearly dreaming in our collective warmth. I was only half watching the television, one of those shouting and hair-pulling talk shows.

Then there was Uncle Bob and a delicate, dark-haired man who looked something like my second wife. They were sitting on a stage, surrounded by an audience on risers. The title card for the next segment of the show suddenly slammed across the screen in bullet print:

UNIONS OF FREAKS!

THE WOMAN WHO BECAME A MAN AFTER MARRYING OVER

A HUNDRED MEN AND HER BROTHER-LOVER!

My wife was lying against me, half asleep, rubbing my chest.

"You married one hundred and two men, is that right, sir? And you performed the services, sir?" The host of the show wore a mask of amazement. His hair was outstanding.

"Yes, that's right," said Uncle Bob, nodding somberly. Jesse crossed and uncrossed his legs.

"And you are also married? You and your sister-brother?"

"Yes, sir," said Uncle Bob.

"Man and wife," said my second wife in a quiet voice.

Uncle Bob reached over to Jesse and patted his hand. "Yes, sir. Man and wife."

The host scratched his head and paced back and forth for a few seconds without saying anything. "Wow," he said finally.

The audience laughed.

"You guys are a couple of real weirdos, aren't you?" The host winked at the studio audience. The audience hooted and howled and stomped. The host did a little jig from one side of the stage to the other; he made sharp fencing motions with his microphone.

Uncle Bob frowned. Jesse shook his head meekly. He looked frail, and old.

"What are you thinking?" my wife asked sleepily.

I reached for the remote control and turned off the power.

"Honey?" She looked up into my eyes. Maybe she recognized something.

"Oh," I said, "I just get tired of those freak shows. They trot those poor people out and laugh at them. It grosses me out."

She nodded sleepily, closed her eyes.

"How did you rescue—" I started, but she put a hand to my mouth.

"I always hated that game," she said.

I watched her drift off and I thought of Starke and Wayne and the guilty hours, of the road and of Appomattox. I had gone mad and experienced visions. Now I was back from the journey and my life was restored. I ran my hands through my wife's hair and whispered that I loved her. I know that Lee must have brushed down Traveler in this way, must have murmured in one of those big sweet ears, must have promised the animal that everything would turn out fine. But had the general ever lowered his own ear, I wondered, and dared to hear the counsel of his truest friend?

Acknowledgments

There are a number of people I need to thank for putting up with me:

The first is my awesome agent, Amy Williams, who never flagged in her confidence in my writing, explained everything, and perhaps most important, drove us to see Dylan.

Several hosannas need to be cast in the direction of my editor, Gillian Blake. Her skillful editing made this a better book, and her enthusiasm made me a happier person. (Sorry again about the couch, GB.)

Among my many wonderful teachers, I want to particularly express my gratitude to Paul Russell, David Plante, and Binnie Kirshenbaum.

Kelly Braffet, Ben Freeman, Barbara Gordon, Lauren Grodstein, Jennifer Guevin, Nathan Hensley, John McNally, Kevin Newman, Christina Saraceno, Daniel Silver, and Scott Snyder provided friendship, criticism, inspiration, and the occasional cold drink.

Thanks are also due to Matthew Elblonk, Arthur Greene, Marisa Pagano, Surendra Patel, and Greg Villepique.

Finally, I want to say that none of this would have been possible without the support of my family: Mom, Dad, Joe, Leo, and Naomi. I love you guys.

A NOTE ON THE AUTHOR

Owen King grew up in Bangor, Maine. He is a graduate of Vassar College and holds an M.F.A. from Columbia University. His stories have appeared in *Book Magazine* and the *Bellingham Review*. He has been nominated for a National Magazine Award and is a recipient of the John Gardner Award for Short Fiction. He currently resides in Brooklyn.

The text of this book is set in Linotype Sabon, named after the type founder Jacques Sabon. It was designed by Jan Tschichold and jointly developed by Linotype, Monotype, and Stempel, in response to a need for a typeface to be available in identical form for mechanical hot metal composition and hand composition using foundry type.

Tschichold based his design for Sabon roman on a font engraved by Garamond, and Sabon italic on a font by Granjon. It was first used in 1966 and has proved an enduring modern classic.